There

A man.

A *savage.*

Naked, but for a loincloth. He clutched a gleaming black knife in strong fingers, but Tory couldn't make herself concentrate on the weapon.

He didn't move, and yet he kept changing. It was, she finally decided, the way the sun greeted him, lent light to his dark flesh and made his ebony hair glisten. He stood too far away for her to make out his features. Still, if the truth was in his broad shoulders, the flat plane of his belly, the proud way he held his head, he was a man in his prime.

She stepped over the rocks, freeing herself from the confinement of the sacred dance ring where she stood, not so that she could run, but because...

Because her legs had decided to walk *toward* him....

Dear Reader,

Happy Valentine's Day! And as a special gift to you, we're publishing the latest in *New York Times* bestseller Linda Howard's series featuring the Mackenzie family. Hero Zane Mackenzie, of *Mackenzie's Pleasure*, is every inch a man—and Barrie Lovejoy is just the woman to teach this rough, tough Navy SEAL what it means to love. There's nothing left to say but "Enjoy!"

Merline Lovelace concludes her "Code Name: Danger" miniseries with *Perfect Double*, the long-awaited romance between Maggie Sinclair and her boss at the OMEGA Agency, Adam Ridgeway. Then join Kylie Brant for *Guarding Raine*. This author established herself as a reader favorite with her very first book—and her latest continues the top-notch tradition. *Forever, Dad* is the newest from Maggie Shayne, and it's an exciting, suspenseful, *emotional* tour de force. For those of you with a hankering to get "Spellbound," there's Vella Munn's *The Man From Forever*, a story of love and passion that transcend time. Finally, Rebecca Daniels wraps up her "It Takes Two" duo with *Father Figure*, featuring the ever-popular secret baby plot line.

Pick up all six of these wonderful books—and come back next month for more, because here at Silhouette Intimate Moments we're dedicated to bringing you the best of today's romantic fiction. Enjoy!

Yours,

Leslie Wainger
Senior Editor and Editorial Coordinator

Please address questions and book requests to:
Silhouette Reader Service
U.S.: 3010 Walden Ave., P.O. Box 1325, Buffalo, NY 14269
Canadian: P.O. Box 609, Fort Erie, Ont. L2A 5X3

THE MAN FROM FOREVER

VELLA MUNN

Silhouette®
INTIMATE™ MOMENTS®
Published by Silhouette Books
America's Publisher of Contemporary Romance

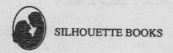

SILHOUETTE BOOKS

ISBN 0-373-07695-9

THE MAN FROM FOREVER

Printed in U.S.A.

Books by Vella Munn

Silhouette Intimate Moments
The Man From Forever #695

Silhouette Shadows
Navajo Nights #58

VELLA MUNN

grew up the daughter and granddaughter of teachers, and from childhood on was in love with the written word. She turned to writing when her first child was born and now has twenty-nine contemporary and historical romances to her credit. She is the mother of two grown children and lives in southern Oregon with her husband.

Although Loka and Tory are fictional characters,
The Land of Burned Out Fires and
the Modoc Indians are real.
Located in northern California,
the Lava Beds National Monument stands as a
testament to the resourceful Native Americans who
once made that fascinating land their home.
I am honored to dedicate this book to the spirit,
the essence, of those people.

Prologue

The warrior's body woke, one slow, gliding movement at a time. He became aware of sound—a distant, half-remembered whisper of wind sliding its restless way over the land. He remembered—remembered closing himself in the cave's darkness beside his dying son, swallowing the shaman's bitter potion, feeling strength flow out of his body, losing control of his thoughts. Losing the thoughts themselves.

How long ago had that been?

He lay on the bear pelt he'd spread on the ground for his forever sleep. The air moving almost imperceptibly over his naked body felt warm, yet not quite alive—ancient air. He was in Wa'hash, the most sacred of places.

Strength flowed into his war-honed muscles. He gave thanks to Eagle for the power in his body. Cho-ocks the shaman had been wrong. The mix of ground geese bone, bunchgrass and other things unknown hadn't ended him after all. He couldn't stay in the underworld with his son; something—or was it someone?—had brought him back.

Back to empty-bellied children, despairing women and men ready for battle.

The anger that had fed him and his chief and the others during that cruel-cold winter of 1873 returned in powerful waves. They were Maklaks—the Modocs—proud people living on land given to them by Kumookumts, their creator. The white skins had had no right to bring their cattle and horses and fences here. The army had had no right to force them to live on a reservation with their enemy, the Klamath. But those things had happened.

Sitting, he tried to hold on to his anger, but his body tightened into a brief, pain-filled knot. He breathed through it, kneaded his calves and thighs, then forced himself to stand. His belly felt utterly empty, his flesh unwashed, but those things didn't matter. Soon his eyes would make the most of the sliver of light coming in through the small opening.

Another kind of hunger touched him with hot, familiar fingers. It pulled him away from urgent questions about what had brought him back to life. His manhood signaled a message that he'd learned to master during the long, cold months of hiding and fighting. Either he'd forgotten how to keep need reined in or something was—

Something or someone.

Like a wolf after a scent, he left his son's bones and went in search of light, taking with him the knife his grandfather's grandfather had created from the finest black rock. His legs unerringly led him down the narrow tunnel that led to the surface and, hopefully, understanding. When he reached the place where surface and tunnel met, he picked up the ladder, but the rawhide that held the wood in place was dry and brittle. Although he had never cowered from an enemy's bullet, he shuddered now. It took many seasons for rawhide to become useless.

After freeing the sturdiest pole, he used it to shove aside the rock that covered the hole. Then he sprang upward, hooked his hands over the rocky ground and pulled himself up. Bright sunlight assaulted his eyes. The wind brought with it the sweet, endless smell of sage, and for a moment he believed that nothing had changed. Peace didn't last long enough.

The enemy.

Cautious, he rose to a low crouch. The Land Of Burned Out Fires was as it had always been, stark and yet beautiful, home to the Maklaks, rightful place of things sacred and ancient. He could see nearly as far as he could run in a long day, the horizon a union of sky and earth. Knife gripped in fingers strong enough to build a fine tule canoe, he balanced his weight on his powerful thighs and spun in a slow circle. Shock sliced into him, almost making him bellow.

The mother lake that had always fed his people had shrunk! Shock turned into rage, then beat less fiercely as the emotion that had brought him out here reasserted itself.

The enemy.

Only, if he could believe his senses, this unknown thing wasn't a soldier or settler. The knowledge tore at his belief in who and what he was in a way that had never happened before. The morning the army had set fire to the tribe's winter village, he'd felt as if the energy of a thousand volcanoes had been unleashed inside him. This, too, was a volcano—heat and fire.

Sucking in air, he forced himself to seek the source of the heat. For a heartbeat he thought he'd spotted a deer or antelope, but his keen eyesight soon brought him the truth.

A woman was out there, so far away that he could tell little about her except that she was unarmed, lean and long, graceful. She walked alone, stepping carefully and yet effortlessly over lava rock and around brush sharp enough to tear flesh.

The enemy, this woman?

She stopped, head cocked and slightly uplifted. Her arms remained at her side, yet there was a tension to them that struck a familiar chord inside him. He viewed the world of his childhood and his ancestors' childhood through untrusting eyes. She was doing the same, trying to make sense of something that kept itself hidden from her.

Let her be afraid.

He slipped around rocks and bunchgrass until he was close enough that if he had bow and arrow, he could bring her down. She was too skinny to survive a harsh winter, and yet he found something to his liking about that. He imagined her under him, arms and legs in constant motion. She would wrap herself around him, nipping, digging her fingers into his back until the volcano she'd turned him into exploded. She'd absorb his energy, share hers with him, her cries echoing in the distance.

Angry, he forced away the dangerous thought. This was no willing Maklaks maiden. The strange woman wore clothes he'd never seen, her sturdy shoes made from an unknown material. She didn't belong here, was so stupid that she stood alone and vulnerable on land fought over by Indian and white.

Didn't belong here? Yes, her bare arms didn't know what it meant to be assaulted by winter cold and summer heat, and yet she looked around her with wanting and loneliness, her eyes and soft mouth telling him of the turmoil inside her, tapping a like unrest inside him. Had *her* emotions reached him somehow and pulled him from the place where he believed he would spend eternity?

Why?

Chapter 1

Six months later

Home.

No, not home, but understanding, maybe.

It was going to be a glorious day—hot but unbelievably clean—the kind of day that made a person glad to be alive and put life into perspective. At least it did if that person had a handle on herself. On that thought, Victoria—Tory—Kent opened her car door and stepped out. Although night shadows still covered the land, the birds were awake. Their songs filled the air and made her smile.

This land was so deceptively desolate, miles and miles of blackened rock. When she'd first seen the Lava Beds National Monument of Northern California, her impression had been that the country was a harsh joke, a massive, lifeless testament to the power of volcanic eruption and little more. But it wasn't lifeless after all. She would have to share it with other visitors and park personnel. At least it was too early for anyone else to be at the parking lot near the site

that had been named Captain Jack's Stronghold, after the
rebel Modoc chief who once lived here. For a little while, her
only companions would be the deer and birds and antelope
and scurrying little animals that somehow found a way to
sustain themselves on the pungent brush and scraggly trees
that found the lava-strewn earth, if not rich, at least capable of sustaining life.

A distant glint of light caught her attention, pulling her
from the persistent and uneasy question of what she was
doing here when the opportunity of a lifetime waited on the
Oregon coast. Concentrating, she realized that the rising sun
had lit distant Mount Shasta. Although it was June, snow
still blanketed the magnificent peak. This morning, the
snow had taken on a rosy cast, which stood out in stark
contrast to the still-dark, still-quieted world she'd entered.

What was it she'd read? That the Modocs who once
roamed this land, and who had murdered her great-great-
grandfather, considered Shasta sacred. Looking at it now,
she understood why.

"Are you still around, spirits?" she muttered softly, not
surprised that she'd spoken aloud. Ever since her too-brief
visit last winter, the isolated historic landmark had remained on her mind—although *haunted* might be a more
appropriate term.

While at work, she'd managed to keep her reaction to
herself, but no one was watching her today. In fact, even her
boss, the eminent and famous anthropologist Dr. Richard
Grossnickle, didn't know what she was doing. She'd tell him
once she joined him at the Alsea Indian village site, maybe.

After making sure she had her keys with her, she locked
her car and started up the narrow paved path that would
take her through the stronghold, one of the high points of
the monument and where some one hundred and fifty Modoc men, women and children had spent the winter of 1873.
She'd taken no more than a half-dozen steps before turning
to look back at her car for reassurance. It was the only vehicle in the parking lot, the only hunk of metal and plastic
and rubber amid miles and miles of nothing. Behind the car

lay a surprisingly smooth grassland and beyond that the faint haze that was Tule Lake. The grasses, she knew, existed because years ago much of the lake had been drained to create farmland out of the rich lake bottom.

Ahead of her—

The land tumbled over on itself, a jumble of hardened lava, hardy sagebrush, surprisingly fragrant bitterbrush, ice-gray rabbitbrush. The plants' ability to find enough soil for rooting here made her shake her head in wonder. She knew they provided shelter for all kinds of small animals and hoped her presence wouldn't disturb the creatures.

It probably would. After all, this time of day—fragile dawn—belonged to those who lived and died here, not to intruders like herself. *Intruder? If your ancestor had fought and died here, his blood soaking into the earth, did that give you some kind of claim to the land?*

Was that why she hadn't been able to shake it from her mind and had to come back? Because she had some kind of genetic tie to this place?

After a short climb, she found herself at the end of the paved area. Day was emerging in degrees, as if one layer after another was being lifted to reveal more and more detail. From the relative distance of the parking lot, the stronghold had looked like nothing more than a brush-covered rise, but she'd reached the top and was fast learning that depth and distance here obeyed different rules. One minute she was walking on level ground with nothing except weeds to obscure her view. Then, after no more than a dozen or so steps, she'd dropped into a lava-defined gully. The rocky sides trapped her, held her apart from all signs and thoughts of civilization.

There'd been a box filled with pamphlets at the beginning of the trail, and after depositing her twenty-five cents, she'd taken one of them. A wooden post with a white number 1 on it corresponded to a paragraph in the pamphlet. She was standing at the site of what had been a Modoc defense outpost. From strategic places like this one, the Indians had been able to keep an eye on the army. As a result, a fighting force of no more than sixty warriors had held off close to a thousand armed soldiers for five months.

A stronghold. It was aptly named.

As the day's first warmth reached her, she stopped walking and concentrated so she could experience everything. In her mind, it was that fateful winter. Settlers had been living in the area for years, slowly, irrevocably encroaching on land that had always belonged to the Indians.

A fort had been built some miles away and the Modocs and Klamaths had been forced onto an uneasily shared reservation. Some of the Modocs under the leadership of Captain Jack had fled and taken up residence on the other side of Tule Lake. When the army, charged with recapturing the rebels, attacked one frozen dawn, the Modocs had scrambled into their canoes and paddled across the lake to take refuge here in what they'd called The Land Of Burned Out Fires.

Peace talks had been tried, and tried. Thanks to indecision on the part of the government and opposition from the Modocs, it had taken months to decide who would try to wrangle out some kind of settlement. Her great-great-grandfather, a distinguished veteran of the Civil War and commander of the troops stationed here, had been a member of that commission. On April 11, 1873, General Canby had been killed a few miles away, the only true general to die during the struggle.

Such a simple scenario. Wrongs committed on both sides. Forceful, clashing egos. An impenetrable hiding place. A hellish winter for everyone. Her ancestor's blood spilled on nearly useless land.

The birds hadn't stopped their gentle songs. Occasionally, they were interrupted by a crow's strident call that made her smile. The wind had barely been moving when she arrived, but it was increasing, an uneven push of air that sent the brush and grasses to murmuring. She wondered what it had been like to be surrounded by little more than crows and other birds and wind for five months, to constantly listen for the sounds of the enemy. Thanks to the correspondence between Alfred Canby and Washington officials, she had a fair idea of what that winter had been like for the army troops, and looking at the land now she could understand why so many had deserted.

It hadn't been that easy for the Modocs. They couldn't leave.

Something in the sky distracted her. Looking up, she spotted an eagle floating in great, free circles over her. Not for the first time, she thought that birds had an ideal life. If it wasn't for mealtime, she wouldn't mind being an eagle. To spend one's days playing with the wind, drifting high above the earth like a free-spirited, tireless hang glider, unconcerned about taxes, an aging car, job politics... Her contemplation of the eagle became more intense when she realized it was slowly but steadily coming closer. She could now make out the details of its proud white head, imagine its sharp eyes were focused on her. Were there such things as rabid eagles? Surely the creature hadn't mistaken her for breakfast, had it?

Its circles became tighter, more focused until she had absolutely no doubt that she was what held its attention. Those talons would make short work of her cotton shirt and the flesh beneath. Her car keys were no match against its killing weapons. To be attacked by a bird of prey—

With a scream that sent a bolt of fear through her, it wheeled away, disappearing in a matter of seconds. Still shaken, she waited to see if it would return, but it must have decided that a mouse or snake would taste better. After longer than she cared to admit, she dismissed the bird and its unusual behavior and went back to her history lesson.

Captain Jack, she thought with a grim smile. The Modoc chief had had an Indian name, but she couldn't remember it. From the pictures she'd seen of him, he looked like a peaceful enough man, but something had snapped inside him and his followers, and they'd gone to war against the United States Army, although she doubted he'd known the sum of what he'd been up against. Still, in 1873, after years of coexistence with whites, the Modocs of his time hadn't been primitive savages, nothing like the cultures she studied as an anthropologist.

What brought the eagle back to mind she couldn't say. Maybe because on a subconscious level she'd been asking herself how far the Modocs had come from their prehistoric beliefs. Surely they'd no longer perceived eagles and other creatures as gods.

There was, she admitted, a fine line to be walked between giving primitive people's beliefs the respect they deserved and not laughing over the notion of coyotes who told tall tales, snakes that were thought to be immortal because they shed their skins, warning children not to harm a frog for fear of causing the closest stream to dry up. Despite six years of studying and working with Dr. Grossnickle, she'd been unable to determine to her satisfaction what had given birth to such legends. Certainly she understood early people's need to make order out of the uncertainties of their lives, but talking animals or the belief that the Modoc creator went around disguised as an old crone... Well, to each his own. She'd talk the talk; she knew she had to do that if she intended to keep her job. But beyond that ... well, let's get real.

Still, she admitted as she moved on to the next marker, there was something about standing on the actual land in question that made logic and professional dispassion a little hard to hold on to. Thinking of everything the Modocs had lost, she stared at the magnificent nothingness of land that stretched out around her. Except for the trail and occasional markings, the stronghold hadn't changed.

That's why she'd come out here before visitors started arriving, so she could more easily capture the essence of that earlier time. She began walking again, a slow gait that hopefully diminished the likelihood of losing her footing. Although it took some doing, she managed to read a little more from the brochure. She was surprised to learn that the naturally fortified stronghold itself was little more than a half mile in diameter. The land for as far as she could see was so awesomely vast and rugged that where the Modocs

had entrenched themselves seemed larger than it really was.
Back then, Tule Lake had dominated the area to the north
while most of the south was barren volcanic rock. The
chance of sneaking up on the Modocs—

A sound overhead caused her to again stare at the sky. She
spotted what she thought must be the same eagle silhouetted against the blueing sky, but this time it was far enough
away that she didn't feel uneasy. "What do you see up
there?" she asked. "Are your eyes keen enough that you can
spot the Golden Gate Bridge?"

Looking as if it weighed no more than a feather, the great
bird dipped one wing. Sunlight caught the tip and gave her
an impression of glistening black. "Forget the Golden Gate.
You don't want to get any closer to civilization than this.
And if you stay up there, the two of us are going to get along
just fine."

As if taking her suggestion to heart, the bird floated away.
When she looked around, thinking to reorient herself, the
stronghold seemed to have lost a little of its definition. It
was, she thought, as if night had decided to return. After
blinking a few times, she dispelled that possibility, but the
wind had picked up and the sound it made coated her
thoughts, allowed her to dismiss everything she'd experienced in her life before this moment.

Not only that, she could almost swear she was no longer
alone.

There was such a thing as too much solitude, Tory told
herself a half hour later. You'd think that a person who
could see so far that she was aware of the earth's curve
wouldn't be looking over her shoulder.

Only, it wasn't just the aloneness, and she knew it, damn
it. Something—someone—*was* watching her. It could be the
eagle, a rabbit, maybe even one of the antelope she understood made their home in the park.

"Say," she whispered because she didn't want to disturb
the lizard staring at her from a rock. "Whoever you are, I
don't suppose you brought some coffee with you, did you?"

Silence, but then she didn't really expect any different.

According to the pamphlet, she should be approaching one of the dance rings the Modocs had used during their shamanistic rituals, but because she'd veered off the trail while seeking the best vantage point to study Captain Jack's wide, shallow cave, it took a little while to orient herself. She'd been right; it was going to be a clean day. Clean and clear and utterly beautiful in the way of a sky unspoiled by pollution. Just the same, she couldn't help but be a little uneasy.

Grass grew between the large rocks that had been placed in a crude circle over a hundred and twenty years ago. She tried to imagine what the spot looked and sounded like back when the shaman—Curly Headed Doctor, the pamphlet said—strung red rope around the stronghold and then sang and danced through the night to ensure that his magic remain powerful.

A red rope to hold back an army. How simplistic. She'd seen a picture of the shaman and had been surprised by how young and untested he appeared, but apparently most, if not all, of the tribe had believed in him—at least they had until the army trampled his rope.

She sat on one of the rocks and faced into the center. If there'd been someone beside her, their shoulders would have touched, and she didn't see how there would have been enough room for dancing in the middle if every rock had had an occupant. An incredible bond must have been forged here. All right, there'd been political squabbling, conflicts between Captain Jack and some of the more militant rebels, but on a cold yet peaceful night, surely the leaders had come here with a singleness of thought, a shared dream for freedom.

She rocked forward and rested her elbows on her knees, eyes closed to slits that blurred her vision and freed her from the question of who or what shared this place with her. To belong, to be part of a large clan, to put aside petty differences in order to survive, to have learned the necessity of depending on one another...

How long she'd been sitting here she couldn't say. She didn't think it had been more than a couple of minutes, and yet she was surprised by how quickly she'd gone from wondering if she should have brought along a can of Mace to losing herself in sensation.

She was suddenly restless, so uneasy with herself that she wasn't sure she'd be able to conquer the emotion. It came at her more and more often these days—quiet and yet, rough questions about where her life was heading. She'd felt like that sometimes back in high school when warm spring nights and loud music and a grin from a boy sent her heart spinning out of control. She'd weathered those adolescent emotions, smothered them under work goals and ambition and the excitement of knowing that she and Dr. Grossnickle and the university that employed them were on the brink of the anthropological find of three decades. Colleagues, the press, even the bureaucrats and legal types she'd been butting heads with over excavation rights assumed she spent every waking moment immersed in exploring this primitive civilization.

What they didn't know about was the search, a goal—or something—she couldn't define.

She needed hard-driving music, to be behind the wheel of a speeding convertible with the wind screaming through her hair. She needed—all right, she needed a man to quiet her body.

After sucking one lungful of air after another into her, she managed to conquer the worst of her energy, but she knew it would only erupt again unless she started moving. Standing, she reached for the brochure, thinking to continue the history lesson. Then she froze.

There was someone out there—a man. Naked but for a loincloth. He clutched a gleaming black knife in strong fingers, and yet she couldn't make herself concentrate on the weapon.

A savage. Savage.

The word slid inside her, solid and yet misty like a vivid dream that fades upon awakening. But this was no dream.

She stepped over the rock, freeing herself from the dance ring's confinement, not so she could run, but because—

Because her legs had decided to walk *toward* him.

He didn't move; she would swear to that. And yet he kept changing. It was, she finally decided, the way the sun greeted him, lent light to his dark flesh and made his ebony hair glisten. She couldn't say how old he was; he stood too far away for her to make out his features. Still, if the truth was in his broad shoulders, the flat plane of his belly, the proud way he held his head, he was a man in his prime.

Prime. Savage. Warrior.

There wasn't enough air at The Land Of Burned Out Fires. If he'd stolen it, she would soon have to demand he return it to her, but maybe—probably—the fault lay in her.

This wonderfully lonely land had remained locked in the past. She didn't care why that was, didn't care whether she ever left it. Somehow—although it was impossible—she'd found a primitive brave, and he was staring at her, and the space between them had become charged.

She moved closer, a skill so complex that it should have been beyond her, because her need to touch him, to look into his eyes, to feel his hands on her, was like an explosion inside her. She should say something, ask him to explain the impossible, but if she spoke, he might evaporate, and she needed to stretch out this moment, enlarge it until it became enough to last a lifetime.

One step, two, three, and still he remained. She could now see that he had a small scar over his right shoulder blade and the fine hairs on his arms and legs were as dark as the back of Captain Jack's cave. His thighs—the loincloth exposed every inch of them—looked as strong and durable as the lava that dominated the land. Those legs could, she knew, lock a woman between them.

They could take her places only imagined before, awaken a gnawing beast of hunger that could only be filled by passion—raw and unadorned passion.

The air was gone again. She had to fight to breathe. The effort did something to her, snapped something deep inside and reminded her of who and where she was.

This man couldn't be. He couldn't!

Chapter 2

Eyes narrowed against the sun, the warrior watched the woman race for her wagon, her car. The urge to bury the ancient knife in her and avenge what she'd done to him was powerful, and yet, now that he'd seen her up close, looked into her eyes, anger and rage had to share space with another emotion.

She'd returned. He wanted to grab her and insist she tell him why. Most of all he'd demand to know whether her presence was what had awakened him.

Belly empty, he cast around for a rabbit or other small animal, but even as he thought he detected a furtive movement, his attention returned to the woman. She'd reached her car, and although she was too far away for him to see anything of her expression, her body language told him a great deal.

She was afraid of him. Even though he was no longer near her, she continued to carry herself as if fear rode deep and full and low inside her. She might call others of her kind to her. If she did, they'd hunt him with powerful weapons and his blood would join that of his ancestors who'd died here.

But he didn't see that as something to avoid. Death, maybe, would bring him the peace he'd known as a small child.

Once again he tried to put his thoughts to finding something to eat before the strangers started swarming over what had once had been his land, but she hadn't yet left in the fast, loud wagon he'd heard her kind call a car. Until she had, all he could do was watch. She'd stopped running, but probably only because she'd become winded. She now walked as fast as she could, an awkward and jerky movement that used much more energy than it would have if she moved with her hips.

What did he care! Let her break her leg on the ungiving rocks. If she did, the green-clad men and women who were today's soldiers would come and bear her away. Except then she'd tell them what had made her run, and his uneasy peace would be shattered.

She'd reached her car. It took her a long time to open the door, and he guessed her fingers shook so that the task was nearly impossible. It was too late to bury his knife in her back and silence her. She'd gotten away!

A sound like a bear's deep growl escaped his throat. Turning his back on her, he stepped around the dance ring and stood where she'd been just before she ran. What fools the strangers were! Those who didn't laugh and whoop like stupid children, walked slowly, reverently around it. At first he'd been mystified by their actions but finally he'd decided that they must think this weed-clogged circle of rocks was something to be revered. It had been, once. But the enemy had defiled it with their presence and Cho-ocks's magic had long ago left.

Left like everything of his time except for him.

Another growl threatened to break free, but knowing it would only tear through him like what he'd felt at his son's death, he stifled the sound. Looking down, he imagined the exact spot where the woman had placed her boots.

She was responsible! She had brought him to this time he didn't want, where he didn't belong! Thinking to grind her prints into nothing, he lifted his foot, but before he could lower it, something on a nearby bush caught his attention. It was a single hair, long and rich, the dark color of a wolf in his prime. Freeing it from the bush, he held it between thumb and forefinger. Despite his roughened fingertips, what he felt reminded him of goose down. The hair belonged to the enemy-woman. In the hands of a powerful shaman, it could be used to bring sickness and maybe death to whoever it belonged to.

He'd been wrong to do nothing but follow a warrior's way. Cho-ocks had been willing to teach him his shaman's magic. He should have stilled his impatience and anger against the enemy and listened and learned. If he had, he could . . .

Soft. Soft as the down on a newborn chick. Touched with light from the sun. He brought the hair close to his nose and inhaled, but couldn't smell anything. His need to understand what had happened to his world had brought him close to a number of women, always without their knowledge. He hated the way they smelled, their scents so strong that they overpowered the sage even. But this woman hadn't covered her body with anything that assaulted his nostrils, and he liked that.

Enemy-woman.

She had a name. And she *would* tell him what spell she'd cast over him. Once he understood, he would . . .

Eyes big and dark. A soft and gentle mouth. Long, strong arms and legs. Slender waist and hips that flared to accommodate a child placed within her. Hips and breasts made to taunt a man. To remind him of how long he'd slept alone.

Breathing more rapidly than she should have a need to, Tory sped around yet another turn. The landscape whipped behind her on both sides, but although she'd come out here for the express purpose of observing the land before she had to share it with other visitors, she couldn't put her mind to concentrating on it.

She'd seen—what? A Modoc warrior? She'd been asking herself the same stupid question for the past fifteen minutes until she was sick to death of it. Unfortunately, she still hadn't come up with an answer. At least now that she was no longer staring into eyes as dark as night, the stark and unreasoning fear that had sent her running had begun to fade.

It must be some kind of joke.

Slamming her fist into the steering wheel, she again ordered the stupid words to stop ramming around inside her. Hand stinging, she again tried to find a logical explanation. Unfortunately, as before, her mind didn't want anything to do with logic.

He'd looked so innately primitive, not at all like those so-called savages Hollywood slapped makeup on. She'd never been able to watch Westerns because the Indians looked so phony. Yes, she supposed that a lot of them actually *were* Native Americans, but they hadn't belonged in the wilderness they'd been thrust into for the sake of the movie. Despite war paint and bows and arrows and little more than loincloths, there'd been something self-conscious about the way they presented themselves.

This man, this warrior, was as natural a part of his rugged environment as the eagle had been. That was what she couldn't forget. That, and something in those ebony eyes that had found and ignited a part of her she hadn't known existed.

A park-service vehicle coming from the opposite direction shocked her back to the here and now and away from absolutely insane images of herself willingly following the Indian back to wherever he'd come from. She thought about trying to flag the park employee down, but what would she say? That she'd had a hallucination about a nearly naked, absolute hunk of a man and wanted to know if it was a common occurrence around here?

There must be some kind of an explanation, logical and practical, so clear-cut that she'd be embarrassed for not having thought of it before.

Yeah, right.

After traveling another ten miles, she reached park headquarters, only then realizing what she'd done. She'd intended to spend the day poking around the lava beds.
Instead, tail tucked between her legs, she'd hightailed it for
civilization. Angry with herself and yet unable to come up
with the fortitude necessary for turning around and going
back the way she'd come, she eased her vehicle into one of
the parking slots. The rustic cabin she'd rented was not quite
a mile away, isolated but accessible via a well-maintained
footpath. It came equipped with a two-way radio to be used
in case of an emergency.

Some of the park personnel lived here year-round. While
wandering around at dusk last night, she'd happened upon
the paved road leading from headquarters to the small collection of houses within shouting distance of where she now
sat. Although she hadn't stayed around the residential area
because she didn't want to invade anyone's privacy, she remembered seeing a couple of satellite dishes. Two girls riding bikes had waved at her, and when she'd asked them, they
explained that they went to school in the town of Tulelake,
which was "only" thirty miles away. They were on their way
to the nearby campground to see if there were any kids their
age staying there tonight. The girls were friendly and eager
to talk; they'd argued with each other over whether they'd
want to stay at the campground or where she was. One had
always wanted to spend a night at the cabin. The other
wasn't interested because it didn't have a TV or electricity
and what would she do once it got dark.

Tory hadn't bothered to tell them that once she got to the
Oregon coast, she expected to spend months camping out
without electricity. Because it hadn't been the first time, she
hadn't had any trouble falling asleep last night with nothing except coyotes and owls to keep her company. Tonight,
however—

She deliberately hadn't told anyone of her ties to one of
the central players during the Modoc War because she didn't
want to risk someone deciding to exploit that. Still, in the
back of her mind rode the question of whether she'd

thought she'd seen a survivor of that time because her great-great-grandfather had died here.

Like that makes any kind of sense.

"Will you stop it!" she muttered, and got out of the car. A strong breeze brought with it a hint of the day's heat, the pungent scent of sage and lava and an almost overwhelming desire to walk away from this spot of civilization and out into the wilderness where *he* might find her again.

When she checked in yesterday, the parking lot had been filled with dusty, crammed vans, cars with out-of-state licenses, even a group of senior citizens on expensive motorcycles. This morning, hers was the only vehicle not belonging to park employees. She was surprised to see them here. Shouldn't they be out doing whatever it was they did to maintain the lava beds?

She opened the door to the small visitors' center and looked around. There was a small collection of Modoc artifacts behind glass on one wall, a large, rough-finished wooden canoe against another wall, shelves filled with a display of books, pamphlets and postcards. A sign above the information desk, unmanned at the moment, informed her that anyone interested in exploring the caves that honeycombed the area were encouraged to sign in here so they could be issued hard hats and flashlights.

There was nothing flashy about the room, no plastic trinkets. Still, it helped her put her incredible experience behind her. This was a place of telephones and probably even fax machines. There'd be computers somewhere, a park director whose credentials would put hers to shame. None of the dedicated professionals who worked and lived here would have seen a mirage from another time.

And neither had she.

Then what did you see?

Someone had played a joke on her—that's what it had been. An elaborate and very good hoax.

Try telling your nervous system that.

Hoping to squelch her thoughts, she opened her mouth to call out when she heard voices coming from somewhere be-

hind the information desk. She guessed there was a room
back there. Maybe park personnel were having a meeting.
If that was the case, she didn't want to disturb them. Besides, what would she say?

A tiny tentacle of fear inched down her back, causing her
to look toward one of the little windows. All she could see
were weather-stunted trees and dark lava rocks—nothing to
be afraid of.

What was she doing here?

Instead of forcing herself to answer what she hoped to
accomplish by taking shelter under a roof when she should
be out looking for a piece of her roots, she picked up one of
the books about the Modoc War. She'd done no more than
read the back blurb when the sound of raised voices caught
her attention. Before she could decide what to do, she heard
a door being opened. The voices became more distinct.

"People will see right through it. You can't get away with
something that cornball in this day and age. They'll laugh
us right out of the water."

"No, they won't. People love the unexplained. Besides,
you already admitted you don't have a better suggestion."

"Only because I haven't had time to come up with one."

"The hell you haven't. We've been staring at a budget
shortfall for the better part of a year now. That's what I'm
here for. Why you're being so..."

Two men came around the divider that separated the
public area from the rest of the building. They stared at her,
their conversation trailing off to nothing. One of them, a
tall, balding man probably in his late fifties, wore the stan-
dard green uniform and a name tag that identified him as
Robert Casewell, acting director. Tory guessed that his had
been the deeper of the two voices, the one who'd told the
other that his suggestion wouldn't hold water. The other
man, closer to her age, wore civilian clothing. If he'd been
sent here to deal with the budget in some way, he apparently wasn't a park employee.

"I'm sorry," she said when the two men continued to stare at her. "I should have let someone know I was here, but I didn't want to disturb anyone."

"It's all right," Robert Casewell said. "The meeting's over." He jerked his head at the other man. "You and I need to get together, Fenton. Come up with something that makes sense."

"What I proposed makes sense. You just need to open up your thinking."

The director muttered something under his breath, nodded at Tory, then walked out the door. Not sure what she was supposed to do now, she gave Fenton a tentative smile. "I heard a little," she admitted. "I know what you mean about budget problems. They never seem to go away, do they?"

"They will if I can get people to listen." Fenton, who was maybe three inches taller than her, with the slightest bit of thickening around his waist and a thatch of windblown hair, smiled down at her. "I'm not a walking encyclopedia about the lava beds, but if you've got a question, maybe I can answer it."

Can you? Can you tell me whether I really saw a man who must be at least a hundred and fifty years old, who looked at me with the most compelling eyes I've ever seen? Stammering a little and hating herself for sounding half-bright, she explained that she'd been out on her own this morning but had decided she needed a map and game plan so she wouldn't risk getting lost. "I love hiking, but I have the suspicion I could get disoriented in short order around here. It's amazing. From a distance everything looks so level, but once you really look at it, you see all those hills and valleys."

"Yeah, there's enough of them, all right. You're here alone?"

Wary in the way of a woman who has learned to navigate the world on her own, she simply shrugged. She should grab a map, ask a couple of questions and get out of here, but after what she'd experienced this morning, a roof felt inordinately comforting.

"So am I," Fenton was saying. He introduced himself as Fenton James and she felt obliged to introduce herself in turn. When he stuck out his hand, she did the same. "I've been here about three weeks now," he said. "I thought everyone came as part of a group, mostly families on vacation, sometimes college students or history buffs. Couldn't you find anyone who wanted to stare at nothing with you?"

Something about Fenton's tone didn't sit right with her, but she didn't have time to analyze what that was. "I'm on my way to a job," she said, dismissing the understatement. "I just have time for a day or two of poking around."

"Two days. Most people are in and out in an afternoon, unless they take in the caves, which I can't understand why. Where's this job of yours? I can't imagine anyone having to go through here to get to a job."

Why Fenton cared what she was up to remained beyond her. However, talking to the man had already taken her thoughts miles away from what she'd seen, or thought she'd seen, earlier. Even if he was trying to hit on her, setting him straight gave her something to do. Besides, he said he'd been at the lava beds for three weeks. If he'd noticed something unexplainable, maybe they could compare reactions. But she doubted that he'd been left feeling as if a huge chunk of what she thought of as her civilized nature had been sucked from him. Keeping the telling as brief as possible, she let him know she was part of the team selected to study some Native American ruins on the Oregon coast.

"How did you accomplish that?" he exclaimed. "My God, that's the find of the century! The opportunity for—what are you? An archaeologist?"

"Anthropologist."

"Whatever." He shrugged. "I never understood the difference."

She could have told him that an archaeologist dealt with the physical world while anthropologists concerned themselves with things social and spiritual, but what was the point? "You've heard of the Alsea discovery, I take it," she said instead.

"Who hasn't? I'd give anything to be part of it. The chance for making one's mark, well—say, maybe you can explain something for me." He rested his arm on the counter, the gesture bringing him a little closer to her. Although the air still held a high desert morning chill, she thought she caught a whiff of perspiration. "The site was discovered over a year ago. What's the holdup? I mean, I'd think everyone would be hot to trot getting their discoveries written up in the press and all. There's Pulitzer Prize potential there, you know."

Maybe. Maybe not. At the moment that was a moot point.

"What's going on?" he persisted. "Why isn't everyone up to their eye teeth in pottery and weapons?"

"It isn't that easy." The sun had reached the window to her left, inviting her to come outside and experience the morning. If she did, would she find only other visitors, or would a look at the horizon reveal someone who couldn't possibly exist? "There's an incredible amount of red tape."

"I suppose so. What is it, the government wanting a piece of the pie?"

There'd been concern about impact on the environment expressed by both state and federal agencies, as well as more than one politician trying to make a name for himself. And the Oregon Indian Council had insisted that they, not university staff, should be responsible for safeguarding artifacts, only they weren't interested in the artifacts so much as protecting what they insisted was sacred ground. Once, the strip of land between ocean and mountains had been sacred to the Alsea Indians, but the culture that had lived there no longer existed. That was what she'd argued alongside Dr. Grossnickle during three trips to Washington, D.C. Finally, after more legal maneuvering than she wanted to think about, the Indians' claim had been dismissed.

Things were now clear for work to begin. That's what she told Fenton, the explanation as brief as she could make it.

"At least we don't get much of that around here." He gave her what he must think was a conspiratorial smile. "There's an Indian council, but they don't care what we do here. At least if they don't like something, I haven't heard about it. Not that I'd have time to deal with any opposition. I've got my hands full trying to put this park on solid financial footing."

She listened with half an ear while Fenton explained that because of governmental cutbacks, the park was hard-pressed to match last year's budget, let alone plan for the future. He'd left a "choice position"—his words—with a San Francisco bank to spearhead a budget drive here, but so far all he'd met with was opposition. "Casewell calls my plan manipulation. Deception. I call it a stroke of genius. You tell me, what's wrong with capitalizing on a few ghost sightings?"

She'd been glancing at the window, both eager to be outside and grateful for the room and its proof of normalcy. Now Felton's comment captured her full attention. "Ghost sightings?"

He shrugged, his gesture casual when she was on edge. "Spirits. Ghosts. Whatever you want to call them." Although they were alone, he leaned closer and would have whispered in her ear if she hadn't pulled back. "I'll tell you because you're in the same business, so to speak. Most people, they come here, take a look around and say how amazing it is that the Indians held out so long, then go on their way. But some of them, particularly those who walk around Captain Jack's Stronghold, say they feel something there."

"Something?"

Again he shrugged his maddening shrug. "You tell me. I've never felt anything, but I'd have to be fourteen kinds of a fool not to realize there's a potential in this. The way I look at it, people with overactive imaginations stand where the Indians stood and they convince themselves that the Modocs left something of themselves behind when they were hauled off to the reservation. I think folks want to believe that. That way they don't have to feel guilty about what was done to the Indians.''

"Maybe." She hedged. "But you're not talking about something that actually exists." *Or does he?* "How can you capitalize on that?"

He gave her what she thought might be a sly wink. "The power of suggestion. A few well-placed leaks to the press and we'll have people swarming here, either because they want to believe, or because they're determined to disprove the rumors.''

"But when they don't see anything, it won't take long for them to decide they've been duped.''

"You're assuming they'll come away disappointed. But if they don't—''

"What are you saying?"

For such a brief period of time that she might have imagined it, Fenton lost his self-confident air; she could almost swear he'd started to glance out the window. Then, smiling deliberately, he briefly touched his hand to her shoulder. "I'm telling you this because, like I said, we're in the same business. We're both looking to make a name for ourselves, you through what you can gain from an extinct culture, me from what it'll do to my career if I turn this park around. Anything and everything is open to different interpretations. For example, those who have been working here for years either count themselves tuned into something— shall we call it otherworldly?—or they don't. Whatever it is, none of them quite know what to make of what's been happening lately.''

"What are you talking about?"

"You've got me. I'm not the one going around admitting I've been seeing things, but there have been sightings.''

When he stood there staring at her, she nearly screamed at him to tell her what he was talking about. But there was no way she was going to let him think she believed in this ghost or spirit or whatever he was rattling on about; neither would she do anything to discourage him from talking. Finally he shrugged and moved to the window and looked out as if assuring himself that their conversation would remain private. "What gave me the idea of capitalizing on things is that all of these sightings, or whatever you want to call them, are the same."

"Are they?"

"Yep. A warrior, brave, whatever you want to call him."

"A warrior?" She thought her voice squeaked a little at the end, hoped it didn't.

"Good-looking stud, at least that's what some say. Damn imposing, too. He's always way off in the distance so no one can ask him what the heck he's up to, but those who do see him are convinced he's real."

Convinced he's real. "You say he's always a long way away."

"A real shy fellow. Not that I mind, because that keeps the mystery going." He ended that with another of his winks, this one lasting longer and punctuated by a slight upward turn of his mouth. "That's what I'm trying to get the director to understand. We don't have to come up with anything folks can either prove or disprove. In fact, that's the *last* thing we want. But if every once in a while people see something or someone they can't explain, that'll keep them coming."

Could Fenton have already put his plan into operation? Was that what she'd seen, nothing more than some actor Fenton James had hired to perpetrate this elaborate hoax of his? If that's what it was—and she wanted the explanation to be that simple—she could tell Fenton that the actor was very, very good.

"It's certainly different from anything I've heard," she said and moved away as if to leave.

"It's more than that. It's a stroke of genius, if it works."

"If it works? It sounds as if you've done more than just presented the idea to the director."

"Maybe I have. Maybe I have."

Chapter 3

Five minutes later, Tory had finally extricated herself from the talkative Fenton and had started toward her cabin. By now people were beginning to arrive at park headquarters, their voices following her until she'd traveled a good quarter of the way. If the heat kept increasing, she'd have to change to shorts before going out again. She should have brought her camera this morning; she wouldn't make that same mistake again because—

Biting the inside of her mouth, she stopped the errant thought. She'd been about to tell herself that a camera was absolutely necessary if she was going to prove the existence of a ghostly warrior for all concerned when there was no such thing.

By effort of will, she forced her thoughts on nothing more complicated than the best place to search for ground squirrels and other scurrying creatures. Looking around, she became aware of her isolation in a way she hadn't been last night. True, she could see the faint jet trail left behind by a plane, and it was a simple matter to get in touch with someone via the walkie-talkie at the cabin, but she doubted that anyone would hear if she screamed.

Scream? Why would she do that? Hadn't she asked for the remote cabin because she wanted a little time with her own company, a welcome change of pace from the hectic meetings and yet more meetings?

After unlocking her door, she stepped inside the single room. She'd left her small duffel bag on the couch because there didn't seem to be much purpose in settling in if she was only going to be here two nights. Thinking to change into shorts, she started rummaging through her belongings. She stopped when she came across the folder filled with newspaper clippings. Although her own role in the Alsea project was essentially a supportive one, she'd been quoted numerous times and had had her picture taken on more than one occasion. Dr. Grossnickle teased her that she was robbing him of top billing, but that wasn't true and they both knew it. Still—

Frowning, she opened the folder and studied the most recent articles. Not only was she photographed alongside Dr. Grossnickle, but two paragraphs of the accompanying article were about her successful effort to discredit the Oregon Indian Council's claim that they alone had the right to excavate and record. Not only was the article one of the most accurate ones that had been written about the project, it had appeared on the front page of a recent Oregonian newspaper. If Fenton James had read the article and seen her name on the guest register and decided—

Decided what? To convince a high-profile anthropologist that something unexplained lurked around the lava beds? Taking the argument as far as it would go, he *had* struck up a conversation with her and immediately introduced the subject of ghosts or spirits or whatever he wanted to call them.

But he'd also told her straight out that he was trying to come up with a way to capitalize on people's overactive imaginations and mine them for the park's financial benefit. There'd been nothing veiled about his intentions.

Warned by the threat of a headache, she turned her thoughts to the less weighty question of whether to stay with boots or change into more comfortable shoes for her next trek into the wilderness. When she started unlacing her boots, she told herself it was *not* because she could run faster in tennis shoes.

It was dark by the time Tory returned to her cabin, and she needed to use a flashlight to find her way home. Throughout a long and eventful day, she'd gone through three rolls of film while documenting the park's wildlife and had eaten both lunch and dinner with vacationers who'd insisted she share burgers and hot dogs with them. True, she hadn't put up much of an argument when the invitations were offered. It wasn't that she was a great fan of stale buns and wilted lettuce, but being around people kept her from thinking about that morning. And if there'd been times, like when she was trying to get close enough to capture a small herd of antelope in her telephoto lens, when she felt as if she were being watched, she'd chalked it up to that overactive imagination of hers.

At least she tried to; only now, surrounded by night and alone with her thoughts, she couldn't shake the suspicion— all right, the conviction—that something, or someone, had had his eye on her.

Warrior. Although she barely whispered the word, it took on a life of its own, existed beside her in the small, kerosene-lit cabin, floated just beyond the two windows.

Warrior—a man willing to give up his life for freedom.

Unexpected emotion touched her, but she didn't try to argue it away with twentieth-century logic. Once, men who answered to no name except "warrior" had roamed this land; that evocative word had spoken of what lived in their hearts.

She'd seen their land today, at least what had once been theirs. The past year of her life had been taken up with one legal and political maneuver after another, all of it aimed at unlocking the key to a way of life that no longer existed.

Consumed by those documents and studies and strategies and jockeying for position, she'd forgotten to take the time to focus on the actual people who had once lived the life she was so determined to record.

But here at The Land Of Burned Out Fires not enough had changed. Although the wolves and grizzlies were gone, the deer and antelope that once sustained the Modocs still roamed free. The eagles they had turned to for guidance continued to soar through an unspoiled sky. And because ancient volcanoes had rendered it inhospitable to so-called progress, most of the land remained as it had always been. Only the Modocs had left.

Feeling a little overwhelmed, she turned on the battery-controlled radio and chose an all-news station. While she did what cleaning up she could, she caught up on the outside world. By the time she changed to an easy-listening station, she'd gotten back in touch with what she'd long believed herself to be—an up-and-coming cultural anthropologist with more than thirty years of productivity ahead of her. Sentiment didn't get the job done.

She'd intended to do a little reading, fiction for a change of pace, but had read no more than five pages before hours of walking and fresh air caught up with her. She turned off the radio and climbed into the double bed with its sagging mattress. An owl kept hooting. She heard what seemed like a thousand crickets, and if she listened carefully, she caught what must be a few frogs somewhere in the sound. Just before she fell asleep, she asked herself when she'd last heard nothing except the sounds of nature. She couldn't remember.

He came into her dream, a whispering presence, heat and weight. She was standing in the middle of a ring of rocks, but this time there were no weeds obscuring the dance area. A sound that was part crickets and owls and frogs and part something else spread over the night breeze like music from an ageless source. Bare toes digging into the sparse soil, she lifted her head so she could pull the incredibly clean air deep înto her lungs. She felt her hair sliding over her shoulders and realized with no sense of shock that she was naked.

He walked toward her. This man, this warrior, wore no more than she did, and yet there was nothing vulnerable about his body. He strode out of the desert as if pride were as vital a part of him as the blood coursing through his veins. His mouth, firm and yet strangely gentle, briefly held her attention and kept her from losing her sanity in the rest of what he was. If he hated her for intruding on his land and his ancestors' land, his mouth gave nothing of that away. Although her need to take in his entire body and commit it to memory was all but overpowering, she deliberately turned her attention to his eyes.

His fathomless eyes.

She felt herself begin to shake, knew her reaction had nothing to do with cold. The moon emerged in the space of a heartbeat. It bathed the warrior with white-silver rays, feathers of light that slowly and sensually revealed muscle and bone, strength and power. Still, she couldn't stop staring into his eyes.

They were black. More than black, they seemed to have been alive forever and born at the earth's core. She wondered if he had his grandfather's eyes, maybe the eyes of the first Modoc to walk this land. In them she saw generations of a proud and resourceful people who understood the seasons and land and sky in a way that had been lost. His mind held the knowledge to gather and hunt throughout the summer so there would be enough to sustain the tribe through the harshest winter. His eyes knew to scan the horizon for the first glimpse of the winter birds that came to the vast waterways.

This warrior with his war-hardened body had hands made for hunting and fighting, for wrestling what he needed for life from land that offered nothing to more civilized people. Although they now hung along his naked thighs, the fingers curving in slightly, tendons standing out in stark relief beneath deeply tanned flesh, she imagined them cradling a child.

What would those hands feel like on her?

Made breathless by the question, she tried to step outside the dance ring, but the rocks expanded until she was trapped within the walls they'd become. Despite that, she could still see him and shrank a little from a gaze that told her he had the power to control these hard stones. She gaped in amazement and yet acceptance when he used his powerful hands to push one boulder aside so he could step inside.

She couldn't take her eyes off his thighs; a dusting of black hair draped flesh that had known years of heat and cold and physical life. Beneath the sheltering skin lived muscle and bone. His calves and ankles and feet were like the rocks that held her, made for eternity. She saw in them the runner he must be, the tireless hunter, protector of women and children.

He hadn't said a word. Still, she knew what had brought him here. The answer lay in the way he used his body, the arrogant strength of him, the blatant sexuality. Although she shrank from him, at the center of her being she wanted what he was. She faced the challenge and danger, the volcano. Their coupling would be as rough and wild as the land he called home. There'd be no gentle whispers, no lengthy foreplay. Instead, he would take what he needed from her, and she would do the same to him. Again and again until her strength gave out.

He lay on his back on his bear-pelt bed. Since awakening—he could think of nothing else to call it—he'd cleared the brush from the slit of an opening above him. Although it was too narrow for him to get his body through or give the enemy access, it allowed enough sunlight to enter during the day that he could easily study the countless etchings that were his people's history. At night, especially when the moon was full, the cave took on a silver cast.

Staring at the opening, he tried to imagine how the land his people called The Smiles Of God had looked when it was painted in the colors the creator had used to bless the moon. But although he gave thanks to Kumookumts for his generous gift to the Maklaks, he couldn't keep his thoughts on what the world must have been like when Kumookumts was creating it.

The woman filled him. He'd watched her today. Often her car—how he hated the harsh word—took her far from where he was, but she seemed to have no purpose to her wanderings, and several times came close enough that he could truly study her. Like so many of her kind, she carried that thing they called a camera. He would like to know what they did with their cameras once they were done pointing them. At least they didn't make a noise like a gun, and he guessed they weren't weapons because they often pointed them at each other.

She'd come here alone. He'd seen loners before, but there was something about her that made her stand out from the others. He'd tried to tell himself it was because he held her responsible for his awakening, but tonight, with Owl foretelling of death and his body restless with his man-need, he knew it was more than that.

He wanted her. He'd been awake for six moons and looked at women with lust and then acknowledged that he couldn't have them. He'd spent his lust-need by running until his lungs screamed. But what he felt for her was different. Like the power of a volcano, it held him in its fiery grasp and warned him that if he didn't run until his legs gave out, he might take her. If he did, she would alert the army men and they would kill him.

Was that Owl's warning? That his need for this woman would mean the end to him?

A growl of anguish rolled up from deep inside him and pushed its way past his lips. Shaking his head, he tried to deny the depth of his craving, but it was no good. He'd had a wife, a woman chosen by his family because of her social standing in the clan. Although she'd been older than him with interest in little more than digging camas bulbs and drying and storing them for winter, she'd let him climb atop her and he'd spent his energy inside her. She'd given him his son. For that he would always be grateful to her.

But she was dead and energy fed upon him the way lightning-born fire feeds upon trees and brush.

When another cry threatened to find freedom, he shoved himself into a sitting position. The moonlight now slid over his head and shoulders, carved his legs in shadowy relief. Gripping a calf, he thought about the great distance he'd walked today, not hunting as he should have, but searching for the woman again.

She carried herself as few of the enemy did. Instead of lumbering like a grass-fattened cow, she walked with an ease that drew reluctant admiration from him. She must spend much of her life, not in a small, cramped house, but where her legs could find exercise. She was tall, slender. Her hair flowed long and straight and dark down her back; the wind loved to play with it. He wondered where she'd come from, where she would go when her time here was done. He wondered what had brought her here. Most of all he asked himself what she'd thought when he showed himself to her.

She'd known he was watching her today. He'd seen the truth in the way she looked around, the wariness in her bear-brown eyes. After spending the morning pointing her camera at anything that moved, she'd joined some of the enemy. Even when she was surrounded by them, there were times when she scanned the horizon, and although he was so far away that he couldn't read the truth in her gaze, he'd sensed it in what her body said to him.

Her body, her hated woman's body.

He flopped back on his pelt but a moment later scrambled to his feet and strode to the nearest wall. Although it lay in complete shadow, he placed his hand flat over a drawing of men herding elk into a brush-and-rope enclosure. When the settlers came bringing their hungry cattle with them, the elk had fled to the mountains and there had no longer been a use for the enclosures. Still, this drawing, like others of Eagle and Bear and Frog and Weasel, of generations of Maklaks life and ways, remained. As long as they did, as long as he devoted himself to their care and protection, he wouldn't be alone.

Guided by instinct, he ran his hand over his people's entire history, ending with the winter when the army burned a small village and forced them to take shelter in caves under land capable of sustaining only rabbits and mice. The men, himself included, had searched for food to fill their families' bellies and when, in desperation, they'd killed some of the enemy's cattle, they'd known they were doing something that would never be forgiven. There were no drawings of that because what today's enemy called Captain Jack's Stronghold was far from this sacred place. There was only what he'd created last winter—proof that the Maklaks weren't all gone after all. He remained.

Alone.

She should have come to Canby's Cross yesterday. Loaded down with fresh film and a container of water, Tory left her car at yet another of the areas designated for vehicles. As she'd done yesterday, she'd chosen early morning so she could absorb the area's essence without interference from her fellow travelers. Yesterday, compulsively taking pictures and finding people to talk to, she'd kept this particular site at the back of her mind. However, as she was waking this morning, she decided to make coming here the first order of business. After all, this was why she'd come to the lava beds, and activity, particularly this activity, should bury last night's dream.

Maybe.

It took no more than a couple of minutes to walk the short distance to a large white cross designating where General Canby, her ancestor, had lost his life. She stood looking up at it, reaching out with her senses for something of the man. Out of the corner of her eye, she spotted distant Mount Shasta, the rising sun painting it gold and red. She became aware of closer landmarks, such as the rocky outcropping to her right, where armed Modocs had hidden while peace talks took place in the flimsy tent General Canby and the other peace commissioners had set up.

The army's headquarters, a hastily erected tent city, was several miles away. Even farther away was Captain Jack's Stronghold. From what she understood, the site where she now stood had been chosen because it had been seen by both sides as a neutral location.

But appearances were deceptive. The land lay in desolation all around her, perfect for friend and foe alike to conceal themselves while the principals argued and postured and tried to find grounds for compromise.

It hadn't worked. The Modocs, led by their chief, Captain Jack, and the young killer, Hooker Jim, had ambushed the whites. In a matter of minutes her great-great-grandfather and a minister had been murdered, and former Indian superintendent Alfred Meacham left for dead.

Not sure of her emotions, Tory turned in a slow, contemplative circle, trying to imagine what the general had seen and felt during the last morning of his life. She couldn't recall when she'd first heard of his role in history. As a child, she'd thought that being killed during an Indian war was a noble way to die. As she grew older, she occasionally thought of him with a sense of sadness because he hadn't lived to see his grandchildren. But most of the time he never entered her mind. Standing here now, she knew he would always remain a part of her.

Although she'd brought her camera with her, it dangled from her fingers. Taking a picture would reduce the experience to something one-dimensional when she wanted to keep her senses alive and alert.

Once again she turned to take in her surroundings, this time not so she could gain a greater perspective on her ancestor, but because *that* feeling had returned.

The wind blew across the grasses and flattened them until they reminded her of a vast gray carpet. Dark lava rocks punctured the carpet and created the only contrast in color. A faint gray haze coated the sky and made it difficult for her to gauge the height of the hills surrounding Canby's Cross. Still, driven by something she didn't quite understand, she imagined she could hear the impatient sounds of waiting horses, the clang of weapons, men's angry or nervous voices.

And through it all she knew she was being watched.

Chapter 4

Crouched behind a boulder, he watched the young woman run her hand over the white cross. When he'd first seen her car, he thought she might be leaving. If she did, he would be able to dismiss her from his mind, his thoughts, and think only of staying alive and safeguarding his people's legacy. If she did, he would never know what she smelled like, sounded like, felt like under him. Never know her name, or why his life had been linked with hers.

She hadn't left. Instead, she'd come to where the army leader had lost his life. More of the enemy than he could count had walked to the cross to aim their cameras at it, but she was simply standing beneath it, alone, looking sad and cautious, her eyes taking in her surroundings.

She sensed he was here. Everything about the way she moved and looked told him that. He could walk away from her, leave her with nothing except her suspicions. Or he could approach her and see if she again ran in terror.

Instead, he simply watched and absorbed and learned as she crouched at the cross's base and ran her fingers over the dried grasses growing there. She looked, he thought, almost as he must when he touched his son's blanket. Knowing that twisted his heart in a way he didn't want. She was the *enemy*. It was his right to hate her. But how does a man hate a woman who has crawled into his dreams?

Confused, he moved a little closer so he could study her features without being watched in return. As he did, she sprang to her feet and looked warily in all directions, her long, straight, shiny hair floating on a breeze. She was like others of her kind, stupid in the ways of the wilderness. If she had spent her life hunting, she would know to watch for birds or rabbits frightened from their hiding places. The birds and small creatures always told when something dangerous was about.

Still, he didn't ridicule her for her lack of knowledge; her body's language told him that she sensed something few did. Yes, many came here, but instead of letting the land tell them what had happened that cold morning, they read the talking leaves they'd brought with them or the plaques that had been placed in the ground back where they left their cars. As a consequence, they knew nothing.

She understood that yesterday waited in the wind, and for that he admired her. He wondered what she heard, whether everything was being revealed to her or whether she knew only the army's side. For her to truly understand this haunted place, she needed to hear the beating of Maklaks' hearts, feel their fear and anger. There was only one way she could know all that; only one person who could tell her— him. In his mind he imagined himself looking into her soft, dark eyes while his words brought his people back to life.

What was he thinking? She was evil! Muscles taut, he touched his hand to the knife strapped to his waist.

He'd been here that long-ago day, a silent and somber shadow among other shadows that had come to watch this meeting between his chief and the army leaders. Keintepoos had had no faith in the words the army men spoke because those men were ruled by their leaders who lived far away and made decisions about things they didn't understand, who hated and feared the Maklaks, who they had

never shared meat with. His voice hard with anger and
frustration, Keintepoos had agreed with the shaman Cho-
ocks and the killer Ha-kar-Jim that if the army lost their
leader, the others would flee in disarray. That was why
Keintepoos had killed the army man, but instead of going
back to where they'd come from, the army's strength had
grown until there was no escaping them.

Why did today's enemy grieve over the army man's
death? General Canby was one of those who'd helped bring
destruction to the People.

The woman was still looking for him, her attention split
between the cross and whatever she was trying to find in the
horizon. With her every movement, his awareness of her
grew, until it was as if she stood beside him, her hand extended to him in invitation and challenge. He felt his body
weakening, knew that if she placed her fingers on his flesh,
he would forget everything except his need for her.

Sucking in sage-sweet air, he gripped his lower thigh with
all the strength in his fingers until hunger for her was replaced by pain. Still, he knew that once the pain was gone,
she would again crawl inside him. For a moment of awful
and total weakness, he wanted nothing else in life.

Then, because he was a warrior in a world where it was a
lonely thing to be a warrior, he pulled hatred from deep inside him and fed upon it.

"*Blaiwas!* Eagle! Hear my cry. I seek your wisdom.
Should the woman live?"

Although he scanned the sky, he saw nothing. Again he
sent out a plea, secure in the knowledge that the wind
pushed his words behind him where she couldn't hear.
"*Blaiwas.* Eagle. You are my spirit and the truth lives within
you. This woman beats upon my body with fists I do not
understand. I must know. The owl call I heard last night. Is
it the cry of a mortal bird or Owl himself sending his warning? Am I to die? Is she?"

The sky remained clean and clear, hazed only slightly by
the morning, but as he continued to study it, he saw a small,
dark and familiar shape. Closer and closer the shape came

until he had no doubt that his spirit, Eagle, had answered. Directly overhead now, Eagle rode the wind in large, graceful circles until it was so close that he easily made out the knifelike tips of its talons. It flew with its head lowered, not because it sought food but because it had locked its eyes on him.

Eagle. *Blaiwas.*

Aware that the woman had taken note of Eagle, he sent out a silent message of thanks that his spirit had answered his call, then repeated his question. As if absorbing the whispered words, Eagle aimed its magnificent body upward in a powerful thrust. The coal-black bird with its pristine white head and tail nearly disappeared before jackknifing and heading down again. This time it aimed itself at the woman, coming so close that she ducked. A cry that seemed to come from the depths of the earth burst from Eagle and held, echoing.

"I see, heed your message. She is danger. I will not forget. Now go! Leave this sorrowful place. Return to Yainax, your mountain."

Eyes still intent on the eagle who she feared might attack again at any moment, Tory couldn't be sure whether or not she'd heard a male voice. Given the state of her nerves, anything was possible. An eagle, the largest she'd ever seen—heading right toward her! Coming so close, she swore she'd felt its body heat! Impossible, just like the voice. Then, taking her eyes off the disappearing eagle, she caught a movement near a boulder some fifty yards away. Except it was more than a movement, it was reality.

The warrior had returned. Standing in stark relief against the muted background, he seemed otherworldly and yet . . . Unconsciously using her researcher's senses, she took in his hard and healthy body, his sure stride, the proud lift to his head. He seemed unaware of anything except her, and as he came closer, her awareness of the rest of her world faded into nothing.

He might be a hoax—had to be a hoax. Still, her heart and nerve endings hinted at something very, very real. As yesterday, only a single strip of material stood between him and nudity. His slender weapon rode low and secure along his right hip, and his hand hovered scant inches from it, warning her that a sudden movement from her might propel it into his competent fingers. His long ebony hair absorbed the sun and played with the wind and made her ache to bury her fingers in it.

She tried to judge the speed of his walk to gauge how much longer she had before he was close enough to touch her, but she couldn't tear her thoughts from his body's beautiful flow. He seemed to be not arms and legs and shoulders and hips, but a single and perfect meshing of everything a man needed to be. His muscles came from the earth, from wrestling life itself from that earth. Watching him walking sure and flat-footed over hostile ground, she believed him totally in touch with his world. In winter he must have to dress to protect himself against the elements, but this wasn't a man for expensive wools and high-tech synthetics. When the elements drove him to shelter, he would clad himself in what the land around him provided. Remain part and parcel of the land, of eternity.

Through flared nostrils, she breathed of the virgin air and felt herself a virgin—waiting for the man who would take her.

"What do you want?" she asked when only a few feet separated them. *Why me?* Her entire being hummed with awareness.

He stared, not blinking, eyes like night and the distant past and maybe the future, as well.

"What do you want?" she repeated in a voice that shook and carried no strength. He had it all; maybe he had everything she would ever need.

"You do not belong here. Go."

His words were thickly accented, hard and rusty as if he hadn't spoken in years. She tried to concentrate on that, but what he'd said demanded her complete attention. "Don't belong?"

"I am *la'qi*. I say you must leave."

"La'qi?" She stumbled over the foreign word.

"Chief. Chief of this place. I say you do not belong here."

A hoax. Someone's idea of a huge joke. Except no laughter waited in his eyes, and she didn't see how even the finest actor could master his speech pattern, or look as if he'd been forged from the wilderness. It was as if his English came from a half-forgotten source, as if it had been years since he'd had anyone to talk to. "I don't understand."

Instead of saying anything, he placed his hand on her shoulder, the grip not quite painful but nothing she could escape. She swayed and then grew strong from his grasp. He, a stranger, had no right touching her. He would know that if he obeyed the laws she'd obeyed all her life, but his incredible eyes spoke of a world beyond her comprehension.

"What do you want?" she asked, although the weight and warmth and warning of his touch made talking all but impossible.

"For you to leave."

"You—you can't mean that." His fingers were heat and barely contained strength. It was as if he were pulling her into him with the contact, and if she didn't soon put an end to it, there wouldn't be anything left of her. "I—I have a perfect right."

"You are evil."

Evil? This wasn't funny. She'd tell him that just as soon as he released her thoughts, her everything. "Why are you following me?"

"You came to my land. Walked where you had no right."

"No right? Look—" She tried to slide out from under him, but he increased the pressure just enough to warn of pain should she resist. She still felt as if he'd wrapped invisible chains around her, but she was now beginning to put herself back together. No longer did she feel as if she might shatter. "Look, this is public property. I don't know what your game is, what you've been paid to pull this stunt, but it isn't working."

"I do not play games. I will know the truth. I *must* know. What is your name?"

"My name?"

"Yes. What do they call you?"

On the verge of telling him, she reached deep down inside for the tenacity that had taken her to the top of her profession. Risking a wrenched shoulder, she rocked back and ducked at the same time, effectively freeing herself. Still, she was left with the unsettling awareness that she now stood alone only because he knew he could recapture her whenever he wanted.

"You are the enemy." His voice rumbled over the words and made her hair stand on end. "Your presence is not wanted on Maklaks land."

"Maklaks?"

"Your people call us Modoc but we are Maklaks." He punctuated his words by tapping his broad, hard, dark chest.

Telling herself that this was an Oscar-winning performance, she quickly judged the distance between her and her car. Even if she'd been an Olympic sprinter, there was no way she could reach safety before his long legs ran her down. Her hands, dangling helplessly by her sides, felt like totally useless appendages. In truth, she wanted to clamp them around her throat to protect it from the deadly looking knife strapped to his hip.

"I ask you one more time. What is your name?"

"Victoria Kent," she said in a rush, her voice squeaking a little at the end. "Everyone calls me Tory. What—what does it matter? Look—"

"Victoria? Queen Victoria?"

He was talking about the queen of England. But the woman had been dead, what, nearly a hundred years? "N-no," she stammered. "It's a family name. My great-great-grandfather's daughter—"

"Kent? What is that?"

"My father's family's name. Look, I don't know what you're pulling, but it isn't funny. I've had—I've had just about enough of this.'' She made what she hoped was a decisive move toward the path leading to the parking lot, but before she'd taken more than two steps, he blocked her progress.

She looked up at him, struggled against the sense of size and strength that flowed around him and lost the battle. There wasn't an ounce of flab on him, no pale patches of flesh untouched by the sun. His arms and legs told of a man capable of any physical task demanded of him. She gauged his height at around six feet, an imposing piece of knowledge given that he was barefoot and still loomed over her. She glanced down at his feet; at least she tried to, but her gaze snagged on his perfectly molded thighs and calves. Tarzan couldn't hold a candle to him. He seemed utterly impenetrable, a tree of a man capable of withstanding the fiercest storm.

He took a step toward her and leaned down. When his nostrils flared and his eyes narrowed, she realized he was using all his senses to gain a better understanding of her. She shrank from his scrutiny but didn't try to escape again, not because she didn't want to, but because as long as he wanted it, he could keep her here. She wasn't up to the battle, especially not one with a man who made her feel newborn and weak and hungry simply by looking at her.

What did he see? Arms and legs, slender body, hair usually kept out of the way with a ponytail or braid, no makeup.

Rocking back on his heels, he again settled his hand on her shoulder. As before, lightning arched through her, and for a moment it took everything in her not to collapse. She opened her mouth, stood there with it hanging open, questions without words crowding what remained of her brain. She felt his fingers exploring, half panicked when his search brought his hand dangerously close to the swell of her breast. When he pulled back, she let out a sigh of relief; still, the loss left her feeling empty. He placed his thumb against the base of her throat. When she swallowed, it was as if a part of him had slid into her.

"What . . ." *Run! Yell for help!*

"You are part of him."

"Wh-what?" she stammered. He'd been silent for so long, communicating on another and utterly primitive level, that she'd forgotten he was capable of speaking.

"General Canby. You are part of him."

That, more than anything that had happened so far, chilled her. She fought the urge to slap his hand, fought to keep a grip on what little of her separate self remained. "What—I don't know what you're talking about."

"You carry his blood in your veins."

"Who told you that?"

"It is in your eyes and the beating of your heart."

Shaking, she ordered herself to wrench out of his grip, but her body refused to obey. Or maybe the truth was, she needed to feel his fingers on her more than she needed freedom and sanity. "It can't—you can't possibly know—"

"That is why you stood so long at the white man's cross. And why your eyes said things better left hidden."

"What things?"

"You are looking for a piece of yourself, Tory Kent. But you are wrong!" His grip increased. Then, before even more fear assaulted her, he relaxed his hold but still didn't free her. She felt wedded to him somehow, as if forces greater than both of them had determined that they would stand like this and say the things they were. "This man." He jerked his head in the direction of the cross. "He knew nothing of the hearts of the Maklaks. He had no heart, not one that understood those whose land this was."

"I—I don't know who you've been talking to or what they told you, but I don't appreciate how you're using a confidence."

"Con-fidence?"

The way the word rolled off his tongue turned it beautiful, rich and tantalizing. But that might be a dangerous deception she didn't dare let herself get lost in.

He *had* to stop touching her. That was the trouble—a stranger was taking liberties with her, breaking through that invisible and yet necessary space that surrounds a person and is broached only when intimacy is wanted. Amazed by her perceptiveness in the face of this—this, whatever it was—she took a deliberate step backward. As before, he let her go. Relief flooded through her and yet she felt lost, as if she'd lost her rudder in life somehow. An avalanche of words boiled inside her, but she couldn't sort them out enough to string any of them together. Her thoughts snagged on the eagle she'd spotted a few minutes ago, veered off into a memory of the one that had bedeviled her at the stronghold yesterday, splintered and resettled themselves on his knife.

His knife. Why hadn't she paid closer attention to it before? She studied the dusty black, opaque weapon now; concentrating on it was easier than gazing into his ageless and yet ancient eyes or learning how he had knowledge of her that he couldn't possibly. Although some of the knife was hidden by the cord holding it in place against his warm flesh, she saw enough. No machine had made it; she was sure of that. Thin chunks had been sliced from it to create something long and deadly. It lacked visual symmetry and yet she had no doubt that it was perfectly balanced. She guessed it was possible that this man or whoever he was in cahoots with could have found a slab of obsidian and gone through the laborious task of turning rock into a knife, but there was no reason for them to go to that much trouble.

Unless, this ancient-looking weapon was what the man used to keep himself alive.

Cold sweat coated her body and forced her to concentrate on what he'd just told her about herself. "Look," she began with less force than she wanted, "I don't know why you're doing what you are, but it's time for the joke to end. It's good—believe me, you're very, very good." *Too good.* "But—but I don't like it."

"You came here looking for a part of yourself in the wind and rocks."

What? How could he know . . . ?

"He is dead. You cannot find him." The warrior took a single, telling step toward her. "Leave me alone, Tory Kent. Your presence ended my forever sleep and I hate you for it. You had no right!"

He was saying that her coming here had brought him into the present? It was insane—insane and yet unshakable.

"This—this isn't fair," she blurted. "Please, at least tell me your name."

His features contorted, briefly revealing raw anguish. He glanced upward, and she wondered if he was looking for the eagle. Then, the gesture reluctant, he again settled his attention on her. "You are not Maklaks. You will not understand."

But I want to. I need to. "I'll try to pronounce it." She stumbled through the words, only dimly aware that she was no longer trying to tell him that he couldn't possibly be who he said he was.

"Not that." He sounded angry. "My name has meaning the enemy cannot understand."

The enemy. So that's what she was to him. "Try me," she whispered. "At least give me something to call you."

"Loka. I am Loka."

She took his name into her through her pores. It settled uneasily, a word from another time and culture, part of a proud and defiant people. "Loka." She still couldn't bring her voice above a whisper. "Is that all?"

"It is enough."

Yes, it was. Although the syllables felt harsh on her tongue, she found something solid and right about it. The whites of her great-great-grandfather's time had called the Modocs such things as Curly Headed Doctor, Hooker Jim, Captain Jack. She'd thought those tags both sad and obscene, was glad this man had escaped the demeaning labels.

"Loka." His name crawled even farther inside her. "Did your father call you that after you had your vision quest? Is that how those things were done?"

Although she'd asked as gently as she knew how, his body instantly became tense and hard and remote. "You know nothing of the Maklaks. How can you stand on our land as if you have a right?"

"I'm—I'm trying to learn."

"You cannot! Go. Now!"

But she couldn't. Something as old and permanent as the rocks themselves held her here. "Why do you hate me?"

"Why? You are part of the man who put an end to the Maklaks."

"No, he didn't!" She felt on the edge of losing self-control and couldn't think how to change that. "Your people killed him. Murdered a man of peace. That's why he was here, don't you understand that? He came to this awful place because his job was to try to put an end to the war. He didn't want any more killing. Do you think he wanted to jeopardize the lives of the young men under him? To be responsible for sons and sweethearts and fathers—he was doing everything he possibly could to keep things from getting any worse. And what happened? Some hothead—"

"Enough!"

The single word stripped her of the anger she didn't know she had until he'd unleashed it. Although she wanted to tell him that she hadn't said enough yet and might never fully expel her anger at a good and dedicated man's untimely death, Loka had leaned closer, and his eyes—his unbelievable eyes—were a tunnel to his soul.

"Were you here?" she asked, her voice so calm that it had to belong to someone else. "Did you kill him?"

Chapter 5

Silence spread between them like a slow-moving river. Tory stared up at this man from the past, thinking not of his role in history, but of the way the sun caressed his ebony hair. His eyes were morning and darkness, danger and challenge, and yet she wanted to experience everything about him. Yesterday she'd wished she was behind the wheel of a speeding vehicle because, maybe, that would kill the energy eating away at her.

Today he was what she needed.

No! The denial reverberated throughout her, coating everything except the truth about her emotions.

"Loka. Did you kill him?"

He hadn't taken his eyes off her, making her think there was no way he couldn't know what was going on inside her. She felt surrounded by him, but although she should want to run from his impact, the thought barely flitted through her before fading into nothing. "No," he said.

"No?" she repeated dumbly.

"My chief ended him."

My chief. "Were you there?"

"Yes."

Yes. The word had a life and strength of its own. It bore its way into her, but she gave no thought to trying to fight it. "Where?" she asked as if that mattered. "Where were you?"

Instead of pointing at the spot where she understood the peace tent had been, he indicated a rocky bluff maybe a quarter of a mile away. "The army said we were to stay in our camps, but we didn't."

What did you see, Loka? On that spring morning in 1873, what did you hear? Instead of giving voice to the questions pounding at her, she waited him out. It seemed as if he were drawing into himself, looking for the memory so he could spread it out in front of them. Looking up at him with the vast sky behind him and the wind and birds the only sounds in this universe they shared, she felt herself losing whatever grip she still had on the world she'd always known.

"The warmth felt good on my back. Cho-ocks and Kein-tepoos said that soon we would be able to move into the mountains because the snow was almost gone. I'd come with my brother and father and two cousins. We hid behind the rocks—the army men were too stupid to know where to look for us."

With every word, his voice sounded less raw and unused. There was music to it, a deep drumbeat that pulsed around and into her. She held on to the sound, the words, knew nothing except him and what he was telling her.

"Keintepoos came armed to the peace talk. He and Ha-kar-Jim had already decided what they were to do."

"Keintepoos? Ha-kar-Jim?"

"My chief and the brave your ancestor knew as Hooker Jim."

The Modoc chief. The man who'd killed her great-great-grandfather. She remembered a little about Hooker Jim, enough to know that the young Modoc had been almost single-handedly responsible for turning a tense situation into war. "Your chief listened to Hook—to Ha-kar-Jim? Loka, he was a killer. He murdered innocent settlers."

"Only after the army burned our winter village."

They weren't going to get anywhere arguing over who carried the greatest blame. "I'm sorry that happened," she whispered.

"So am I."

His tone carried a deep regret, making her wonder if he understood that that single act had eventually brought about his people's defeat. "The killing that took place here... Why didn't you try to stop it?" she asked.

"Stop? It was my chief's decision. I would not argue with him."

"But you knew he was wrong, didn't you? I mean, it's insane to think that killing a general would make the army scatter."

"Insane?" He frowned, then looked away as if tired of this conversation. "I tell you this, Tory Kent. Our children's bellies were empty. Our women cried themselves to sleep. A warrior does not close his ears to those cries. Cho-ocks said that an army without its leader will leave. We believed because we had nothing else to believe in."

Swayed by the force of his speech, she swore she could hear those despairing women, see the look of hunger in children's eyes. "Cho-ocks? Who was he?" she asked when it didn't really matter."

"Our shaman."

Curly Headed Doctor, at least that's what the soldiers and settlers had called him. "I—I read that he tried to protect the stronghold with a red rope. Did you really think that would stop an army?"

"You do not understand," he said forcefully. "Cho-ocks was a powerful shaman."

Not powerful enough, she thought, but didn't risk his anger by saying anything. How could she be arguing religious theory with a primitive? With someone who couldn't possibly exist, or be who he said he was? She wanted to look over at her car and assure herself that she hadn't fallen into some kind of a time warp, but would gazing at a hunk of metal make any difference?

"You do not believe me. You think Cho-ocks was like your leaders—weak. But you are wrong."

"I didn't say—what's happening here? Damn it, what's going on?"

He laughed at her outburst, the sound hard and filled with something that might be hate, but she thought went further, deeper. Frightened by the intensity of his emotions, she took a backward step with the half-formed thought that she needed to run.

He stopped her by planting himself between her and freedom. He'd done that before, and she remembered the mix of fear and anticipation that had filled her. The same emotions coursed through her, leaving her without the strength to do anything except fight them—and him.

"What are you?" he demanded. "Are you a shaman? Why did you end my forever sleep? Why?"

"Forever sleep? What are you talking about?"

Without doing more than shifting his weight from his left hip to his right, he put an end to her outburst. She waited, not wanting to hear what he had to say but sensing that this was why he'd approached her. "I do not belong here. This is not my time. But you walked onto this land, and somehow you reached me."

"Not—your time?"

"I do not want to be here. I want back my forever sleep."

A deep-felt melancholy rode his words. Irrationally, she wanted to fling it away and gift him with something to make him smile. "But you have destroyed that," he continued before she could think what she possibly might say. "And now I know why."

"You—you're not saying you were dead? Please don't try to make me believe that."

"How little you know! Death or life. That is all your people understand. But there is more. The magic of a great shaman."

Insane. Insane. But no matter how many times the words echoed inside her, she knew she'd never say them. Unbelievably aware of his presence, she waited for him to continue. "I was undead but not part of this time. I slept, the endless sleep of one who has taken the midnight medicine. It was what I wanted."

"Midnight medicine? What—"

"And then you came." Although the day was rapidly growing brighter, his eyes seemed to be getting even darker than they'd been at the beginning. "With *his* blood flowing in your veins, you stepped on Maklaks land and robbed me of my peace."

He'd been in some kind of suspended animation; was that what he was trying to tell her? The logical part of her mind screamed at her to tell him he was crazy for saying this, but she had no explanation for what and who he was—none that made any more sense than the explanation he'd just given her. Despite her undiminished fear of him, excitement began building inside her. It left her both weak and unbelievably strong. She was an anthropologist, a trained professional dedicated to unveiling the mysteries of the past.

This morning she stood face-to-face with the past.

She didn't realize her mouth had gaped open until he pressed the flat of his hand against it. "Stop! You will not laugh at me!"

"I'm not laughing," she said around the hard, warm prison. "I—Loka, I don't know what to think. To say."

He blinked. If he'd done that before, she hadn't been aware of the gesture. By the time he'd focused again, it seemed to her that he'd lost some of the anger that had nearly overwhelmed him. His hand dropped back by his side, briefly taking her attention to his knife—his ancient knife.

Nothing of today's world had touched him; that's what she couldn't deny.

"I want to understand," she whispered. "You don't— maybe this means nothing to you, but I'm an anthropologist." When he gave no indication that he had even heard the word, she shrugged, dismissing six years of college and another six years spent exploring and documenting extinct cultures. Loka wasn't extinct; that was all that mattered. "I want—'' She pressed a less-than-steady hand to her forehead. "You're the key. Loka, you're the key to the past."

"Let me go." When he sucked in a deep breath, his chest expanded until there seemed to be no end to it. "That is what I want of you. The only thing I want. Let me return to my son."

"Your son?"

His nostrils flared and she sensed he regretted telling her that. Fighting the cloud now swirling around her, she groped for him, touched her fingertips to his chest, pressed until his body's warmth became hers. While in college, a field project had taken her onto the empty land east of the Four Corners area. Through binoculars she'd watched a doe giving birth. For those few minutes the rest of the world had ceased to exist, and she'd never forgotten that she'd been privy to one of nature's wonders.

Loka was a wonder.

Although she'd already removed her hand from him, she had no idea how she could diminish the impact of that brief contact.

"I don't understand any of this. It's impossible. Impossible. And yet—'' She had to stop while the need to touch him again raged through her. "If you're who you say you are— What's locked inside you? What do you know of your people's legacy? Their legends and stories? I . . .'' A million fragmented thoughts continued to bombard her, but she couldn't make sense of any of them. She might be looking history in the face, and yet this man was no dry history lesson. He'd watched her great-great-grandfather being killed and celebrated his death. He'd listened to Modoc children crying from hunger, must have felt despair and hate beyond anything she could ever comprehend. "You—you say I had something to do with your being here? How can—''

"Silence! You do not know how to accept. You throw out stupid questions while I face the truth. I am here. I do not want to be. You have done this to me."

"No." She shook her head until she felt dizzy. "I didn't. I had nothing—''

"You carry his blood!"

As if that was all the explanation needed, he whirled away from her and stalked to a slight rise before turning around. "You are my enemy."

Tory had no idea how long she'd been driving, but if her gas gauge was any indication, she must have been behind the wheel for hours. Relying on instinct, she pulled into the parking area closest to the path leading to her cabin and cut the motor. Although there were a number of people about, she was aware of little except for a succession of dust devils being kicked up by an erratic and playful breeze. The hot afternoon made her feel lethargic, but she didn't dare stretch out on a bed because if she fell asleep, the questions she'd been battling might overwhelm her.

Loka.

A man who couldn't be and yet was. Who had become an integral part of her.

Feeling both vulnerable and charged with energy, she slipped out of the car. Thanks to the land's natural dips and curves, she couldn't see the park headquarters or campground. Yes, she shared the parking lot with a number of other vehicles, but it was all too easy to dismiss them and concentrate on the landscape.

It wasn't lifeless land. She'd learned that in a way no one else here possibly could. Because she was related to General Canby? Because, somehow, her presence last winter had awakened Loka?

Of course not! What was she thinking?

Hoax. The greatest hoax of all time.

But he'd known about her heritage, and his eyes had carried a message about a once-proud and now-defeated people.

When she heard her name being called, for a moment she thought that Loka had somehow overtaken her. Determined to take her back to his time, he would wrap his powerful arms around her and she'd be stripped of a will of her own.

Instead, the voice belonged to Fenton. "I've been look-ing all over for you," he said breathlessly. "Just got back from your cabin. I don't know why they built that thing way off in the sticks like that, or why anyone would want to stay there." He took another deep and slightly shaky breath. "I hate to say this, but you look as if you've been on a hard run."

She wasn't at all surprised by that. The last time she'd glanced at her reflection in the rearview mirror, she'd caught an image of too-bright cheeks and a too-pale mouth. She wondered if her eyes gave away anything of her turmoil and what she could possibly say if he brought that up. "Hope-fully I'm smarter than that," she said with what she hoped was a convincing smile. "I'm afraid that if I went jogging this afternoon, I'd wind up giving myself heatstroke. It sure is hot. What were you looking for me for?"

"You got a phone call. The way he talked, I knew it was important. That's why I've been trying to find you. His voice isn't as deep as I thought it would be. A man with that much prestige—well, I guess I've given him a larger-than-life image. Don't tell him I said anything, will you? I thought I handled myself pretty—"

"Dr. Grossnickle left a message for me?" she broke in when it looked as if Fenton would never run down.

"About an hour ago, maybe a little more. The connec-tion wasn't that good. Anyway—" Fenton pulled a piece of paper out of his pocket and handed it to her "—here's the number. Maybe you have it already."

She did but hadn't committed it to memory because she hadn't thought she'd need to get in touch with her boss during the few days she'd planned on being away. Glad for the reminder of a world she understood, she looked around for a pay phone. When Fenton said she could use the one in his office, she had a momentary hesitation about indebting herself to him, but the pay phone was close to the parking lot. It might be difficult to carry on a conversation.

Unfortunately, Fenton wasn't content to simply lead her to the cubbyhole at the rear of some kind of storage build-

ing that he referred to as his office. Showing absolutely no
hesitancy about what he was doing, he leaned against a wall,
watching her as she dialed the number.

The phone rang so many times before Dr. Grossnickle
came on the line that she was about to give up. As was usual
with him, he wasted no time in small talk. Yes, he was sorry
to inconvenience her, but she had told him where she was
going to be. He knew she'd want to hear this.

She listened while Dr. Grossnickle brought her up to
speed about the Oregon Indian Council's latest attempt to
block the university's involvement in the Alsea excavation.
Although the district court had ruled that the council had no
exclusive right to the site because it was on federal land,
they'd drawn up an appeal based on their original contention that the artifacts were sacred and thus should be entrusted to Native Americans, not outsiders.

"What really worries me is the way the press is reporting
things. They were so excited by the discovery—well, you
know what they were calling it, a vital key to the past. It
looks like they've changed their tunes and are saying we'd
be exploiting the site instead of giving it the reverent treat-
ment the Indians would. Can you believe that?"

Dr. Grossnickle continued detailing his objections, but
because she'd heard them so many times during the pro-
tracted legal maneuvers, she listened with only half an ear.
The university's official stand—with Dr. Grossnickle as its
spokesperson—was that only trained professionals should
be allowed to document the Alsea culture. Knowing what
could happen to a site if someone who didn't know what he
was doing trampled over it, she had no argument with any
of this. But there was more at stake than uncovering an ancient village. Whoever headed the project would see his career take a giant step forward. Already they'd been
approached by national magazines, and the three major TV
networks had all sent representatives. She wouldn't hazard
a guess at the chance for a Pulitzer, but she also had no
doubt that Dr. Grossnickle was in part motivated by what
this project would do for him professionally. All right, she

admitted. She had been motivated by the same thing: ambition. After all, it wasn't every day that a twenty-eight-year-old woman got her name linked with something that rivaled the locating of the *Titanic*.

As Dr. Grossnickle rambled on, she found herself staring out the tiny window to the left of Fenton's office. She couldn't see much, just a small chunk of the horizon and a butte so far away that it lacked definition. Still, the butte held her attention.

Did Loka ever go up there? If he did, what could he see? Loka—a key to the past.

Something was softening deep inside her. She couldn't put a name to it, could barely face the reason for its existence. She tried to tell herself that she'd been on a killer pace for so long that she hadn't had time for herself, but it was more than that. Loka had touched her. Left something of himself. That was what had crawled inside her, might never leave.

Barely aware that Fenton was still watching her, she walked from one side of the desk to the other so she was closer to the window. Dr. Grossnickle's voice was part and parcel of who and what she was as a professional. She'd been on the same fast track to success, so single-minded that the notion of having a personal life was a joke. Her mother had stopped asking about boyfriends. Her sister no longer teased her about getting into the baby business.

Coming here had put distance between herself and her professional goal. Now that it was no longer within reach, it seemed unimportant. Unnecessary. *Wrong.*

"Tory? Are you there?"

"What? I'm sorry. It must be the connection," she told Dr. Grossnickle.

"I said, when are you going to get here? We've got to work on our strategy. I'm meeting with the rest of the team tonight, but you're our spokesperson. We need you on-site."

She was their spokesperson because she was young and reasonably attractive, intelligent and articulate; she'd never had any delusions about that. But something had been missing from her life during these months of feverish activity, legal posturing, publicity and dreams of prestige. That *something* waited just beyond her reach, might exist in the distant butte.

Might have everything to do with a warrior named Loka.

"Give me another day or two," she heard herself say. "I promise I'll get there as soon as I can."

"Two more days? Damn it, Tory. This is important."

"I know it is," she said, although at the moment, if anyone had asked her why, she wouldn't have been able to answer. She tried to concentrate on what he said in response, but between the poor connection and the way a cloud now hovered over the butte, she lost his words. She repeated her promise to wind things up here in the next day or two and then ended the conversation.

Aware of Fenton's scrutiny, she hung up the receiver. But her gaze remained on the horizon. Her great-great-grandfather had looked at that same butte during the last months of his life. Had he, like she, wondered if it was worth dying to protect that hunk of rock, and why the Modocs had been willing to fight for it?

"I can't believe what I'm hearing," Fenton said. "He's depending on you. Dr. Grossnickle himself is depending on you."

"I know he is," she agreed before weighing her words.

"And yet you're going to hang around here?"

The sun would be setting in a few hours. When it did, the park would quiet down for the night. Creatures who spent the day asleep or hiding would venture out. Did Loka know that world as well as he did the one they'd already shared? A wave of sorrow raced through her with such strength that she felt sickened by it. Loka belonged in his time. With his son.

"What is it?" Fenton pressed. He'd shifted so he, too, was looking outside. "Rocks and weeds. That's all I've looked at for too long. There's got to be more than what we can see out there keeping you here."

"More?" she muttered, then forced herself to try to satisfy Fenton's curiosity. "I haven't had anything approaching a vacation for nearly two years. I'm beat."

"Yeah?" He didn't sound at all convinced. "Well, fine, but why here? If it was me, I'd be on my way to some resort for a little pampering."

"Maybe next time." She winced at how inadequate her response sounded, but The Land Of Burned Out Fires had wrapped itself around her heart and soul, and she had no will to try to break free. Loka, alone.

Maybe thinking of her.

Maybe hating those thoughts.

Chapter 6

The underground tunnel cared not whether it was day or night. Its temperature remained nearly the same in winter or summer, and there was an ancient smell to the air, which kept Loka from staying in it any longer than he had to. However, the long, narrow corridor led from Wa'hash, the sacred place, to another that had once also been sacred. He needed to stand in what the enemy called Fern Cave, needed to place his hand over ancient drawings and seek wisdom from his ancestors, so—maybe—he would understand the woman who'd touched his today.

When he reached the barrier Cho-ocks had blessed so long ago, he easily pushed the boulder aside and stepped into the large underground room. Because it was nearly dark, only the faintest amount of light reached the thick mound of ferns growing near the opening in the cave's ceiling. Although he'd told himself not to, he stared up at the metal bars the enemy had placed over it. When he first saw what had been done, he had wondered if someone had learned of his existence and was foolishly trying to keep him out. Now he believed that those who thought they owned this land feared that other strangers would come into the cave and steal the ferns. He still hated that the small opening had been imprisoned, but at least the enemy came here only infrequently and in small numbers.

It didn't matter. What had once been a holy place, a place of reverence, had been destroyed. From his hiding place, he'd watched the enemy stare at the drawings that ringed the rock walls or walk to the cave's dark corners. He'd heard some of them speak in awe of what they saw and felt here. They knew nothing. And Tory? Would she understand?

Confident that no one would drive out to the isolated area so late in the day, he crouched at the base of the ferns. They had been growing here for generations; his grandfather had told him so. They were part of Kumookumts's blessing, put here by the creator because he knew the Maklaks would care for them. He'd been coming here since his awakening, praying over them and asking Eagle to safeguard the fragile growth. Seeing the low rock barrier around the ferns, he cursed the enemy who'd placed it here. If they'd left this place they had no right to alone, there would be no need for barriers. And no risk to both the ferns and drawings.

Leaving the plants, he returned to the wall and touched a strong nail to the outline of a figure with its arms outstretched. He'd heard the enemy say many things about what it might be and had shaken his head at their stupidity. The answer was so simple: Telshna, the power of vision, had been granted to only a few since the beginning of time. This was the first Telshna, a man who'd brought his people to The Land Of Burned Out Fires because Kumookumts had told him what he'd created. Eyes closed now, Loka took his thoughts back through time to when the Maklaks ancestors came here. How blessed they must have felt when they gazed at the mother lake and uncounted birds that made the lake their home. His ancestors had dipped their hands into the cold, clear water for camas and wocas, dug into the soil for sweet epos, gathered fruit and berries to dry for winter, turned their attention to the mountains where deer and elk and mountain sheep roamed.

The world had been good then. Good and safe.

Fists clenched now, he sent up a prayer that was half anguish, half desperate hope. His people's heart still beat in his
breast; he alone understood the meaning beneath the ancient drawings.

Was it enough? Was that what Kumookumts wanted, for
him to safeguard the treasures of the past for as long as he
lived? But when he died—when he died, the legacy of the
Maklaks would die with him because he was the last, the
only believer left alive. Maybe it would no longer matter so
much if he could share this with *her*.

His sensitive fingers reaching automatically for the tunnel walls for guidance, Loka made his way from Fern Cave
toward Wa'hash until he reached the spot where the tunnel
broke through to the surface. Because he'd built a new ladder, he easily climbed out and into the night air. Although
a little of the sun's memory remained in the distance, he
could already see the first star.

"Yainax! Mountain of the gods. Do you hear me tonight? Do you know of my uneasy heart, thoughts without
answers? Yainax. I pray to you and wait for your guidance.
What do you want of me? Why am I alive? Alone. Why am
I here?"

He watched as several bats swooped and dived around
him. Bats were creatures of little consequence. Although
their presence meant that the land was healthy with insects,
they carried no wisdom in their tiny bodies. Knowing they
would sense his presence before flying into him, he lifted his
arms toward where the moon would make its appearance.
"*Blaiwas!* Eagle, hear me. I have stood face-to-face with the
one who brought me to this unwanted time. I ask you. If her
heart beats no more, will I feel peace?"

Peace. The word, the concept even seemed foreign to him.
His heart hadn't known rest since early childhood, when the
ranchers began allowing their cattle on land that belonged
to the Maklaks. He still mourned everything he'd lost in
life—his son most of all. If he had to walk his time on earth,

at least his heart should be quiet, not full of a woman, of her.

"*Blaiwas*. Eagle, you are my spirit. Wisdom lives deep inside you. When I became a warrior, you gave me your knowledge and guided my feet. In my grief I turned to you for guidance and you showed me that it was right for me to walk beside my son. Maybe he no longer needs me. Maybe that is why I have been torn from his side."

Taking a deep breath, he waited until his throat no longer felt clogged with emotion. He opened his mouth, but nothing came out. The day was gone; in the few moments he'd been here, heavy darkness had fallen over the land. He spotted a few stars, but the moon hadn't yet joined them. He still sensed the presence of bats. Crickets and distant frogs created an ageless hum, which took away a little of his loneliness and reminded him that the enemy hadn't stolen everything. Wolf might be gone. Grizzly might have sought more isolated places to live. But most of the creatures he'd known as a child still existed here, and he was grateful for that. Most of all, when he stepped inside Wa'hash, his son's memory waited for him; the walls spoke of his heritage.

Maybe it was enough.

"Eagle. I want quiet in my heart, for her to leave me alone. If I am to roam alone over The Land Of Burned Out Fires, I will do so. Kumookumts must have plans for me I do not yet understand. I want—I need understanding."

Although he couldn't see it, he gazed in the direction of the great mountain Yainax, where the sun god lived. Tory Kent knew nothing of the high court of heaven that was held there, of the Lemurians who waited on the sun god so he could concern himself with making decisions, with deciding right from wrong. "She does not belong here," he said aloud. "I do not want to see her again. She tempts me, makes it impossible for me to listen for wisdom from Kumookumts. Eagle, tell me. How do I strip her from my thoughts and body?"

Wise in the way of Eagle, Loka didn't grow impatient. Instead, he waited until the moon slid out from behind the night to spread its cool silver light over the land. Bit by bit, shadows took form until he could see Spirit Butte, distant Yainax, until he almost believed he had Telshna, the power of vision. When even individual sage bushes took on definition, he again lifted his arms to the heavens, thinking to call Eagle to him. Instead, he absorbed a sky filled with mysterious stars, the moon's beauty, the song made by crickets and frogs and thought.

She, Tory Kent, wouldn't be about tonight. He'd learned that the enemy feared darkness, that even their man-made lights didn't push back enough of the night to make them feel safe. She stayed alone in an isolated cabin; he'd learned that earlier today. Her fear wasn't as strong as many, and for that he had to admire her.

Maybe she was standing at her window staring up at the moon. Was it possible that the enemy saw beauty in Kumookumts's gift? If she did, what feelings did the night bring to her heart? Although he wanted to deny the thought and throw it from him, he wondered if she felt the same fullness he did when it was only him and this dark-quieted world.

There were many of her kind, so many of the enemy. It was an easy thing for her to reach out to a man. Still, she'd come here alone and would sleep alone. Why?

What would she be like in his arms, writhing under his man's body?

"Eagle! I do not want her inside my thoughts! Tell me! How do I rip her from me?"

His spirit rode to him on a wind known only to the great birds. Not breathing, he watched Eagle turn from shade and shadow into the form he knew so well. Wings outstretched, Eagle hung over him and made him ache with the desire to join him in freedom. "Eagle," he whispered. "You heard. You are here."

One slow circle became another and then another. "Eagle," he repeated, making no attempt to rid his voice of the sense of awe he always felt. "Do you bring your wisdom to me?"

A high, powerful scream forced the other creatures into instant silence. Wondering if Eagle intended the same message for him, he waited. An image of Tory staring upward as he was doing entered his mind; he wrenched himself free.

Again Eagle ruled the heavens with his voice. Loka continued to stand unmoving, absorbing, listening. Learning. When Eagle came lower, he saw that the bird held something in its talons. After yet another circle, Eagle abruptly released whatever it had been holding. It fell to the ground in front of Loka, but he didn't look down until he could no longer see Eagle.

His spirit had brought him a dead mouse. Squatting, he touched the creature to assure himself that it had recently been alive. He imagined its tiny heart beating in fear as the bird of prey clamped its claws around it, felt the same tearing pain the mouse must have felt.

"Is this your message?" he whispered into the night. "I will know peace only if she is dead?"

The question seemed to swirl around him and ignite a fresh pain. Still, because he'd lived his entire life believing and trusting in Eagle's wisdom, he clamped his fingers around his knife and drew it out of its resting place. The weapon felt heavy and sure.

If she couldn't sleep, she should have at least gotten up and read. And if it had been no more than a week ago, she would have used her insomnia to brainstorm what her role in this new wrinkle with the Alsea project should be. But this wasn't a week ago, and she wasn't the person she'd always believed herself to be.

Feeling too unsettled to fit within her own body, Tory threw back her covers and washed up as best she could at the makeshift sink. Because the day already showed signs of being hotter than the one before, she pulled on shorts and a loose cotton blouse with sleeves she could roll up when necessary. As before, she debated between tennis shoes and boots, angry at herself because she didn't seem capable of

making the most basic decision. In the end she chose the
tennis shoes because they were closer to where she sat.

She had to stop dreaming of him.

Upset because she'd allowed the thought to break free,
she filled a thermos, checked to make sure she had enough
film and stepped outside. Although she wasn't sure it would
make any difference, she went through the motions of
locking the front door. It was cooler out here than it had
been inside, and she started walking purposefully toward
park headquarters. It didn't matter how fast she went because her thoughts kept pace.

She couldn't block out dreams of him. He existed inside
her, his presence so strong that she knew fighting him was a
useless battle.

*This isn't like me. I should be logical and practical. I'm a
researcher! I don't want to dream. To feel. To want...*

At the last thought, she stopped and breathed deeply
several times. The smells here had already become a part of
her. She would miss them when she left—which should be
today.

But dry sage and mountain air weren't all she would miss.

What was he doing this morning? She could rummage
through the cooler she kept in her car for some fruit to go
with a granola bar, probably make a sandwich for lunch.
But Loka—she loved the way his name sounded—had never
been inside a grocery store. His food came from the land.
She shuddered a little at the thought of his bringing down a
rabbit or some other animal, but that was the way his people had sustained themselves for generations. Just because
her culture relegated meat processing to something done
behind closed doors didn't change reality.

She looked down, aware that she'd stopped moving. She
gazed out around her, listened to the lava beds.

She no longer questioned the truth of him. She could—
she guessed—argue and discuss and debate until, like a good
attorney, she'd thrown so much doubt on what her heart
accepted that it would be silenced. For hours, days maybe,
she'd go along smug in the knowledge that logic once again

had the upper hand. Loka the warrior couldn't possibly exist.

But eventually her heart would demand that its own brand of logic be heard and she would again believe. How much simpler it was to simply accept.

Somehow, the Modoc, the Maklak called Loka, had traveled through the years, bringing his world with him. He'd joined her in her time.

Only, they weren't truly connected—except by her ancestor, who was responsible for the limbo Loka found himself in. She felt guilty.

By concentrating, she forced herself to start moving again. Still, she wanted to remain in her own brand of limbo. If she spent the day here where no one else seemed to care to come, would she somehow find that channel through time? Could she enter his world? Could she—could she possibly understand the heart and soul of his time?

Tears burned her eyes but didn't surprise her. How was it possible for a dedicated anthropologist to toil at her trade for years without realizing that understanding primitive people had nothing to do with documenting where a shaman stood in a tribe's social structure, what foods they ate, who raised the children? It didn't matter what names those people called their gods, what rituals were performed, who was allowed to be part of spiritual ceremonies and who was excluded.

What mattered was that being alive and believing had been one and the same for the Maklaks who once walked this land. The sun wasn't just the sun; it was life itself. And because it was, everyone revered the fiery heat. A youth went on a spirit quest, not because his elders had done the same thing and it was part of becoming a man, but because he didn't believe himself capable of reaching manhood without his own spirit to guide his journey.

Moaning under her breath, she put an end to philosophical considerations and turned her head so the breeze caressed her cheek. Coming to a slight rise, she spotted the small lot where she'd left her car. There were several vehi-

cles near it, probably belonging to those staying in the
nearby campground. They were strangers; she'd never belonged to a tribe, never been part of a group that depended
on each other for survival.

"I thought," she admonished herself, "that you'd had
enough of philosophy for one day." When she realized she'd
spoken aloud, she looked around, but except for a tiny,
brilliant yellow bird, she was still alone.

Unless Loka was watching her.

She should have known that the rig bearing the park's
logo belonged to Fenton. If she'd been the slightest bit cautious, she might have been able to avoid the man. However,
because she'd been incapable of freeing herself from her
thoughts, she had no choice but to acknowledge him when
he joined her in front of her car.

"You're out bright and early," he said. He glanced down
at her breasts, her waist, her legs, the look coolly apprais-
ing. "Not as easy staying out there as you thought it would
be. Is that it?"

Because the real explanation was incredibly complicated
and not at all his business, she tried to change the subject by
asking why he was already at work.

"I was hoping to catch you before you took off." He
nodded at her camera and canteen. "I thought you might
pack up and get on the road at first light. I was wrong."

"Yes," she said. "You were." She thought about walking around him but guessed that trying to avoid him would
only make him more determined.

"I still don't get it." He sounded as if she'd deliberately
tried to disappoint or deceive him. "What if Dr. Grossnickle
decides he can't wait for you? Can he fire you?"

"He won't," she said although her boss had the power to
do exactly that.

"You sound pretty sure of yourself. What is it? You've
made yourself so valuable that it would never enter his
mind?" Although they had the area to themselves, he leaned
forward and lowered his voice. "That's exactly what I'm

trying to do here. Hey, we've all got to look after number one, don't we?''

She wasn't quite sure what he was getting at but wasn't going to make the mistake of asking. ''It's that kind of world,'' she said, figuring she couldn't go too far wrong with that.

''Ain't that the truth.'' He brushed an insect off the side of his neck. ''The gnats were out in force last night. Damn, I hate those things.''

She hadn't noticed an insect invasion but maybe she'd been too preoccupied. Before she could come up with any observation about things that crawled or flew or both, he gave her what she'd be willing to bet was a calculated smile. ''I'm glad I met you. Really glad. I don't know if I told you, but I majored in archaeology until halfway through my junior year. That's when the light bulb went on and I realized the chance of making a name for myself in that field was somewhere between damn little and none.''

''Well, no. It's not a field to get into if your primary goal is to get rich.''

''And it is. Rich and famous,'' he said with a laugh. ''However, that isn't as easy as I'd like it to be. All I can do right now is hope I come up with the right combination that'll get me noticed, and rewarded. I'll tell you, if I was sitting on the gold mine you are, I'd be jumping through every hoop there is to make sure I'm riding the crest of the wave.''

Fenton's speech was riddled with clichés. She could only hope that his presentations were more original. ''I'm not sure we've reached the crest yet,'' she explained. ''Maybe we'll never get everything resolved.''

''Exactly!'' His eyes glittered as if she'd said the most brilliant thing he'd heard in a year. ''I've been thinking. I know how to grease a few squeaky wheels. Did I tell you, my uncle's a state senator. That's how I got this job—a little pulling of the strings. Not much, I want you to know. I can do it. Damn straight I can. But it doesn't hurt to have someone capable of getting your name to the top of the pile, you know."

"No, it doesn't."

"Sure, my uncle is in California, but Senator Baldwin knows a lot of Oregon's politicians. What I'm saying is, if I ask, he'll tell me who has pull in these kinds of things. A little behind-the-scenes negotiating on my part and that Indian organization will pack up its bags and go home."

Not only didn't she believe that, but she seriously doubted that Fenton had enough clout to influence the politicians who'd deliberately been taking a neutral stand on things. Wondering if Fenton's uncle hadn't gotten him this job because he wanted his nephew out of his hair, she pointed out that this was an issue for the courts, not politicians. Fenton had just begun to tell her she didn't know what she was talking about when a battered, once-blue pickup with a pathetic excuse for a muffler pulled into the parking lot. Instead of turning off the engine, the driver sat behind the wheel of the roughly idling vehicle.

"Damn him. He never gives up."

"Who?" Tory asked, glad for any change in the conversation.

"Him." Fenton jabbed his finger at the driver. "Black Schonchin. He lives over by Tulelake on some farm he and a bunch of his relatives own. He's been nothing but trouble."

Tulelake was the nearest town, a small ranching community with little to show for itself beside a couple of cafés, a hardware store, post office and grocery. Even from this distance she could see that the elderly man was Indian. "Black Schonchin," she said. "That's an unusual name."

"I think he made it up, not that you'd get him to admit it. Apparently some Modoc named Peter Schonchin was the last survivor of the war. Black must have decided he'd rather go by that instead of whatever name his parents had. As for the Black, there was a Black Jim who got hung alongside Captain Jack."

"Then he's Modoc?"

"Oh, yeah. He never lets me forget it. Damn, he's going to sit there until I talk to him. Look, don't leave, will you? I hope this won't take long."

Although Fenton hadn't indicated he wanted her to join him and Black, neither had he told her she couldn't tag along. As they reached the pickup, Mr. Schonchin turned off the engine. After kicking and sputtering for a good half minute, the truck finally fell silent.

Mr. Schonchin kept his attention on Fenton, giving her the opportunity to study him. If she'd been an artist, she'd want to paint him. His sagging, leathery, expressive face spoke loud and clear of a life spent out-of-doors. His eyes seemed locked in a permanent squint. His cheeks looked as if they'd been rubbed with sandpaper until they'd hardened in self-defense. Much of his hair was gray but enough black remained that she could guess he'd once had rich, midnight hair like Loka.

Black Schonchin wouldn't understand the concept of conditioning creams, of sunscreen, of sunglasses. Neither would he see any reason to go inside just because the air had a wind-chill factor of minus twenty. The way she guessed he saw things, if a man made his living from the land, he lived with that land.

"How'd you know to look for me here, Black?" Fenton asked in a tone that showed no respect for the Modoc's age. "I don't have time for you today."

Black regarded Fenton for a long time before moving so much as a muscle. "You say this because you hide from the truth."

"Your version of the truth. Come on, Black. You know how I feel about this nonsense of yours."

"It is not nonsense." Black pointed at the sky, his eyes following the line of his finger. "The truth is written in the stars. You cannot see it because you aren't Modoc."

"You've got that right. I thought we had this out earlier. I'm *not* about to keep people out of certain areas while you and the rest of your group poke around. Restricting tour-

ists in any way, shape or form is the last thing I'm going to
let happen."

"A man who walks blindfolded will never see the sunrise."

"Where do you get these sayings of yours? You must stay
up half the night thinking of new ones. Look—" Fenton
made a show of studying his watch "—I told you the last
time you were here, if you want to talk to me, you've got to
make an appointment. You must have left Tulelake before
dawn to get here this early. Too bad it was a wasted trip."

"Maybe. And maybe I saw *him.*"

"Don't get going on that, Black. I don't have time. I will
not, repeat, I will not close off the butte."

"*He* was there this morning. *He* wants back the Telshna
place."

"Telshna?" Fenton frowned, then waved an impatient
hand at Black. "Never mind. I'm not interested in whatever Modoc word you've conjured up this time. This spirit
warrior business of yours has gone far enough." On that,
Fenton turned away from the pickup. When his gaze landed
on Tory, he repeated his desire to talk to her, then asked
whether she planned on leaving anytime soon. She gave him
a noncommittal answer, knowing all too well that that
would only feed his curiosity. Although he stared at her until she felt uncomfortable, she didn't elaborate, and he finally muttered something about having a meeting to attend.
After getting her to promise to hook up with him later in the
day, he got in his rig and drove off.

Although it took a great deal of self-control to wait until
he could no longer see her in his rearview mirror, Tory
pointedly didn't move until Fenton was out of sight. "I'm
sorry he was so abrupt," she told Black. She wasn't sure
what she was going to say next; what mattered was finding
a way to get him to elaborate on what he'd said earlier. "It
sounds as if he really was in a hurry. Strange, he didn't say
anything about it to me."

"He doesn't want to talk to me."

"Well, I—maybe he doesn't."

"I know he doesn't. It's all right. I feel the same way about him. Actually, I was just trying to bug him."

Tory smiled. She had expected something ancient and profound to come out of the Indian's mouth. "I think you succeeded."

"Good. He doesn't like me, and I don't like him."

"Oh."

"Don't let it bother you, miss. We can't all get along with everyone else. Besides, the less he involves himself in what we're trying to do, the better. I don't trust him."

"Don't trust him. Why not?" she asked although it was none of her business.

"White man speak with forked tongue." Black smiled briefly. "You're staying here, are you?"

She was going to have to revamp her impression of old Indian men. Whatever he was, he was no stoic. She explained, briefly, about having rented the cabin, but said nothing about her ties to General Canby. When Black reached for the ignition key, she placed what she hoped was a casual hand on the open window. "You were talking about someone Fenton referred to as a spirit warrior. What was that all about?"

A moment ago Black had impressed her as a man of today, a man comfortably carrying on his share of a casual conversation with a stranger. Now, although it might only be a trick of the morning light, she swore there was new life in his eyes. His mouth worked, but he didn't say anything, telegraphing to her that he hadn't expected the question and didn't know how to respond.

"It just sounds interesting, that's all." She hated sounding as if she were stumbling through her words, but couldn't think of any way to change that. "I was at Captain Jack's Stronghold the other day. There—" *Careful.* "It's an impressive place with a strong sense of history."

"Hmm."

"Look, I'm an anthropologist. It's in my nature to be interested in these things."

"Anthropologist. What are you doing here?"

This man kept her off-balance with his changing moods. She now swore he didn't think any more of her than he did of Fenton. "A vacation. I've really had my nose to the grindstone lately."

"You're not here to do research?"

The question sounded innocent enough; it was the tone behind his words that warned her that no matter what she said, he wouldn't take it at face value. "I promise. No research. Just call it a busman's holiday. I'm so glad I took the time to—"

"What are you doing?"

"I just told you. I'm on a vacation."

"No." All hints of sociability had been stripped from his voice. His eyes, although still nearly hidden beneath dry, loose flesh, made her feel like a bug under a microscope. "What is your job?"

She could have lied. Probably should have come up with anything except the truth. Except she wanted this old Modoc to know that she wasn't afraid of him. When she mentioned the Alsea project, she swore she could feel his distrust, his hate even envelop her.

"You're one of them. One of those trying to steal what doesn't belong to you."

"That's not it at all. We're all highly trained researchers. We know what we're doing. Do you think we want the site to be ruined? That's why we're determined to do it right, so there are no—"

"It isn't yours. The village belongs to those whose ancestors understood the land."

Halfway through a rejoinder, she forced herself to stop. Not sure what she could say to salvage the conversation, she took a moment to survey her surroundings. People were beginning to stir at the campsites. A dog yapped and a baby squalled. "I don't believe that only Indians can understand the land. When I was at the stronghold, I asked myself what it had been like for the Modocs that winter. Their babies must have cried. Every morning they had to go in search of water. The constant foraging for wood was—"

"And food. Without the cattle they stole, they would
have starved. I've seen the work of anthropologists. Fenton thinks because I am old with dirt under my nails that I'm
a stupid man, but he's wrong. I know what you and the
others are trying to do."

"Then you know we're trying to salvage what's left of the
past. I don't understand why you're against us."

"Because you put my people's heritage in boxes."

"Boxes?"

"The past is not something to put labels on. You write
books that say this and that and the other thing about my
ancestors. That isn't right. My heritage isn't about what my
grandparents' grandparents called their gods and how one
became a shaman. How do you know? Were you there?"

"Of course not, but—"

"You look at a carved mask or boat and decide that those
things were used in a certain way, but because you weren't
there, you will never know. A lie told and retold becomes a
lie believed by all."

"It isn't a lie. We—"

"No! Listen to me. I was educated at a white man's
school. I live in the white man's world. It's not what I want,
not when my eyes and heart are Modoc. But my ancestors
are dead. Because they were torn from this place, I'll never
know the truth about them. The past is not a picture to be
placed in a book. It is belief and nature, the land and creatures living on it speaking to a boy and guiding him into
manhood. History should be free to live in the air and fly
with the wind so each of us can breathe in the air and find
our own truth."

She wasn't sure what he was getting at, and yet it made a
terrible and proud kind of sense. "The truth," she whispered. "Is that why you're here this morning? Because you
want to learn the truth about this spirit warrior?"

Jaw clenched, Black stared over the steering wheel until
she despaired of getting any kind of answer from him. Then:
"Your heart is white. More than that, it's the heart of one

who seeks labels, not understanding that which lives in the earth and on mountaintops. You'll never know the truth about what I seek."

Wouldn't she?

Chapter 7

So many men had died here. Staring out at the windswept expanse, Tory tried to imagine what that long-ago spring day had been like. Historians considered the ambush that had taken place here to be one of the greatest examples of Indian military strategy. But had those historians stood on this spot and thought, really thought, about the young men who had lost their lives on this barren land?

Turning in a slow, deliberate circle, she went back in time to that fateful day not long after General Canby had been killed. The Modocs, for reasons she didn't fully comprehend, had left their stronghold and had scattered—or so the soldiers thought. A number of troops had taken off in search of them. Why they had chosen a gully to climb into was something else she didn't understand. What she did know was that the decision had been a fatal one because the Modocs had snuck up on the soldiers while they rested. The first shots had sent the men into panic. She didn't blame them for trying to run back to headquarters; the tragedy was in how few had made it.

A sense of unease crawled up her spine, and she lifted her hand to shield her eyes, staring intently at anything that might hide—hide what, Loka? It was still early enough in the day that no other visitors had yet made their way out here. The thought that she was over a mile from the road and that the path she'd come on was narrow and rocky increased her sense of isolation. If Loka, man of mystery and intrigue, stood beside her, would she still feel this way? Maybe—maybe it wasn't Loka at all who was filling her with apprehension.

The wind brought history with it. It was as if it had never lost touch with the sounds of wounded and dying men, terrified horses, desperate warriors. If she remembered right, the day of the ambush had been warm, the sky cloudy but not threatening. The soldiers must have thought the war was coming to an end.

Had the solders laughed and sung that day? Surely there'd been talk of what they'd do once they went home. Maybe they were thinking of sweethearts and wives, the relief of being able to go to a more civilized place. And then—

And then death had visited them.

Had Loka been part of that? She'd asked him if he'd been among those who'd attacked her ancestor and he'd told her no. She'd believed him, but what about here at what was now known as the Thomas-Wright Battlefield? Was that what had put her on edge—the memory or soul of a soldier searching for a peaceful resting place?

So many things assaulted her senses and emotions. She felt as if her entire being had been rubbed raw. She was sensitive, so damn sensitive to what had happened back then. She didn't want it this way, didn't want to think about resting men being stalked by relentless braves.

Damn you, Loka. Damn you for being part of this slaughter!

"You do not understand."

A tidal wave of emotion slammed into her, spun her around. She stared up at Loka, not in shock but fascination. That he'd been able to approach her without her knowing didn't surprise her. After all, this land was his, and he was as at home here as any rabbit or antelope. "What don't I understand?" she mouthed as he stepped over a rock. She ached inside, an ache more all consuming than anything she'd ever experienced. She felt starved, a breath away from death. If he didn't touch her—

"Why we did what we did here."

The realization that he alone knew what had compelled the Modocs to commit an act that they must have known would be avenged gave her something other than him and the raw sensuality that was him to enter her mind. "Why, Loka?" she whispered and dropped cross-legged to the ground. He stood over her, a living wall of a man full of challenge and promise. "The Maklaks killed General Canby, but the soldiers kept coming. Surely you didn't believe that killing a few men here would save you."

"You do not understand," he repeated.

She wanted him to sit beside her, but he remained on his feet, dominated her with his size and the power in his voice.

"Have you ever watched a doe with a fawn? If her fawn is being hunted by a predator, she will tell her fawn to run. She will lead the way, pacing herself to her baby's strength. It is not a doe's way to fight—her legs are swift because Kumookumts created her to run. But if a wolf overtakes her fawn, she will turn and fight. We were like that doe."

"But you weren't trapped. You could have gone on running."

"Where? How long?"

He asked his questions so softly that for a moment they didn't register. She looked around, thinking to point at the distant hills, but before she could, full realization sank in. "You're saying—you're saying that your children were like that fawn, aren't you? They couldn't run anymore."

"And some of our women and the old people." He lowered himself to the ground, the movement more graceful than anything she'd ever seen in her life. He sat opposite her on the hard, rapidly heating earth. Morning sunlight caressed his flesh, glistened off his chest and shoulders. An image of her hands gliding slowly, reverently over his flesh settled inside her and refused to leave. She wanted to concentrate on what he was saying. Damn it, it was vital to her understanding of him. But she could barely think around him, not when he looked the way he did. When she reacted the way she did.

"They were exhausted?" she finally thought to ask. "But they hadn't been on the run that long."

"No." The muscles around his mouth tightened and then relaxed. In his eyes, she saw the effort that took. "Not running. But we were a proud people. We built good homes, strong homes to keep us warm through the winter. It was not our way to burrow into caves like bears. To spend moons living underground like frightened animals—" Again his jaw clenched. "We could no longer go to the sacred butte for our spirit quests. The new ways—the things we had been doing since the white men came—they had brought us heartache. We wanted back the old ways, to be close to Kumookumts again, to feel Bear and Wolf's wisdom, but how could we be as we once were if we were not free to live on the land our creator had given us?"

She had no answer for him, or maybe the truth was, she understood him with a depth she didn't believe possible. Yes, they were weary of being trapped at the stronghold, of what must have been a Spartan diet. But it had been more than that. "You had always felt yourselves a part of the land. And now that was being denied you."

He'd been staring at the ground, his eyes unfocused. When he looked up at her now, she saw something she hadn't seen in him before. Was it possible that he trusted her? That she'd said something that resonated deep inside him?

Wanting that, praying for that, how could she not believe in him?

"I met a man this morning," she whispered, not sure what, if anything, she could say. "A Modoc. He said the same thing, that an Indian's belief is part of who and what he is. That the land and sky are as essential to who he is as his strength or intelligence. I don't think I ever understood that before."

"And now you do?"

"I'm trying." He might disappear. If she said the wrong thing, he might evaporate like the morning mist. She didn't think she could bear it if that happened. "You're making it possible."

A darkness that seemed to originate from deep inside him slid slowly over his features. She watched in fascination and fear, desire for him lapping through her body, her mind even. She *needed* to feel his arms around her as much as she needed air in her lungs, and yet it wasn't for her to make the first move. "Please," she whispered. "What are you thinking?"

"How long it has been since I have spoken to anyone."

Desperate to stem the tears that threatened to engulf her, she breathed in deeply. This was his air. He knew its smell as intimately as he knew the land around him. He was sharing it with her this morning, and her gratitude knew no bounds. "What was it like?" she asked. "When you first woke up, what was it like?"

"Sorrow."

Sorrow. "Loka, please." She held out her hand but let it drop without touching him, because if she did, she would be lost. "Tell me everything. Please. You aren't alone. I'm here—you can talk to me. What was it like? You saw what had happened to the land and—"

"No!" He straightened, his eyes so fierce that she thought only of him and the eagle she'd seen yesterday. "It was more than that. So much more."

"I don't understand. I want to understand."

Although he remained silent, she sensed that she'd said something dangerous, something he didn't want to hear.

Fascinated in the way of a bird staring into the eyes of a stalking cat, she watched as he reached for his knife and pulled it free. When he held it up for her to see, the sun briefly kissed it. He leaned forward, challenging her with his body. Somehow she found the courage not to move; or maybe the truth was, she would never be able to pull herself free from him. The knife came closer, an extension of him, keen and ancient, both artifact and weapon. She knew what it was like to be incapable of movement. To have her life held in another's grip.

"Loka," she whispered. "I can't give you back what you had before I arrived. I wish I could." That wasn't the truth. She would never want him to return to the slumber that had been his existence. "I believe in you. It's insane. There's no way you could possibly be who and what you are and yet—"

"Cho-ocks."

The shaman who'd given him whatever it was he'd taken so he wouldn't have to leave his son. She wanted to tell him that that was impossible, remind him that the shaman's red rope hadn't prevented the army from storming the stronghold, but Loka stood as living proof of Cho-ocks's power, didn't he? Maybe—no!

"You should not have come out here this morning. Surely you knew I would find you."

She hadn't known, but she had hoped. "Maybe that's why I came."

He still held his knife in his competent fingers. Looking at the strength in his arm, she had no doubt that her life would end in a single movement if he so desired. But if he'd come here to kill her, he would have already done it—ended whatever it was that existed between them.

"I sensed—" Barely moving, she indicated the barren ground around them. "As I approached, I sensed the presence, maybe it was the ghosts of the soldiers who'd died here. I felt their fear and pain."

"Yes."

Yes. With that single word, he was acknowledging that something brutal had happened on this site. She wanted to leave it like that, to place the burden of the massacre on the Modocs, but she couldn't. "Loka, if it was in my power to give the Modocs back their land, I'd do it. I'd have already done it."

He blinked, said nothing, his essence a living curtain around her.

"But we both know that isn't possible. I want—" No, she couldn't tell him that, couldn't lay herself naked and vulnerable before him. If only she could stop shaking, stop thinking about what could be between them.

As if her hand no longer belonged to her, she watched it reach out to touch his chest. The day had just begun to heat up, but she could already feel its warmth in his flesh. Maybe, she thought, the warmth came from inside him. He was alive then, alive and here. With her.

Made weak by the thought, she increased the pressure on his chest until his beating heart seemed just out of reach. She looked up into the eyes of this man who couldn't possibly exist and yet did. He stared down at her, his emotions unfathomable. It seemed to her as if the world had slowed down, maybe stopped entirely for them. She wanted to run her fingers over every inch of him because maybe then she would understand. Instead, she continued the fragile contact and let her eyes speak for her.

The breeze eased over his flesh, ruffled his long, glossy hair, spoke of unsettled souls and regret, said something about promise and tomorrow. She felt on the verge of tears and yet far beyond that, as if what was happening between them eclipsed any emotion she'd ever known. Life itself seemed to hang suspended between them, waiting—waiting for her to understand.

She heard a sound, dismissed it because only he mattered. But when she saw the look of utter concentration in his eyes, she forced herself to listen. The howl seemed to ride on the wind and yet control it at the same time. She'd seen so many emotions in Loka's eyes. They were by far the most expressive part of his expressive body. He'd become almost childlike in his fascination, a boy-man hearing something essential to his existence.

Again the howl touched her nerve endings, the impact more intense this time. "Wolf," she said, unaware that she'd been going to speak until she heard her voice. "That's a wolf." But it was impossible because wolves had been extinct from this part of the country for decades.

"Wash."

"Wash," she repeated, wondering if that was Modoc for wolf.

"Wash, the trickster coyote. Maybe she . . ." His voice trailed off when the haunting note again rode the windways to them. "No," he muttered. "Not Wash."

A wolf, then? Was that what he was saying? Fighting his continued impact on her senses, she scrambled to her knees. He stood, held out his hand and she took it. He effortlessly helped her to her feet and she waited beside him, feeling proud, feeling part of him and the land he commanded.

"I want it to be like this again," she managed around the great lump in her throat. "For it to be the time of the wolf. If there was any way I could make that happen . . ." She wanted, needed to say more, but nothing sorted itself out inside her. She stood shoulder to shoulder with Loka and looked out into the distance with him. He smelled of the desert, pungent sage, heated lava rock, clean, mountain tainted wind. Until this moment, the rational, logical part of her had continued to disbelieve his existence. He couldn't possibly be who and what he was. He couldn't! But his scent changed that.

That and the wolf call.

Belief as solid and clean as what she now felt toward him seeped into his features, solidified and became something beautiful. He had no doubt about Wolf's existence, not a lean, gray predator that had somehow eluded man's rifles, but a spirit-creature unhampered by the rules that dictated her existence.

Wolf was like Loka, an essence in and of itself.

He hadn't moved a muscle since helping her stand, and she understood his desire to absorb and comprehend what was happening. But she needed more from him. She wanted to take his knife and tell him that there was no need for him to carry a weapon on this peaceful morning, but she didn't.

Couldn't. If someone, anyone, learned the truth about him, he might be in danger.

That thought, more than her body's need, propelled her into action. Lacing her fingers through his, she brought his hand up to cover her breast. The instant she did, a lightninglike shock surged through her. She swayed, unable to hide her reaction. Instantly he stopped listening for Wolf and focused on her. Questions, and a desire that rivaled hers, imprinted themselves on his features, tested her self-control as it had never been tested. "Do you feel my heart beating?" she asked when she could force herself to speak.

He nodded, the gesture languid as if aware that his power over her had no limit. "Fast and strong. Like that of a doe who senses a buck."

A doe who senses a buck. She loved the image his words conjured up in her mind. She indeed felt like a deer being approached by a magnificent stag. But if she allowed the image to continue, she would have no more control over her fate than a small bird caught in a fierce wind. Struggling to remember what she'd had in mind when she'd thought to touch him, she sucked in a deep breath and placed her hand over his hard chest. For a moment she felt nothing, then the beat-beat of his heart pulsed through her fingertips and seeped into her nerves, her brain, her entire being.

"I can feel your heart beating, Loka." It was so damnable hard to speak, to remember why she'd felt she needed to say anything. If he reached for her, she would lay herself open to him. Surrender everything to him. "Your—your heart. That tells me you're alive. Real."

"You did not believe I was?"

He struck her as being a mix of innocence and power, the most incredible man she'd ever met, and the most dangerous. But sometimes a person had to look danger in the eye if she was ever going to fully experience life. "I never— Loka?" She had made her point. There was no longer a need to touch him. Still, she couldn't possibly bring herself to break the contact. "When you first woke up, you must have thought this couldn't possibly be happening."

"Yes," he said softly, and she wondered at the hell he must have gone through before accepting that he'd been thrust into a time not of his making.

"That's the way I've been feeling. Ever since that first day..." His heart pulse was so powerful. It seemed capable of beating forever, of transcending laws of the flesh that mortals had to obey. Capable of capturing her and keeping her with him forever. "That first day when you showed yourself to me—I didn't want to believe in you."

"Why not?"

"Because your existence goes against everything I've ever believed, against all logic. I told myself—never mind what I tried to convince myself of. It doesn't matter anymore because—because I believe in you."

She waited, hoping he would say something, but he only looked down at her with eyes that were a mix of panther-like strength and ageless wisdom. He lifted his hand from her chest, but before she could think how she might survive the loss, he slipped his knife back in its sheath, caught both her wrists and pulled her within an inch of his body. He held her there, challenging her. She couldn't think beyond his nearly naked body, her need to explore and possess and be possessed by that perfect body.

He hadn't touched a woman for well over a hundred years. Yes, he'd been neither alive nor dead during that time, but somewhere deep within him must have been awareness. And he'd been awake for over six months. Awake and alone. A primitive man who knew nothing of today's moral codes.

Who needed.

Frightened by the realization that he might think nothing of taking her, frightened even more by the fact that her body didn't give a damn *how* they came together, she remained where she was, waiting.

He pulled her closer, his strength both relentless and gentle. The fear that had been flickering inside her gave way to a much more powerful emotion. She thought, briefly, of what the wolf's howl must mean. After that, there was nothing except him. She felt as if she were standing above a simmering volcano. At any time, the mass of power and heat would burst free and she'd be consumed by it.

As long as he controlled the volcano, was the volcano, she didn't care.

"I do not want you here," he whispered hoarsely as her breasts pressed against him and his arm around her back held her firmly in place. "You should have left me in peace."

"I know. But, Loka, it's too late."

"Too late." He bent his body over hers. She tried to concentrate on something, anything else, but there was only him. "What does this mean?" he whispered. "You and me together. What does it mean?"

"I don't know."

It didn't matter that he said nothing in return. He was so close that his features had blurred, leaving her to think only of his heat and strength, his control over her. Her primitive need for him. She knew she shouldn't risk losing what little self-control remained, and she drew her wrists out of his grasp. But instead of stepping away from the danger, she wrapped her arms around his neck, pulled his head down toward her, covered his mouth with hers. He jerked back but only slightly, only briefly. He seemed to hang there, allowing her to do with him what she pleased. *Insane,* she thought as she parted her mouth and touched the tip of her tongue to his lips. *Insane.*

"Loka..."

"What?"

"I need to understand."

She waited for him to ask what she meant by that, but he didn't. Instead, he pushed her away, leaving her lonely and yet grateful for this small step back into sanity. When he tensed and cocked his head, she thought he'd heard someone approaching. Fear for him surged through her.

Then she heard the wolf howl again.

Chapter 8

It had always been said that dreaming of the dead meant more death would come, but Loka often dreamed of his son, and in the morning felt comforted because that meant his child continued to live within him. It had also always been taboo to speak the name of the dead, but whispering "Kina'n" over and over again had given him as much comfort as dreaming of the boy.

Maybe, Loka thought, not everything the shaman taught his people had been the truth.

Tory walked behind him, her breathing quick and soft, her shoes making almost no sound. She might never learn how to move as silently as he did, but at least she wasn't like most of her kind, unthinking in the way they traveled over his ancestors' land.

Wolf understood her, maybe trusted her. If he hadn't, he would have remained silent instead of revealing his existence to her. That was why he'd decided to bring her to Spirit Mountain. If she betrayed him, if Owl and Coyote warned him not to trust her, he would heed their wisdom, ask Eagle for the truth behind Wolf's howl. And, if they so decreed, he would end her. Somehow.

"Loka?"

"What?"

"I don't know how you do it. You never get tired, do you?"

He looked back over his shoulder at her. Her cheeks were flushed; sweat glistened on her temples and her lips looked dry. He should have known she couldn't keep up his pace, but when he told her there was something she had to see, she'd agreed and he'd led the way across The Land Of Burned Out Fires.

Maybe the truth was that he should have walked away from her.

But she hadn't fought his embrace, and when she touched her mouth to his, a fierce need for her had taken hold of him and he hadn't been able to think beyond that. He wouldn't take her as a buck takes a doe. He had watched and listened and learned and knew that that was not the way of her people. Even if this was the only day they would spend together, he wanted to step into her world.

Her world? He was taking her into his.

"You do not want this?" he asked when she stopped, planted her hands on her hips and took several long, deep breaths.

"This? Loka, you haven't told me anything. We just keep walking. I thought—I don't know what I thought. But I have to know."

"Wolf lives on Spirit Mountain. We go to find him."

"That's what you said." She shook her head, eyes tired and determined and confused. "But I don't know what you mean. Spirit Mountain." She pointed in the direction they'd been going. "That's Schonchin Butte. At least I think that's what they call it."

"Schonchin Butte." The unwanted words lay heavy on his tongue.

For a long time she said nothing. Then she touched his forearm. "Nothing's the same, is it? That's what you're thinking."

He didn't answer because she'd spoken the truth. Although he knew she needed to rest, he spun back around and began walking again. As he always did, he kept his eyes on the land around him, watching for a sign of the enemy. He saw cars moving along the road far to their right. There were several hikers ahead of them, but they were so far away that they would never spot him. She could call out to them, with a few words put an end to him.

"Loka? I'm sorry. But I need some water. I can't—I'm not as used to this climate as you are."

She would never be. Instead of telling her that, he pointed off to the left, then headed in that direction. She didn't fully trust him. If she had, she would have started walking as soon as he did. Still, he didn't blame her, because he didn't truly trust her and maybe never would.

It wasn't the same for his body, he admitted a few minutes later, as he lowered himself into a cave opening that led to an underground stream, one of several that had once sustained the Maklaks when they couldn't reach the mother lake. His body cared nothing about tomorrow. It knew only that it wanted and needed her.

"What is this?" she asked once she joined him underground. She glanced around her, then her gaze settled on him. Too much white showed in her eyes; he wondered if she was afraid of being beneath the surface. Maybe the cave increased her sense of isolation, her dependence on him when she didn't want that. "I hear water running."

"Earthriver," he explained. "When the great fires cooled, the river was driven underground. In winter it freezes."

"I've heard about that. My God, this land—it's absolutely incredible."

He'd begun walking again, bent over in the confining space, but stopped when he realized she wasn't keeping pace with him. As before, her eyes spoke for her. He knew this place of cool, damp air and the sound of rushing water, but to her it was nothing except darkness. Retracing his footsteps, he reached out and took her hand. She drew back, turned her body toward what she could still see of the opening.

"You are safe," he said.

"Am I? All right," she said with a sigh. "I'll—follow you."

It wasn't far from the cave entrance to where the stream cut its way through rock, but the path down to the water was steep and narrow. Clinging to him, she kept up with him until he brought her to the water's edge. No light ever reached this place, something he gave thanks to because it kept the enemy from invading his privacy. Her breathing had quickened, telling him better than words that she felt trapped and helpless.

He could keep her here. She would have water and he knew of a level spot where she could sleep. He'd bring her food, and she would never leave him. Never betray him. Answer his body's needs.

But if he did, she would hate him just as he hated those who had taken claim of his people's land.

"Loka?"

"What?"

"You were so quiet. I have to admit this, I don't like it down here. I keep thinking how dependent I am on you. I can trust you, can't I?"

"Trust? That is for you to answer."

What did he mean by that, Tory asked herself for the umpteenth time. Thank goodness they hadn't stayed in the underground cavern for longer than it had taken to satisfy their thirst. He seemed to be at home in that claustrophobic place with the unseen stream rumbling and roaring past. Maybe—she stared ahead of her to reassure herself that they were indeed getting closer to the top of Schonchin Butte—maybe her moment of raw fear hadn't been directed at him at all. Given where they'd been, it was a distinct possibility that the place itself had everything to do with her mood.

And maybe he was more responsible than she wanted to admit.

When they emerged from the cave, he'd gestured at her to remain sitting while he scrambled onto a boulder and looked around. She'd caught the echo of far-off voices and guessed that distant hikers had been responsible for his caution. She could have called out to them; they both knew that. But she hadn't—maybe because being with him was more important than life itself.

And maybe because she no longer controlled her own will.

The hikers had gone off in another direction, leaving them to continue toward whatever it was he wanted to show her. She'd had to stop and rest several more times and would have told him she couldn't go on if he hadn't reassured her there was water at the top.

They'd made it. At the moment, that was all that mattered.

"It's all right, Loka," she whispered when he looked around for the third time. "There's no one here. There's so little vegetation, there's nowhere anyone could hide."

Leaving his rocky lookout, he returned to her side. Although the sheen of sweat on his body distracted her from her surroundings and the endless view of what seemed to be a vast chunk of the world, she was glad to see that he, too, felt the effect of their climb. "I must be careful," he said. "Always."

"I know." Were they insane? There was no earthly reason for them to hide. No earthly reason except that he was a man out of his time, a man no one but she understood. "Loka, do you come here much? I mean, there are several trails leading up here. And that structure I spotted. What is it, a fire lookout? People must be around all the time."

"I know when the enemy walks on sacred land. I wait until they are gone."

"Oh." Her reply sounded so inadequate, but what else could she give him? The wind seemed to whistle up here. Maybe it loved the sense of freedom and space and agelessness and that was how it expressed itself. Mesmerized both by the sound and the realization that she and Loka were utterly, completely alone with the world spreading out all around and below them, she slipped closer to him and wrapped her arm around his waist.

At the touch, all her weariness faded, leaving her aware of a man in a way she'd never been before. Instinctively fighting his impact, she struggled to take note of her surroundings. After all, he'd brought her here because this place was special to him.

But he mattered more to her than any place ever could. Claimed her awareness in ways she'd never imagined.

He slid his hand over her shoulder and pressed her against his side. She could hear him breathing, the cadence quick when he should be rested from their climb. So he was no more immune to her than she was to him.

So.

"It's beautiful," she whispered, hoping that was what he wanted to hear. "Stark and yet—I can see forever."

He turned her slowly, their bodies meshing and moving in perfect unison. She'd thought she'd seen everything there was to see while climbing up here, but the butte had always been between her and distant Mount Shasta. Now she could see, fully see, the massive peak. Even though it was so far away that it seemed more illusion than substance, it still dominated the landscape. Yes, the world below stretched out until it seemed to slide off the ends of the earth, but she would put her mind to concentrating on that later.

For now there was only the mountain and Loka, who had brought her here to see it.

"Yainax. Home of the gods," he said softly.

"Y-ainax. Your gods. Of course. It's perfect. Loka, did you ever think what it must have been like for the first Indian who saw this? How overwhelmed he must have felt. How—maybe it frightened him."

Loka's attention had been riveted on the mountain. Now he stared at her, blinked as if still trying to make sense of what she'd just said. "I do not know."

"Think about it. I mean, I'm trying to imagine a small group of people traveling for weeks, maybe months for whatever reasons, finding this place. Their reaction to it. Loka, how did they know that this land had been created by volcanic activity? You call it The Land Of Burned Out Fires, which means your ancestors understood its origin. Those first Indians—were they here during the eruptions or did they come afterward? Why? What brought them and where did they come from?"

She pressed the palm of her hand against her forehead. So much of her professional life had been spent trying to answer questions exactly like what she was now asking Loka. Before, everything had been part of hypothetical observations, a matter of taking bits and pieces of the past and molding them together into a logical, practical whole. It felt different today—not just because she was talking about Loka's people, but because, maybe, he was the link.

"What do you know?" She kept her voice soft and low but couldn't still the excitement she felt. "Your people's legends... What do they say about the first to come here?"

"You want to know this?"

"Of course I do. Please tell me."

"Tell? The Maklaks were created by Kumookumts. That is our beginning."

She reeled from what felt like a door being slammed in her face. She was asking for fact and he was giving her, what, superstition and legend?

Maybe.

"Tell me." She barely did more than mouth the words. "Please. Everything."

"It is not for you to know. You are *sano'tts*. The enemy."

Sano'tts. "If you really believed that, you wouldn't have brought me up here."

He stiffened, started to step away from her, then stopped. Eyes on the horizon, he squared his shoulders and threw back his head as if seeking something in the air, the land, maybe the sky itself. "Without Kumookumts there would be nothing. He was everything."

"Was."

"He is no more," Loka said with no touch of sadness in his voice. "He was The Old Man, the father and creator. When he finished here, he became one with the mist."

"How did you come to believe this? Your parents—did they tell you?"

He glanced at her, and in the brief silence she sensed that he was again asking himself whether he should tell her anything. Then, his eyes probing so deep into her that she felt as if her soul itself had been stripped naked, he continued. "The shamen hold all wisdom. They are the keepers of our past, and we believe what they say."

He was speaking in the present tense. If only it was in her power to make that time real for him again! "Cho-ocks, the shaman who kept you alive. Was he the only one you had during the war?"

He nodded, the gesture slow and even and sensual in a way she could barely handle. Maybe if he wasn't still touching her, she wouldn't be feeling this way, but she couldn't tell him to stop.

"Loka," she said when she realized he hadn't spoken, when desire for him threatened to become a flood. "I—I've been trying to learn more about the Modocs. I, ah, I've read books—every book I could get my hands on—but they contradict one another. I don't know if there's truth in any of it. You believed in Cho-ocks's power? Completely believed in him?"

"Yes."

Yes. "Why?"

"Cho-ocks told me when to climb Spirit Mountain for my vision quest. I did as he said and Eagle came to me."

He made it sound so simple, but maybe it was. From where they stood, she could just make out the thin, dark ribbon that was the two-lane road cutting through the lava beds. Except for that and the diminishing wisp of a jet trail, the small collection of buildings that made up the park headquarters, nothing of the twentieth century existed.

"When the army came," he said. "we could no longer reach Spirit Mountain. My chief died without returning here."

Her fingers had lost all strength, but his words returned it to her. She grabbed his wrists as he'd done to her earlier and hung on to him as if her presence might be enough to end the pain she knew went along with his simple comment. "I'm sorry." The wind seemed to grab her words and fling them outward.

"I am glad that I did not see his end," Loka said. He wasn't looking at her. Instead, his gaze seemed welded on Yainax. "When I learned that my people were sent away from here after Keintepoos was hung, I gave thanks to Eagle that I was not there."

Maybe, if he had been, he would have been hung alongside Cap—alongside Keintepoos. "I don't want to talk about that," she managed. "Not now and maybe never. What was it like before white men came? Please, will you tell me about that?"

He looked relieved at her question, but maybe she only imagined the expression. "This is important to you?"

"Yes. Oh, yes."

"Why?"

She couldn't answer. The need for understanding had become too deep for words. "I don't know your world, Loka, and I want to."

"My world, what was once my world." His voice had become heavy. All she could do was cling to him and pray he could find his way through regret to where she waited for him. Finally: "Kumookumts provided us with everything we needed. Deer and birds, fish and camas. We had the strength to fight the Klamaths. For a long time they were our only enemies."

"Them and sometimes this land."

He frowned at that. She explained that there must have been times when the weather had been so severe that they'd been afraid they wouldn't survive until spring. To her surprise, he shook his head. "If a Maklaks walks the right way, he has nothing to fear."

"The right way? But how do you know what that is?"

"Our spirits, the land and sky, tell us."

It seemed as if she'd been holding on to him forever, feeling the essence of him through the contact. Most of the time it was a battle to concentrate on what he was saying, but his simple statement freed her, at least briefly. "Your eagle spirit?" she asked. "He guides you?"

He nodded and again she was struck by how sensual he could make the gesture. "He always did, Tory. But this is a new time. I need to learn how to walk in today."

Only when pain shot up her arm did she realize she'd been gripping his hands with all her strength. It didn't matter; nothing did except the beauty, the mystery of what he was saying. "I wish—I want to help."

A deep sigh echoed throughout his body. When it was finished, he pulled himself free and stepped over to a low, flat rock. He stood on it, arms outstretched, eyes closed. He began chanting, the sounds hard and discordant and yet hypnotic. She couldn't take her eyes off him, yet she remained aware of the horizon. The setting sun glinted off his dark chest and all but buried flashes of light in his ebony hair. He didn't move. If he breathed, she couldn't tell. He remained silhouetted against the world, a man secure in his belief, at home with an untamed world. If she had a camera—

No! This moment was for her heart and soul, not something man-made.

She felt her lips move and realized she was trying to duplicate the words he was saying, but she didn't know how to make her mouth and tongue work in that way. Because he was staring at Mount Shasta, at Yainax, she did the same.

Something—there was no doubt—was coming their way. Even before it flew close enough that she could identify it, she had no doubt of the bird's identity. The setting sun kept her from making out every detail, but her memory supplied

the missing pieces. Eagle. Because she'd long been fascinated by birds of prey, she knew that its keen eyesight made
hers pathetic by comparison. It had come, she believed, not
because it was looking for something to eat, but because
Loka had called it to him.

"What—" she began and then stopped. The eagle was no
more than twenty feet above Loka's head now. Driven by an
instinct for self-preservation, she slipped behind some rocks,
observing it from that relatively safe vantage point. Its
wingspan had to be at least twenty feet, its eyes clear and
dark and keen. More than anything else, its talons fascinated her. Instruments of death, they hung at the ready beneath its muscular and yet nearly weightless body. The
thought of those weapons digging into Loka's body forced
a cry from her throat, but neither Loka nor the bird seemed
to have heard her. They remained focused on each other, an
invisible linkage forged. She tried to tell herself that it was
impossible. Surely her warrior and this primitive bird
couldn't think as one, but what other explanation was there?

Loka continued to stretch his arms outward. His lips were
slightly parted, his eyes focused on nothing except the black-
and-white bird. He continued his chant, his prayer, whatever it was, and time no longer mattered. He could be doing this tonight or a thousand years ago. The message
remained the same: that bird and man loved each other.

She wasn't part of what they shared, could never fully
understand.

The knowledge made her weep.

"We will spend the night here."

Still numb, Tory nodded. She watched as Loka handed
her a water-filled gourd, some kind of ground meal, a strip
of dried meat. She guessed that at least an hour had passed
since the eagle—Eagle—had left. In that time Loka hadn't
spoken, and she'd been unable to think of a single way to
break the silence. The sun had set, colors spilling out over
the world with such vibrancy that she'd nearly cried again.
Loka had continued to stand on the flat rock, his attention

fixed on distant Yainax until he could no longer see it. She remembered sitting down, rubbing away a cramp in her calf, thirst, the realization that she would be content to spend the rest of her life on this plateau overlooking what had once been Loka's world.

Just before it became completely dark, he'd left his rock and disappeared into the shadows. She'd felt a moment of panic at the prospect of being left alone, but then the first star had emerged, and she'd taken comfort from its cool glow.

Loka had returned with food and water. She'd wanted to ask him how often he came here and met with Eagle, but didn't.

They'd eaten in silence. When the moon came out, she'd studied him as he gazed at the stars. Never, never would she forget how he looked then.

Loka was ageless, wind and sun, sky and mountains. She'd known men who wore their physical strength as if it were a badge, who threatened others with their size, who thought of themselves and their prowess as one and the same. Loka had taken his strength from the mountains. The muscles that roped his body were for one purpose: survival. This land, this harsh and beautiful land, knew no mercy. Only those strong enough and brave enough to face it head-on would live.

Loka was built for survival. And he was looking for his place in the present.

Her mouth dried, and her body felt newly alive. She wished she were stronger, because maybe if she were, Loka would think her more worthy of him. She wanted to watch him hunt. She wished she'd been here when he'd accepted Eagle as his guardian spirit. She wanted to show him her world and yet was glad they were in his, at least for tonight.

For maybe a half hour now the stars had been pushing free of the darkness one by one until they littered the sky. The moon was the last to arrive. It made its appearance slowly, exotically, pulling her attention briefly from Loka and putting her in touch with what had always existed. The moon's color spilled over the top of Spirit Mountain, bathed it in silver and gold and stole her breath.

"It's beautiful," she whispered. Loka stood with his back to her, moonlight shimmering down over him like an endless waterfall. "There wouldn't be anything without the sun, and yet the moon . . ."

"My people knew it was a gift."

"I love it up here." She wanted her words to reach him, but it was nearly impossible to speak aloud, to think of anything except making love to him. "I don't ever want to leave."

"I know."

She watched him turn and come closer. Her mind fixed on arms and legs, hips and thighs and chest. She remembered the feel and excitement and smell and promise of the first day of true spring, thought of sunlight caressing ice and freeing it to run over the land. Her lungs were starved for oxygen and yet she knew air wasn't enough.

Only *he* would be enough.

Ever.

"You're incredible," she heard herself say. "Magnificent."

"Magnificent?" He was less than five feet away, all but naked, armed with a knife that had been in existence for generations. Known only to her.

"It doesn't matter. You're who you are. You belong here. Nowhere except here."

"No longer. The world has changed. I must become part of that, somehow."

She tried to pull the words apart to see if there was sorrow or regret in them, but five feet had become four. She'd never felt so overwhelmed in her life. The reality of being consumed by a man who hadn't so much as touched her spread through her until she could do nothing but accept it.

"Why are we here?" she managed. "Why did you bring me here?"

Chapter 9

In the distance, she could just make out the outline of the structure that served as the fire watch. Although she was grateful that it was there and that people were on duty making sure neither lightning or man-made fire destroyed the beauty below her, she couldn't put her mind to what that other world was like—not when Loka stood over her.

"I'm not afraid of you," she whispered. "Maybe I should be. Maybe I will be before—" No, she couldn't say before this was over, not when he was the only thing she wanted in life, might ever want. "I need to understand where you came from, why you decided to defy the enemy along with Keintepoos and the others, whether you killed—whether you killed any of the enemy."

"They were not always my enemy."

She waited for his simple words to fully sink in, but how could she make sense of them when she knew so little about him? "Why not?" was the only thing she could think to say.

He sighed, a low sound that melted into the backdrop of night creatures coming to life. "You want to hear this? It was long ago—I was only a child."

She tried to imagine him as a child, but the man he'd become dominated her. "Yes, I do. Where were you born? Did you have brothers and sisters? I want—" She raked a restless hand through her hair, aware that his attention never wavered from what she was doing. "I want to hear everything."

She hoped he would sit down. That way at least he would no longer loom over her, but he seemed to need to stand. Moonlight eased away some of the harshness in his features but left so much in mystery that she couldn't read his expression, or his mood. He lifted an arm and pointed off into the distance. "I was born at Gowwa, the Swallow place. After my parents exchanged their marriage gifts, my father built a new wickiup near my mother's family.

"When I was old enough, my father taught me how to hunt. The mother lake was filled with ducks and geese then in numbers you will never know. In the winter, the sky sometimes turned black because so many eagles made their home there. We built canoes and seined for fish." He made a sweeping motion with his arm, and she imagined that he was throwing a net into the water.

"My brothers and I learned to spear fish from watching our uncles. They told us not to make noise, but we boasted and made fun of each other until the fish swam away. It was good then." He sounded wistful. "Innocent children playing at being men. We went to the settlers' houses, and they gave us food. When their horses and cattle strayed, we brought them back to them."

"You got along with the settlers?"

"For many years. Until there were too many of them."

She couldn't imagine this area being considered overrun with people, but Loka was used to sharing it with antelope and bears, not more human beings. "When you were around the settlers before things went wrong, what was it like?"

She couldn't tell whether he was frowning or not, but something in the way he held himself told her she'd asked something he didn't want to answer. His arms hung at his sides. Still, she sensed a tension in him that might explode at any moment. Irrationally, she wanted to face that tension, feel the explosion.

"I was a child, Tory. I did not see the world in the way my grandfather did. Now I know he was the one with wisdom."

"He was afraid of the settlers?"

"Not afraid. My grandfather never knew fear."

She wasn't sure that could be said of anyone, but Loka was remembering the man from a child's perspective. "What then? What did he say when you and the other children went to the settlers?"

"That we were foolish for not heeding the call of the owl."

The call of the owl. Turning his comment around in her mind, she was struck by how smoothly Loka bridged ancient and modern worlds. "What does that mean?"

"That someone will die. Owls, coyotes, loons all carry the knowledge of death within them. In those days their cries filled the night air as never before and the grandfathers sat listening to them. But the young people, foolish children like myself, cared only that the settlers would give us sweets and other foods that we had never tasted. We thought that no harm could come from someone who let us ride their horses, who welcomed us into their homes."

"Don't blame yourself for what happened, Loka. You were only a curious boy."

"A boy! I had known eight winters when I first asked a settler to place me on his mule. I thought it was a wonderful thing, that this settler had wealth far beyond that of my parents. I saw my parents as less because of that. I was wrong."

She could hear him breathing and knew that he was, not for the first time, asking himself how he could have been so blind. "You didn't know—there was no way you could have known the Modocs would go to war with the whites. It— there was so much misunderstanding."

He turned away from her, presented her with the faint outline of his back. He was looking at what he could see of the moonlight-bathed world below them. Getting to her feet, she stood as close to him as she dared. The landscape seemed endless, timeless. Except for the distant blip of light that was the fire lookout, she might have been transported back in time thousands of years.

Was that why Loka had wanted to come here today, so he could escape all signs of today's world? Had he brought her with him because he wanted her to be part of this misty time? Because he'd decided she could be trusted?

She wished she believed that. "You speak English very well," she whispered. She didn't want to break the charged silence, but if she didn't pull as much as she could from him now, the opportunity might be lost. "Who taught you?"

He'd glanced down at her, but now he went back to staring at what seemed to be an entire universe. "I did not stay a foolish child, Tory. I saw things which I did not like—soldiers taking Modoc and Klamath women for their pleasure. Indian men selling their wives for liquor. Hearing my chief being called by a name not his own. I asked my grandfather why this was, and he said that both soldiers and Indians were playing a dangerous game."

"One side is never totally right or wrong."

"No. It is never that simple. I thought much on what he had said. I came here, sought Eagle for my spirit because Eagle is filled with wisdom. I prayed and he came to me. I opened my heart to him, and he showed me cattle who had died because they were trapped at the end of a canyon. They could have turned around and gone back where they came from, but they did not have the wisdom to look another way. That was when I knew I had to learn all I could about the white man. So I would never be trapped by him."

He'd made the telling sound so simple; she had no doubt that he'd seen a lesson for his own life in what had happened to the cattle. Surrounded by night punctuated only by stars and the moon and song from unseen throats, she stared up at him, recorded his dark form to her memory, knew she would never forget tonight. Or him.

"I went to a rancher, a man who treated Maklaks children with kindness. I asked him to teach me his words. And when he had, I asked him to show me the meaning of his talking leaves."

Talking leaves? She nearly asked him what he meant before remembering that that was what the Modocs had called writing. Loka looked as if he had stepped out of a primitive piece of history, but because she'd heard his wisdom, she knew he wasn't. Now, knowing he was literate, she asked herself if he was capable of bridging the gap between his time and hers. He wanted to; he'd already told her that.

"What did you think of what you read? Did it open up a new world for you?"

He glanced over his shoulder at her, but she couldn't see enough of his features to understand his expression. "I had my world," he said. "I did not need another one to open."

"It's an expression. I just meant—what kind of things did he have you read?"

"His Bible. Books. Newspapers. I did not understand everything that was in them, but I tried. I was eager to learn. Sometimes the things in the talking leaves frightened me. To know that the white men were like the winter snow, endless... Jerome was a patient man. He said I should take what I was learning back to my village. I think he knew I was not just a curious child, that what he was giving me should not be kept inside him."

"It sounds as if he became your friend."

"Friend?" Loka whispered the word. "Yes. And then Ha-kar-Jim killed him."

"Ha—Hooker Jim you mean?"

"That is what your people called him."

"I remember the name. He was there the day my great-great-grandfather was murdered. And before that, he was the leader of the young braves who avenged the burning of your winter village by killing every settler they could."

"Yes." Loka turned and started toward her, once again he dominated her world. "That was when Jerome was killed."

"How did that make you feel?"

"Feel?"

Was she pushing things too far? Ripping apart a fragile relationship? She had to know where he'd stood emotionally when war broke out. Keeping her voice as calm as possible, she asked if he thought Ha-kar-Jim had been right in leading the attack on unsuspecting settlers.

"He wanted me to go with him."

"Did he? Did you?"

"No."

She felt weak with relief, but it wasn't enough to let things end this way. "Did you want to?"

"A part of me, yes. The soldiers burned our village, destroyed our winter food, turned us into fugitives living in caves because we could not live with the Klamaths. When I heard children crying in fear and hunger, when my son clung to me asking why he couldn't return home, yes, my heart was full of hate."

"But one of those men had taken you into his home." Why was she doing this to him?

"Yes." He held up both hands as if balancing a weight in each one. "There were two of me then. One Maklaks, one white. But my blood is Maklaks. I could not kill my friend, but I could hate those who set fire to our village."

Much as she wanted to go on looking at him, she couldn't prevent her head from dropping forward. For Ha-kar-Jim, the decision to attack had been an easy one. Maybe it had been no different for the young brave when he aimed his rifle at the members of the peace commission, but Loka had been ruled by reason, and by his heart. "Was that what it was like for you throughout the war, feeling as if you were being torn in two directions?"

"No."

Surprised by his answer, she looked up. He'd come closer. Power and strength surrounded him, blocking her from every other emotion. She continued to stare at him, once again shaken by how much a part of his world he seemed. She'd always enjoyed exploring new areas, learning about different parts of the country, but never before had she thought in terms of whether she blended into wherever she went. She'd come close to feeling at home when she was on the coast, but nothing she'd experienced could possibly touch the way Loka meshed with his surroundings. She wanted—needed—to share that belief with him. The only way she possibly could was by touching him.

It was harder to stand than she thought it would be. True, she was tired from the long climb, but physical weariness had only a little to do with the way she felt. Once she was standing in front of him, she felt a little stronger; her body had somehow tapped into his seemingly endless strength.

"You do not like my words?" he asked. "You do not want to hear that my heart remains Maklaks and that stepping into today may be impossible?"

"No. That's not it."

Then what? Although he remained silent, she sensed his question. She couldn't provide him with an answer, couldn't speak the words that would let him know how vulnerable she was to his presence. But maybe she didn't need to.

She couldn't say which of them reached for the other first. It might have begun as a reaction to the sound of an owl hooting; it might have been the moon. And then maybe the world beyond the two of them had nothing to do with her reaction.

She fit inside the shelter of his arms. She hadn't known, had thought that surely people from two different worlds wouldn't be able to mesh. The air had begun to cool, but with his body shielding her from the breeze, she was no longer aware of the chill that had been nipping at the edges of her consciousness. The faint light from the fire tower seemed to wink in time with the stars. The sounds of animals, birds and insects became part of her sense of isolation.

Her awareness of Loka.

She wanted to hear his voice rumbling out from his chest, but if he spoke, she might be reminded of how incredible it was that they'd found each other, how impossible to ask that it might last beyond tonight.

Tonight was all she had. She would take from it as if she were starving.

She sensed that he was looking down at her, felt his hands running slowly up and down her arms. The message in his caress was simple; he, too, felt awed by what had happened between them. She needed to taste his lips and show him— show him what? How things were done in her world?

Despite the dark, she easily found his mouth. She clung to his neck and sealed her lips to his. She wanted to slide her tongue between his teeth but held back because maybe things hadn't been done that way in his world, his time. He might be shocked or feel invaded. It was so important to share herself with him in the right way, but what was right?

What did he want from a lover?

Lover. Still holding on to him, she fought the impact of that word. She had no idea what had happened to the mother of his child, whether he'd loved and now mourned her. He'd spoken of sexual relations between Modoc and white. Everything she'd ever read about primitive people made her believe that the need to ensure the survival of the species and family and societal demands dictated the role and expectation of marriage. If that was true, then people married because it was expected of them, not because of something as vague as the notion of love.

Was Loka capable of loving a woman?

When he laced his fingers through her hair and held her head firmly in place, she felt trapped and willing and on fire. What did love matter? *Making* love was enough—making love with a warrior from another era.

"Have you been promised to a man?" he asked, his lips still against hers.

"No."

"A woman and yet not promised?"

She pulled back a little, tried to read what was in his eyes. "It's different for my people, Loka. Today men and women marry only when they love each other."

He grunted but said nothing. She waited, hoping he would press his mouth against hers again, but he didn't, and in the few seconds apart, she lost her courage. Afraid to do anything that might not please him, she stayed where she was, aware that he could wrench her head in any direction he wanted simply by increasing his grip on her hair.

She wasn't afraid of him—nothing that simple. Rather, she felt as if she'd stepped inside a cave to find a fully grown grizzly there. The bear, secure in the fact that this was his domain and his strength far outstripped hers, simply stared at her.

Loka was doing the same. She didn't need daylight to know that.

"What—" She swallowed and tried again. "What are you thinking?"

He didn't answer. Whether he didn't have a reply or had chosen not to share it with her didn't matter; at least that's what she tried to tell herself. His manhood, ready for lovemaking or sex or whatever he chose to call it, pressed into her. He had to be battling need; the fact that he didn't simply take her should have helped. It would have if she hadn't needed him so much.

Nothing mattered. Nothing except the two of them.

Although it took two tries, she finally remembered how to command the muscles in her arms to move. Reaching out blindly, she found his waist. It put her in mind of granite, yet was covered by deceptively silken skin. His flesh should be rough, but it wasn't. It was almost as if the elements had known his life wouldn't be an easy one and had been gentle with him.

She couldn't be gentle.

She ran her fingers up his side, rolling the tips over one rib after the other while his muscles jumped and his breath caught. His grip on her hair increased; she felt the need to control him as he controlled her. Inch by inch she explored

and sought to command him. Waited for him to take her.
Wanted that. Risking everything, she leaned into him and
lapped her tongue over his naked breast. He shuddered, released her hair, caught her around the waist and held her
against him. She imagined herself struggling, fighting and
yet not fighting his advances, playing a game for which there
was only one end. She had no fight in her, only hunger.

The thought of laying herself out on the hard ground under him filled her with new excitement. He would mount
her. She would look up at him with eyes that held back
nothing, which begged him to take her.

And they—and they...

A sound teased at the edge of her awareness. When she
first heard it, she tossed it aside, but it returned again, familiar and wild. Part of everything she felt.

"Wolf," Loka whispered.

Wolf. A creature as impossible as he was. "He—he's still
here?"

"Wolf," Loka repeated and after that, she couldn't understand anything he said. Still tight and dangerous and
alive against him, she heard and felt the sharp, guttural
sounds that was his language. Loka was speaking to Wolf.
And by the changing cadence of the animal's howls, she had
no doubt that Wolf was responding.

Man? Warrior? No. Loka was more than that. When he
stepped away from her, she didn't try to follow him.
Whether it was because she now feared him she couldn't say.

Wouldn't admit.

Chapter 10

Long after he'd released Tory, Loka sat looking out at the night. He knew she was watching him. He felt her gaze along his backbone, sensed it searching beyond muscle and bone and wondered if she was trying to reach his heart. Still, he didn't acknowledge her.

Wolf had come to them—to him—again. Wolf with its wisdom and warnings. If Cho-ocks had still been alive, Loka would have brought gifts to the shaman and asked him to explain the meaning behind the haunting howls. But Cho-ocks had been taken far from here, along with the rest of the Maklaks. There was no one to speak to—except for Tory, who had touched his soul and left it weak and hungry when he didn't dare let that happen.

Wolf wasn't the only one who had found them. No matter how often he tried to tell himself that owls and coyotes always called out at night and thus did not always foretell death, he couldn't ignore the warnings of danger.

He had brought a white woman to this place where warriors for untold generations had come to complete their spirit quests. It angered him to watch the enemy climb up here, but he'd been helpless to stop them. Now he'd done what he never believed he would. More than that, he'd come within a heartbeat of surrendering himself to this woman who carried General Canby's blood.

Enough! In the morning, he would take her back down to where she belonged. Never again would he tell her of ancient beliefs. No more would he give her access to his heart.

He would be strong. And the next time Owl and Coyote sang of death, he would not ask whether the song was for him. If it was, it was because he had no place in today.

No longer would he search for the tunnel from past to present.

Daylight was just beginning to touch Mount Shasta—Yainax—when Tory sat up. Every muscle in her body ached from trying to sleep on rocks and brush, but it wasn't physical discomfort that brought her to her feet.

Something had taken Loka from her. Whenever she thought of Wolf and his cry, she came close to convincing herself that the warrior had been pulled from her side by whatever message the predator brought with him. After all, Wolf no longer lived here. He couldn't possibly be, and yet he was. The sound must have come from another time, been so compelling that Loka with his ageless wisdom had been unable to ignore it.

But it wasn't just Wolf. Maybe—she stretched and looked around for Loka—maybe it was the relentless sounds that Owl and Coyote had made throughout the night. Loka believed that those creatures warned of danger and death; if she shared his belief, she'd have been distracted, too.

But she didn't and she hadn't and therein lay the difference between them.

One of the differences.

Loka lay curled on his side, his body half-hidden by a rabbitbrush. If she'd been thinking, she would have found some sage to sleep under because the ground looked softer there. He could have pointed that out to her but no, he'd left her alone. Wanting to keep distance between them?

She should have walked to the fire lookout.

As the first rays of morning touched Yainax, she again thought about what Loka had told her. His people believed that Kumookumts had been sitting on top of the massive peak when he decided to make the mountains and valleys, streams and lakes, animals and humans. If she'd run to the lookout and spent the night with a roof over her head, she'd have missed this.

And maybe inadvertently jeopardized Loka's safety.

Making sure she kept a fair amount of distance between herself and Loka, she climbed over rocks until she had an uninterrupted view of the world below. It remained sheathed in darkness, waiting for the sun to wake it. Although it was summer, a thin frost clung to the ground at her feet. She probably wouldn't warm up until the sun reached this spot, and it first had to kiss the mountains dominated by Yainax. Cold as she was, she couldn't help thinking about what Loka and the other men must have seen when their searches for manhood brought them here.

As she watched and waited, she thought of Dr. Grossnickle, the four years she'd spent at the university as an undergraduate and then two more while she pursued her master's degree. Everything had seemed so logical then, short-term sacrifices made so she could prepare herself for a career she loved. She'd deliberately avoided any serious personal relationships, and although she was sometimes lonely, she usually didn't have roommates because she didn't want to be distracted from her studies. Her father had applauded her dedication; her mother had worried she was letting her chances for a personal life slip by.

Her mother had been right. She was sitting here—alone— looking at a display of nature that took her breath away.

She felt as if she were splintering into a thousand pieces, becoming little more than the tiny particles of dust being borne along by the wind. Fighting to hold on to reality, she tried to remember what her apartments had looked like, the route she usually took from the library to the anthropology department, how she felt the day Dr. Grossnickle chose her as his assistant. She couldn't hold on to any of that. This land, this morning, had too powerful a hold on her.

She was wrong; she wasn't alone. She couldn't say when she first became aware that Loka had joined her. What she did sense was shivering anticipation, fear that a single word from her might destroy this moment.

He sat beside her, his shoulder briefly brushing hers, warming her. Heating her. After the way he'd left last night, she didn't expect him to sit beside her. His body, cool and yet already being warmed by the summer sun, called to her in ways both subtle and blatant. Bit by glorious bit the day became brighter, the world below and around them more sharply defined.

She deliberately kept from looking at the fire tower because she wanted to experience this morning exactly as Loka had when he'd come here seeking Eagle. Some of the natural trenches on the valley floor were coated by a fine mist, which had the effect of sanding away the land's hard edges. She wondered if birds of prey saw the same thing she did, wondered if Loka had ever brought his son up here.

Tory knew she would never forget this moment.

"I feel so peaceful," she whispered when she could no longer hold her reaction inside. She looked over at Loka, half-afraid he would get up and leave. Instead, he simply nodded. "It's as if time has no meaning. As if we could come here a thousand years from now or have been here a thousand years ago and it would be the same."

"The same and yet different."

It struck her that she no longer had to concentrate in order to understand him. "Different because it isn't Modoc land anymore? Is that what you're saying?"

"*Eh.*"

"*Eh?*"

"Yes. This is no longer Maklaks land. I am the only one left."

No! Don't say that. She wanted to talk to him about Black Schonchin, the old Modoc man she'd met, but she'd tried before, and he hadn't wanted to listen. Thinking to

make him feel less alone, she took his hand and placed it on
her knee. The moment she did, she knew she'd made a mistake; the weight of his hand on her increased her awareness
of him tenfold. "The Land Of Burned Out Fires," she
managed. "Looking at this—" she nodded at the lower hills
now coming into sharper definition "—I can't help thinking it should be called something else. There's nothing dead
about this. Nothing—"

"The Smiles Of God."

"What?"

"That is what my father and my father's father and his
father called this land. The Smiles Of God."

"Oh. That's beautiful." She blinked back tears and concentrated until the panorama below was no longer blurred.
"I don't think I've ever heard that."

"The enemy do not understand everything."

"There's a lot we don't know about your world, Loka. So
much."

He gave her a sharp look, but she didn't care. Maybe
there would always be a schism between them. If that was
true, it might as well be faced full-on right now, before she
gave any more of herself to him.

"There is much I do not know about your world," he
said.

"Do you want to?"

"Yes. I must. You know that. But not this morning." He
turned his attention back to the flowing, golden sunrise. He
didn't say any more, but he didn't have to. His eyes and the
way he held his body told her he was thinking about what it
had been like when he'd come here with others from his
time.

As the shadows lifted, she was able to pinpoint the park
headquarters, which looked like a child's toy because it was
so far away. She wondered if anyone had noted that she
hadn't spent the night at her cabin. Probably Fenton, she
thought ruefully. The man's attempts to use her as a go-
between for an introduction to Dr. Grossnickle were less
than subtle, not that she could think of anything different

he might have done. He would want to know where she'd been. And if he found out—

"I live in an apartment in Seattle," she said softly. "I'd like to buy a house, but I'm not sure I'm going to stay in the same area. Until things settle down for me, it doesn't make much sense to—"

"Apartment?"

How could she possibly explain about one living quarter stacked upon another when he had all this to roam? But he wasn't as free as she wanted him to be. "Where I sleep and eat when I'm not on-site." She shrugged. "It doesn't matter."

"You do not like it?"

"No," she answered thoughtfully, "I don't. Not really. I need my own piece of land, some dirt to call my own."

He gave up his study of the landscape. "That is what I will never understand," he said. "That one believes he can own land."

Because she knew most Indians had had no concept of land ownership, she wasn't sure she could ever get him to fully comprehend what she was trying to say. "I want to put down roots. I'm not a nomad, although I enjoy seeing new places. Loka, this butte is where you came to find Eagle. He gives you a sense of peace, doesn't he?"

"Yes."

"I think, for me, having my own property would do the same thing. The world has changed since your time." The words, highlighting how little remained for him, made her shudder. "Your first time. These days, there's no way a person can so much as claim a rock or clump of grass without paying for it."

"That is not right." He leaned down, picked up a chunk of lava and held it out to her. "This was created by Kumookumts. He also created the first Maklaks, the first bear, all lakes and streams. If I say this is my rock, then I am saying I am more than a rock or bear or lake, and that is not so. We are all the same. I honor this rock and it honors me.

Those are things about me that I cannot change. This is why I am not sure I will ever find my place in today."

A few days ago she might have laughed at the notion of honoring a rock. All the time she'd been studying anthropology and then earning a living putting anthropological theory to use, the cynic in her had stood off to one side. It no longer did. "What else do you believe?" she asked. "What did your parents and the shaman teach you?"

Something dark flickered in his eyes. She'd asked a great deal of him; he had to weigh the wisdom of revealing more of his world. Would it make it any easier for him if she told him that having him sitting beside her, hearing the sound of his voice, watching expressions dance in his eyes, meant as much and maybe even more than any words?

"Wolf?"

"What?"

"Wolf," he repeated. "He trusts you."

"I want *you* to trust me," she whispered. Dangerous as she knew it to be, she wanted to lay her head on his shoulder. "Trust me enough to tell me more about your beliefs. If I understand, it'll help me bridge the gap for you."

"Bridge the gap?"

"Walk into the present."

He straightened. The gesture brought him so close to her that she felt the fine hairs on his upper arm brush against hers. Something like a low electrical current hummed into life.

"You will not ridicule?"

"No. Why should I?"

"Because others did."

Missionaries and religious fundamentalists had tried to convert the Modocs. Loka must have bitter memories of being told that his traditions and beliefs were nothing more than primitive superstition. "I'm not them, Loka," she insisted. "Remember, I've seen Eagle. I've heard Wolf."

He was silent for so long that she thought she'd lost him, said something wrong. Then, dividing his attention between her and the horizon, he told her about Ga'hga the

heron, who had been brought into being by Kiuka, the first
and most powerful of all medicine men. Kiuka had fash-
ioned Ga'hga as a joke, believing the Maklaks would be so
busy laughing at the long-necked bird that they'd never
catch it. Kumookumts had exploded with anger when he
saw what Kiuka had done and created Tusasa's the skunk
and then commanded Tusasa's to crawl into bed with Kiuka.
The next spring, hoping to improve their relationship,
Ga'hga had asked Kumookumts to create a mate for him.
After Kumookumts demonstrated his superiority by fash-
ioning many herons from the mud at the bottom of the
mother lake, he took a small handful of mud and turned it
into Gowwa' the swallow. Kiuka hadn't known what to say,
how to react, but from then on the medicine man never
challenged Kumookumts.

Tory listened in awe. According to what little had been
pieced together of the Modocs' early beliefs, she knew they
believed Kumookumts was responsible for all creatures, but
the mythology had lacked specifics. Now Loka was telling
her that Ke'is the rattlesnake had come into being because
Kumookumts had known his time on earth was coming to
an end. Ke'is had been the result of Kumookumts's anger.
Somehow, the Modocs discovered that if they left a swallow's egg outside a den of rattlesnakes, the snakes would be
placated and leave the Modocs alone.

She settled a less-than-steady hand on his arm. "No one
knows this, Loka. The things you're telling me, they've all
been lost."

"Because I am the only Maklaks left."

"No, you aren't!" Her grip increased. She couldn't help
it. "A lot of Modocs died when they were sent to Okla-
homa. It was tragic, all those lives lost to disease—and to
heartbreak. But they didn't all die. Eventually the survi-
vors were allowed to return here. I told you about the old
man I talked to. There are others. They—"

"They are *not* true Maklaks! Their hearts have never
known the old ways. They will ridicule what they do not
understand."

She couldn't argue this with him again, not with his life force seeping into her through her fingertips. She should let go, now, before it was too late.

But it was already too late.

Running her thumb over his forearm, wishing it was her lips instead, she said, "I know how you feel. The way they dress and act and talk, I don't blame you. But they carry Mo—Maklaks blood just as I carry General Canby's blood."

He grunted.

"Loka, I don't want your people's heritage to end with you. You can't want that, either. You keep saying you want to be part of the present. But part of that means you have to bring the past along with you."

"I will not speak to them."

"You're speaking to me."

He stopped her hand's restless movement by clamping his over it. When she tried to pull free, he increased his grip. "What are you—"

"I do not want you."

"Want? Loka, what are you talking about?"

"You do not belong in my world. Near me. I must walk this journey alone—find my way alone."

He surged to his feet, pulling her along with him. She tried to fight him as he dragged her to a ledge overlooking a steep drop, but even as she struggled, she knew her strength was no match for his. When less than a foot separated them from the edge, she sucked in a frightened breath. "Loka! What—you can't! Loka!"

He stopped, looking at her as if just now aware of her presence. A groan that seemed to come from the depths of his being burst from him and he shoved her away. She managed to catch herself before losing her balance. Still, her legs felt so weak that she slumped to her knees. Arms wrapped around herself, she watched in disbelief as he perched on the very edge of the cliff. Her throat filled to bursting with the need to scream, but she couldn't force anything out.

Seemingly oblivious to any personal danger, he lifted his arms to the sky. "*Blaiwas!* Eagle! I cry out for your wisdom. Show me the truth. The way!"

"*Blaiwas!* Hear me. Where do my feet stand? With my people? But they are no more. No more, while I live—while I search . . ." There was more, a deep torrent of words she didn't understand. As before, she was mesmerized by the sound of his native language, but could barely concentrate because her heart pounded painfully and she was terrified Loka might misjudge his footing.

He stood on tiptoe, eyes half-closed, arms extended as far as they would reach. He seemed to have turned to stone. She wondered if he was aware of anything, or anyone, except the bird he put such faith in.

And why shouldn't he, she asked herself as a distant speck came closer, became larger. She held up her hand to shield her eyes from the sun. She didn't really need to see because she already knew.

Loka's eagle.

Loka's tone changed from a chant to something less singsong and yet just as compelling. She tried to concentrate on him to see if anything in his posture might give her a clue to what he was saying, but the bird continued to command her attention. She'd seen it yesterday, become convinced that it was who and what Loka said it was—his spirit. And yet yesterday had been filled with so many shocks, so much discovery about herself and this warrior, that the eagle's appearance had been relegated to the back of her mind. It seemed larger today, darker somehow. When it shrieked, she clamped a hand over her mouth to keep from screaming.

This was no oddity trapped behind some cage, no picture in a book, not even a distant object brought into one-dimensional clarity with the help of binoculars. This was a magnificent bird of prey, eyes keener than any other, talons and beak capable of killing anything he captured.

Deadly.

She should have realized it was coming for her, but maybe she'd been hypnotized by the bright, piercing eyes. Loka's voice vibrated against her ears, pounded inside her skull. She heard another shriek, watched the massive wings stretch and then contract as it began its downward dive. Instinctively she placed her hands over the top of her head, but even as she did, she knew they were no defense against those killing weapons.

''Tory!''

Loka's bellow spun her toward him. She saw him catapult himself toward her, started to tense. Then he slammed into her and she felt herself being dragged under him. From the shelter of his body, she watched the eagle make a shuddering halt in its dive. It seemed impossible that the great bird could stop in time; if she'd still been exposed to it, she had no doubt it would have completed its attack. But it couldn't get to her, only Loka, and Eagle wouldn't attack him.

''*Blaiwas!* No! Do not kill her.''

The eagle screamed, the sound even more chilling than it had been before. It made an impact deep inside her; she knew she would ever forget that primal cry. A rock dug painfully into her side. She squirmed under Loka, trying to get him to move, but he only grabbed a flailing hand and caught it against his side. She stared up at him.

''*Blaiwas*. Eagle! *Nu-nen-wade-hanoks. Sho-te-tonko. Kasker. Sho-te-tonko.*''

The eagle hovered for a moment before shooting skyward. As it did, two large tail feathers floated to the ground just out of her reach. She thought the bird must be leaving and dared to take a breath. She'd just begun to try to free her hand when Eagle began a slow and absolutely graceful circle above them. One rotation became another and then another. She had no doubt the bird was staring at Loka and him at it. There was something almost sensual about the unspoken communication. She felt lonely and frightened because Loka understood something she didn't, accepted what couldn't possibly be, and it had become reality.

"Sho-te-tonko. Kasker. Nu-nen-wade-hanoks."

Sho-te-tonko. The sounds were anything but musical and yet she didn't want them to end. If they did, she would have to seek the answer to whether Eagle had tried to kill her.

Chapter 11

"Where are you going?"

Loka looked down at her. "Home."

"Where is that? Please, I don't know where you live."

He nodded but said nothing. She should be used to that by now. After all, in the hour it had taken them to descend Spirit Mountain, he hadn't said a single word to her, and she hadn't known how to break the silence. He'd taken her within a hundred yards of where she'd left her car yesterday. She had no doubt he meant to leave her—maybe forever.

"Loka? We can't end it like this." She hated that her voice sounded as if she were on the verge of crying, but how could she deny the truth? "At least tell me what happened up there."

"Eagle."

"I know Eagle." Her hand hovered over the two feathers she'd woven into her hair. "But that isn't enough."

"He answered me."

Answered what, damn it, what? "Please tell me. I have a right to know, don't I?"

His right hand began fingering his knife. She tried not to think about that, but it was impossible. This man frightened her as she'd never been frightened in her life, and yet the prospect of never seeing him again was more than she could bear. He made her feel so alive! "I won't tell anyone. If that's what you're afraid I'll do, I promise you I won't."

"It does not matter."

"Why? What are you talking about? Loka?" She grabbed his wrist and yanked his hand away from the knife. Turning his hand over, she studied the deep lines in his palm, imagined herself tracing them over and over again, covering them with kisses. "I have a right. Damn it, I have a right. Why did Eagle do what he did?"

"I asked if you could be trusted. That was his answer."

Legs threatening to collapse under her, she clung to his arm for strength. "He wanted to attack me."

"Yes."

Yes. "Loka, how do I make you understand? I—" She heard a car. Although the sound was still distant, it might mean someone was planning on coming to the site of the Thomas-Wright Battlefield. "I would never hurt you."

"Eagle does not lie."

"Neither do I!" She hated the desperation in her voice. "Won't you please listen to me?" She tried to turn him so he was forced to look at her, but he resisted; he was a rock, a massive tree. "Why would I want anything to happen to you?" she demanded. "You're the most incredible human being—"

"You want me to show myself. To tell the truth of the ancients to disbelievers."

She couldn't deny that. And she wouldn't lie and tell him that she'd changed her mind, not when he was the only link to an entire tribe's heritage. "If they knew the truth, they would believe."

"Do you?"

He was asking if she believed Kumookumts had created the world and put skunks here because his ego wouldn't allow a medicine man to best him? "I believe in Eagle—" was the best she could give him. "Loka, you stopped him from attacking me. Why?"

"I do not know."

Didn't he? She hadn't imagined his sexual energy, his need for her. "That wasn't the only thing you said to him." She shut her eyes, trying to concentrate. "I can't remember the words. *Nu-nen-wade-hanoks.* What does that mean?"

Loka's body stiffened; she pushed away the sound of the wind and concentrated. Still, when she heard a car door slam, she knew their time together was almost over.

"I gave Eagle another question. I asked if I could forgive you for carrying your ancestor's blood."

"And?"

"He gave me his answer."

She remembered Eagle's graceful circling, the way its beak had closed. The talons had been pulled back against its body. *Thank you, Eagle. Thank you.* "In other words, Eagle told you to put the past behind you?"

"Yes."

"And have you?"

"All I have is the past, Tory. I look at the present. I study it. I try to understand. But the step from one to the other is so great. Maybe too great."

How could such simple words hurt this much? She longed to pull him against her, to make love to him, and have her body show him that he wasn't alone. But would their love-making change the simple and harsh fact that the world he knew and loved and embraced no longer existed? "It doesn't have to be." *Did she believe what she was saying?*

"Go." He indicated the trail leading to the parking lot.

No! "Where are you going? Please, at least tell me that."

"I seek Bear."

"Bear?"

"His wisdom runs along the same river as Eagle's."

Did he have any idea how beautiful some of the things he said sounded, the imagery of them? She could now hear the sound of approaching footsteps. But instead of leaving, Loka leaned toward her and drew the feathers out of her hair. Then, the gesture achingly gentle, he placed them in her hand. "Go to your place, Tory. When I am done with Bear I will come to you."

I will come to you. I will come to you. No matter how many times the words echoed inside her, Tory was incapable of reducing their impact. A little while ago she'd been terrified that she would never see Loka again, but he'd made a promise and she believed him.

She couldn't be sure, but she thought she'd at least acknowledged the four elderly people trudging along the path leading to the battlefield. They'd kept staring at her until she realized they'd been trying to figure out how she'd gotten out there so early in the morning. It didn't matter. Nothing did except waiting for Loka.

That and cleaning up, she thought as she pulled into her parking slot at park headquarters. There was a tour bus nearby, but fortunately she saw no sign of whoever had been in it. She spotted the vehicle Fenton had been driving and looked around, hoping to hurry out of sight before he spotted her.

Unfortunately, before she could reach her trail, the bus door opened and Fenton and a distinguished-looking gentleman with long, thick gray hair stepped out. Fenton stared at her, puzzlement and what might be suspicion etched on his features. A thought, half-formed and maybe impossible, took root inside her.

"You're just the man I want to see," she said, hoping her smile didn't look as phony as it felt. "I've been thinking. You remember that Modoc man you introduced me to yesterday? Do you have any idea how to get in touch with him?"

Leaving the other man to stand beside the bus, Fenton walked over to her. "You're still here? When I didn't see your car this morning I thought you must have taken off—without giving me a chance to talk to you again. Sure am glad you didn't. I'm serious. If there's any way you can get me an in with Dr. Grossnickle, I've got some ideas on how he can make this hassle from the Indian council work to his advantage."

"I'll see what I can do," she said, although that was the last thing she wanted. "How about a trade? That Modoc lives in Tulelake, doesn't he? Do you happen to know where?"

The way Fenton kept staring at her, wariness flickering in his eyes, made her uneasy. She held his gaze and after a moment he said he thought he had Black's address somewhere. Then he pointed at her hand. "What's that? Eagle feathers?"

Feeling like a thief caught in the act, she had no choice but to acknowledge them. "I found them," she explained lamely. "Eagle? Is that what they are? I wasn't sure."

"You'd better believe it. It isn't legal for anyone except an Indian to have them in their possession, you know."

Fenton certainly expected her to hand them over to him, but knowing what they represented, needing the memory, she couldn't. "I'll be going out later today. I'll just leave them where they won't be disturbed. That ought to get me off the hook," she said with an easy grin that took more work than Fenton could possibly guess.

"Later today? You're still not leaving?"

"Leaving?"

"Yeah, leaving." His scrutiny of her intensified. "There was a piece on last night's news about the Indians' appeal. We have satellite dishes, you know. We're not as out of touch with the rest of the world as people think. 'Course, being out in the boondocks the way you were, you missed it."

"Missed what?"

"They interviewed Dr. Grossnickle on prime-time news. This hassle over the Alsea site is really capturing national attention, you know." He hung on the words just long enough to make his message loud and clear; he didn't understand her agenda and was determined to learn more. "He said he and everyone else involved in the project were determined to make sure the court decision was upheld. It sounded as if there was a high-level summit being planned.''

He didn't have to say anything more; she knew exactly what he was thinking, that there was something very suspicious about the fact that she was still here. Keeping her attention resolutely off Spirit Mountain—she could never imagine calling it anything else—she told him she wouldn't be here much longer. *Leave? How could she? How could she not?*

"Hmm. You spent the night out there, didn't you?" Fenton waved vaguely at the wilderness.

"Oh, yes." Surely he didn't know exactly where she'd been, or with whom. "It's so peaceful. Nothing except owls and a few coyotes."

"I guess. Me, I'd much rather have a bed. I didn't think you brought any camping equipment with you."

His probing was beginning to make her nervous, and more than a little angry. What she did was none of his concern. Only, how was she going to convince him of that? "It was a kind of a spur-of-the-moment thing." She shrugged and smiled again.

"Fortunately, I had my sleeping bag in my trunk and was able to find a level spot to spread it over. Look, I want to get cleaned up and have something to eat, but there are Modoc artifacts in storage here, aren't there? I'd like to see them."

"Artifacts? Today?"

"Yes, today," she said, determined not to be trapped into explaining further.

"Yeah, some." He frowned, the gesture leaving no doubt of what he was thinking. "You've got to have seen artifacts that would put these to shame. What do you want to look at them for?"

"Curiosity. Busman's holiday. If I'm at headquarters in a little over an hour, do you think someone could show them to me?"

Fenton consulted his watch. "I'll get the key. I'll be in the director's office. The man is so damned entrenched— pounding a new idea in his head is next to impossible. He doesn't care whether this place dries up and blows away. Fine, let the lava beds go to ruin. I'd much rather work with someone who knows the meaning of commercial potential.''

He didn't say it, but he didn't have to. He'd already indicated he believed Dr. Grossnickle to be such a man. He was right; she just didn't feel up to reinforcing his belief—not with the reality that she would soon have to leave staring her in the face.

A little over an hour later, clean and finishing the last of her granola bar, Tory walked around to the back of the visitors' center. Before she reached it, she heard angry male voices coming from behind the closed director's office door. For a moment, she debated turning around and walking away, but this might be her only opportunity to see the Modoc artifacts. That possibility had given her something other than Loka to focus on. She knocked on the door, then stepped back. A moment later it opened and the park director poked his head out. "Fenton said you'd be coming by," Robert Casewell said as he shook her hand. "Too bad you didn't introduce yourself when you first checked in. I could have arranged a tour that would have shown you much more detail than the tourists get."

She wondered how he'd react if she told him that last night had been more revealing than anything anyone could ever imagine, so revealing in fact that she knew she would never get over it. Instead, she acknowledged Fenton, who now stood beside the middle-aged but athletic-looking director. Neither man glanced at the other, not that she blamed them. The air between them fairly dripped hostility; obviously each man wished the other would disappear, forever.

After a moment, Fenton reached in his front pocket for a handful of keys. "It's going to happen," he muttered to Robert. "I've already talked to my uncle, Senator Baldwin. He agrees that opening up Fern Cave is a step in the right direction, a necessary financial step. He wants a formal proposal of all my ideas just as soon as I can get them to him. He says that the timing for getting additional appropriations couldn't be better, what with budget sessions going on, but we've *got* to make people aware of this place. That's the problem—not enough legislators know it exists."

"The lava beds are the responsibility of the National Park Service. There's no way they'd allow that kind of exploitation. The destruction—"

"The National Park Service's budget is set by Congress—a Congress that is feeling a severe financial crunch. Look, Robert, it's a basic matter of the squeaky wheel getting greased."

Guessing the two men had had this argument several times before, Tory waited to see who would come out with the upper hand. To her discomfort, the director had nothing to say in reply to Fenton's sharp comment. After a moment, Fenton touched her elbow to indicate which direction he wanted her to go. She followed him, not sure she wanted to be anywhere near the ambitious, determined man.

The small, climate-controlled storehouse consisted of little more than a series of metal drawers in addition to several glass-enclosed shelves. From the way Fenton opened and closed drawers at random, she guessed he hadn't spent enough time in here to be familiar with the contents. How dare he be so willing to jeopardize the lava bed's future integrity without first learning all he could about its past!

Finally he opened a shelf filled with Indian baskets. He reached for one before she reminded him that the white gloves on the nearby table were to protect fragile objects from body oils. "It just seems like overkill," he said as he pulled one on. "No one ever comes in here. It's not like they're going to get mauled. That's another thing I'm working on. Trying to set up a hands-on exhibit so people can experience life as the Modocs did—at least as much as we know. You know, how they cooked their meals, what their bows and arrows and stuff were like. That's bound to bring more people in than sticking things away in a back room.''

She conceded that it might. Although she wanted to be reassured that Fenton had no intention of letting people handle the genuine article, she couldn't concentrate enough to ask the question. Taking over, she methodically studied each drawer and glass case, appalled to find only a few baskets, a limited arrowhead collection, some ragged clothing. Certainly more than that had been salvaged.

"That's it?" she asked. "I can't believe it—there's almost nothing.''

"I guess there's some stuff over at the county museum. I haven't gone there so I can't be sure. Look,'' he indicated one of the glass shelves "—I've been told that some of these rusty old rifles still work, not that I'm going to take a chance on shooting myself. They weigh so damn much, I can understand why it was hard for the soldiers to make a decent advance on the stronghold.''

She didn't care about the soldiers' weapons, their uniforms, even their personal belongings. The army had been the invader, and yet there was much more of their possessions than what had been part of the Modocs for thousands of years. "What happened?''

"What do you mean, what happened?''

"The Modocs had an entire culture, an ancient and enduring way of life. There has to be more of its physical evidence still in existence.''

"Maybe. Maybe not. People were all over this place before it was made into a landmark, you know. A lot of it was probably carted away.''

He was right, of course. The same thing had happened over and over again at other Native American sites. But although she'd been upset over the destruction and vandalism, it had never before felt like a personal invasion. "They'd been partially assimilated before they went to war,'' she muttered. "That means they'd forsaken many of their traditional materials, like baskets and—and obsidian knives—for what the settlers had. So much was already lost." Although the room was windowless, she looked around for some ray of sunlight, anything to keep her from thinking they'd entered a pathetic repository of the dead.

"It happens. There's nothing we can do about it."

Something in Fenton's tone caught her attention. Concentrating, she wondered if she really had sensed regret in him. Maybe he wasn't as materialistic and insensitive as she'd thought. "No, I guess not."

Although she already knew it was an exercise in futility, she made a systematic search of the room's contents. She had to admit that what had been collected had been carefully preserved. The Modocs, for whatever reasons, hadn't overly concerned themselves with art. She'd been to Petroglyph Point, a nearby high bluff filled with prehistoric carvings and drawings, and had tried to find meaning in the seemingly random symbols, but if they represented examples of the Modoc religion, the truth had been lost to history.

The climate here was such that the Modocs had spent most of their time as nomads who concentrated on food gathering and otherwise preparing for the long, harsh winters. True, they'd been so tuned into their surroundings and what nature provided that they'd been able to live comfortably, but there must not have been enough time left over for such creative endeavors as the totems found on the Pacific Northwest coast, elaborate blankets and jewelry like those the Navaho were known for. Even their language was gone—except for Loka.

"Are you done?"

Pulled out of her musing by Fenton's question, she nodded and left the room so he could lock the door behind them. "It seems so tragic," she couldn't help saying, "to think that a whole way of life has been lost. I . . ."

"There's the library. One of the books was written by Winema's son—you probably know that. I haven't looked at it but I'd think it would be pretty accurate."

She knew about that text, had read it in fact. Winema, the Modoc woman married to a white man during the Modoc

Wars, had played a pivotal role in bringing the war to an end, but her son had been only a child then, and many of his recollections had been disputed. Still, she wandered into the library with Fenton and thumbed through books for several minutes.

To her disappointment but not surprise, everything in the small but complete collection had been written from an outside perspective. She found the personal diaries by soldiers fascinating and wished she had more time to pore over newspaper accounts of the war. Still, there wasn't a single word describing what that time of upheaval and change had been like for the Modocs themselves.

"They're in here," she said at last. "But they've been filtered, disturbed, and too much has been lost."

"Like I said, we can't do anything about that," Fenton said, obviously anxious to leave. "If we could recapture that time, well, that would be incredible. Absolutely incredible. Think of the hoards of people who'd flock here then. It boggles my mind just thinking about it. Well, at least the land is the same, and the more people we can get here to see it, the more who will think the way you do."

Maybe, she thought, but lacked the energy to contemplate that, or the energy to fathom how Loka would be exploited if his existence became known. Now that she'd been up and moving for several hours, she had to admit that last night had been anything but restful. But did she expect it to be any different? After all, she'd spent it with the final living link to the culture she'd been searching for this morning.

But he'd been more than that. Loka was a man, young and healthy, sensual and sexual in a way that defied description.

When she stepped outside, the sun was waiting for her. It lay heavy on her shoulders, heated her hair. She walked over to a stone wall and looked out at miles and miles of beautifully barren land. She sensed Fenton's presence behind her, but couldn't concentrate on him. This was Loka's world,

damn it! His and his people's's! Only, they no longer existed.

Except for him, it had all been lost.

*You have a responsibility, Loka. You can't keep an entire
culture trapped within you! You know that. Damn it, I know
you do. That's why you reached out to me—why you keep
seeking... What?*

A way of life can't die with you. It can't.

Die?

Despite the wind swirling around him, the mother lake
remained calm. For a long time, Loka simply stared at its
peaceful surface, remembering how as a child he'd gone
fishing with his father and uncles. The men had been intent
on spearing as many fish as they could, but he and the other
children had found it impossible to remain motionless for
what seemed forever, not when tiny fish ventured close to
nibble at their toes.

Closing his eyes, he heard again his son's excited giggles
the first time a fish did that to him. At least, he reminded
himself, he would always have that memory.

Memories. There were so many of them, gnawing at him
with hungry fingers. He surged to his feet, belatedly remembering to look around to assure himself that he hadn't
been spotted. Realizing he'd let something come between
him and the need for caution, the instinct for survival made
his temples pound. Still, no matter how hard he tried to remain rooted in the past, thoughts of General Canby's great-
great-granddaughter continued to haunt him.

He'd told her he would seek out Bear and take Bear's
wisdom as his own, but there'd been an even more compelling reason for him to go in search of the wise one. While
they were together, Tory's presence had blinded him to the
truth in the messages from Coyote and Owl, but she was
gone now, and he could no longer ignore certain things.
Coyote's howl had lasted for days while the Maklaks at-
tempted to flee the white men. Now Coyote was back, his
haunting cry so close that Loka knew his life was in danger.

And the only thing that had changed about his life was that Tory had entered it.

"*Blaiwas*. Return to me. Hear the questions in my heart. Give me the answer I seek."

He had to repeat his prayer twice but finally the familiar dark dot made its appearance. Freed from the distraction of Tory's presence, he concentrated on the great bird. If the enemy was about, they would see an eagle and think it had come to the lake in search of something to eat. Only he knew the truth—he and Tory Kent.

"*Blaiwas*. I am yours, as you are mine. I would lay down my life to protect you. Surely you know that. I seek only your wisdom. I walk a dangerous path. I fear nothing, but a warrior who wishes to live another day must understand his enemy. Is it her? Is this the message from Coyote—have I angered Kumookumts by taking her to the sacred mountain? By trying to understand her world? By wanting to take her to my bed? If I expend myself inside her, will she keep my strength?"

As the questions he'd been most reluctant to ask swirled above him, he studied Eagle's awesome wingspan. Eagle's strength had become his during those long-ago days of fighting and trying to stay alive and vowing to do the same for the other Maklaks. If it hadn't been for his son, he would have willingly died a warrior's death. But he hadn't, and because he hadn't, he now found himself alone in a world not of his making, torn between loyalty to the past and a woman from the new world.

"I lost myself in her eyes," he told the circling bird. "My flesh was weak—I took her to sacred ground because I wanted her to see the power of Kumookumts. Because I wanted to see understanding and belief in her eyes. Maybe I was unwise." His fingers clenched. "Maybe I have become a man who has forgotten that he is foremost a warrior. She wants me to reveal everything to her people, to those she calls Modocs but are not. I ask of you, should I listen to her or turn from her? Is there wisdom in her voice? Or treachery?"

Eagle floated lower, a wing dipping so close to the lake's surface that it cast a vivid shadow. Loka felt himself being embraced by the bird. Like a warm blanket, a wing touched first one shoulder and then another.

Eagle's message was clear.

Danger lurked. Eagle wanted to protect him from that danger.

Chapter 12

Tory waited while Fenton unlocked the metal grate over the entrance to Fern Cave. Taking the lantern he'd brought along, he stepped onto the narrow ladder and made his cautious way past the vibrant ferns reaching for what little sunlight made its way into the cave. She followed him, careful not to brush so much as a single frond. Once on the ground, she walked around the large green mound until the narrow path widened enough for her and Fenton to stand side by side.

"Pretty impressive, isn't it?"

Although Fenton was referring to the ferns, which had been growing for thousands of years in this uniquely protected environment where shade and constant moisture made it possible for water-loving plants to grow, her attention was immediately drawn to the drawings on the rock walls ringing the small opening. The markings at Petroglyph Point had been behind cyclone fencing, too far away to touch and high overhead; thus, it had been impossible for her to get close enough to see much in the way of detail. Here, however, was an anthropologist's delight.

Yes, a botanist could and probably had devoted months to studying this anomaly, but although she wanted to know more than she did about soil and water and air conditions underground, this wasn't the time.

When she realized Fenton was watching her, she went through the motions of taking pictures, but although she'd told him she needed to record the drawings to incorporate these with what hopefully would be done on the coast, the truth was much more personal.

Maybe Loka had been responsible for one of these symbols. A number had been placed here using some kind of dye. Other marks had been carved into the rock itself. Although she'd seen markings similar to these ever since she began taking anthropology courses, she knew that interpretations as to their meaning was nothing more than educated guesswork, something she wasn't going to indulge in.

"I don't know," Fenton said. He'd been kneeling near the ferns, studying them intently.

"You don't know what?"

"How much people are going to be interested in this. Sure, botanists, biologists, people into plants get off on this kind of thing, but I've got to look at the larger numbers. If I propose a publicity blitz and we get only a few hundred more people a year coming here because of the ferns, it's not going to be worth the effort. And Robert's right. It won't be long before the ferns are trampled, and then we'll be back where we were, scrambling for dollars."

It was cool down here, not cold enough that she felt the need for a jacket, but after the heat of the lava beds, she knew she couldn't stand still for long. The cave's opening was highest here near the opening. It sloped away behind them until the roof and a massive jumble of boulders in the distance seemed to meet. Between the muted sunlight and Fenton's flashlight, she had no trouble seeing back here, but she could make out little more than shadows at the cave's far reaches. They called to her, encouraged her to step back in time.

Had this been a sacred place? She didn't see how it could have been otherwise.

"What do you think?" Fenton inquired. "Would you pay good money to be brought here?"

She was hardly the one to ask. After what had happened to her life and heart and emotions since coming to the lava beds, no price was too great. "I think you're going to get a lot of opposition, and not just from the park director and board members."

"I've been thinking about that." Fenton walked around to the right of the ferns as far as he could go, then, arms folded, surveyed them again. "There's so little room down here. No way could we get more than a dozen, maybe twenty people jammed in here at one time."

She tried to hold on to what he was saying, tried to convince herself that if she came up with a compelling enough argument, she might be able to stop his potentially destructive plans before they went any further. But something was calling to her, taking her away from today's world just as spending the night on top of Spirit Mountain had. The walls felt alive with history. More than that, they gave out a timeless message of heritage and belief, thousands of years of Modoc tradition just beyond her fingertips.

One of the hard realities of her career was that much of her work was speculative in nature. She could look at what remained of a shaman's belongings and basically guess how he'd used a mix of herbs and other materials plus the power of belief to heal his patients. What she hadn't known—what her generation would never know—was whether a warrior truly believed in and trusted his guardian spirit, and whether that belief gave him courage far beyond what today's so-called sophisticated men could possibly understand.

Loka held that key—Loka whose essence haunted her every thought.

Did she dare tell Dr. Grossnickle about him, she asked herself for what seemed like the thousandth time. She went back to studying the seemingly random wall markings. Dr. Grossnickle was one of, if not *the* foremost anthropologist in the world, and although he was sometimes criticized by the academic community for the way he used the media, he was brilliant. And just as frustrated as she.

Together they could—with Loka they could . . .

Could what?

If she insisted on being in charge of working with Loka, she could guarantee he would remain protected from the media. Dr. Grossnickle would know how to handle that.

Wouldn't he?

What was she thinking about! If so much as a hint of his existence leaked, Loka would become a specimen fought over by hundreds of ambitious researchers, the press, maybe even the government.

If that happened, it would destroy him; he would hate her for as long as he lived.

Maybe he already did.

Head pounding, she placed her hand over one of the drawings. It looked rather like a sun being held aloft by a stick figure. It could mean that the early Modocs worshiped the sun. And it might be nothing more profound than a representation of one of their games.

No, not a game, she decided as her palm warmed. She stared at her hand, at the stone, and forgot to breathe. It wasn't possible! Surely she was letting her imagination get away from her. Or was she? The back of her hand felt cool thanks to the cave's temperature, but she could swear, almost, that her palm had become warmer.

Tearing her attention from what she was doing, she looked around for Fenton. He was down on his hands and knees gazing at the far side of the ferns, which grew up to the cave wall there. She could hear him muttering something but didn't think he was talking to her. Not that it mattered.

Heat? Coming from an unknown source?

Eagle. Wolf howling.

She tried to swallow, but her mouth was too dry. Feeling as if she'd been dropped into a twilight zone, she simply asked herself if she'd become privy to something that couldn't possibly be and yet was.

Loka existed. Being who she was had awakened him. That in and of itself was a miracle—only there was more to it than that. She couldn't let this link with the past, this link between a man and a woman—remain locked within her.

But Loka would hate her if she told anyone, and a word from her might jeopardize his life. No wonder he'd remained separate from everyone. If she, who was a supposedly competent member of the here and now, couldn't figure out his role in it, how could she expect more from him?

But he'd been alone, shut off, for so long. He hungered for some sense of belonging. Wanted to be touched by a living, breathing woman.

"It'll work." Fenton's unexpected comment shook her from questions without solutions. "I'll just have to make sure there's plenty of signs around telling people what they can and can't touch. We'll have to have someone around to guide the tours. I thought I might be able to get away without tying up a ranger for that, since no one puts restrictions on other activities around here, but having an employee on hand will give people the clear message that vandalism won't be tolerated. Yeah, I think it's going to work."

She didn't realize she still had her hand over the drawing until she felt numbing cold seep into the bones of her fingers. Shocked, she drew back and held her palm up to her mouth. There was no denying it; her hand was as cold as stone.

"You're not saying anything. You think I'm wrong, don't you?"

"What?"

"I said—never mind. I've got to get back to headquarters. Are you about done?"

She nodded because she didn't trust herself to speak. She took a single, tentative step and then another. If only she could tell someone what had happened. But what, if anything, had she experienced? And who, or what, if anything, was responsible?

Fenton started up the ladder. She gripped the railing, telling herself that sunlight and fresh air might bring herself back to reality, but couldn't make herself leave. For a moment, her attention remained fixed on the drawings, but then, slowly and relentlessly, she felt something at the rear of the cave call to her. Turning, she stared into shadows. Fenton had told her the cave ended back there, that if there'd ever been another opening, boulders shaken loose by a long-ago earthquake had sealed it off.

She and Fenton were alone down here.

Or were they?

As her eyes became accustomed to the dark, she saw something in the shadows. Something—some*one* who stared back at her.

Loka.

Hours later, Tory sat in the only chair in her cabin and stared out the nearest window. After returning to park headquarters, she'd tried to get in touch with Dr. Grossnickle, but had reached only his voice mail. She'd left a message that she now regretted, a disjointed comment about having discovered something she had to try to understand better. She was sorry about this delay in getting back to work and would be there as soon as possible.

What would she say when Dr. Grossnickle demanded an explanation as she knew he would?

It was the strangest thing. I met this Indian who fought the army here in 1873. He's got this pet eagle and we heard a wolf; you know, wolves haven't been here for years. I—he touched me and I changed. I want him, need him.

No! She couldn't say a word; it might risk Loka's life. Certainly her emotions, splintered and dangerous and overwhelming, were too private to share.

But if she kept her secret, everything he represented—a proud and noble way of life—would remain locked within him.

Sighing, she leaned her head against the back of the chair and tried to think of nothing. Unfortunately, that didn't work.

Darn Fenton, he'd refused to give her any privacy, and she'd been forced to call Dr. Grossnickle with him hanging on to every word. And the way he'd looked at her as she made her way out of the cave—it was as if her expression had given something away.

There wasn't enough air moving in the cabin. She supposed she could go outside, but it seemed like too much of an effort. Maybe she'd spend the rest of her life sitting here listening to insects buzz and chirp and make other insect sounds. And maybe she had no choice but to head into The Land Of Burned Out Fires, The Smiles Of God, and ask Loka to make love to her.

As thoughts of his hands on hers grew stronger, she easily dismissed everything else. She wanted to know what his chest and back and arms and legs felt like, ached to lose herself in his embrace.

Needed to feel him entering her.

Her mouth parted; she didn't care. Eyes closed, she allowed herself to be swept into a world of imagination and imagery. Loka would be waiting for her. It didn't matter whether she went back to Fern Cave or climbed Spirit Mountain or took the trail through Captain Jack's Stronghold, he would find her.

He would know why she was there.

Her fingers began moving restlessly up and down the chair's wooden arms. They needed not hard wood, but a man's flesh. It didn't matter how he took her; she didn't need foreplay. To come together in heat and need—to reach for and find that sensual explosion, to—

She wasn't alone.

Sitting up, she looked around, but the cabin hadn't changed. This wasn't Fern Cave and Loka wasn't staring at her from the shadows. Still, she had no doubt that he was near. After kicking back into her shoes, she stood and walked over to the window. Although she peered in all directions, she saw nothing that hadn't been there before. Just the same, the belief that he was here intensified.

She opened the door and stepped outside. The insects became noisier. The afternoon's heat should have made her feel lethargic. Instead, anticipation and raw hunger surged through her.

"Loka? Where are you?"

Nothing. Slightly apprehensive now, she looked around more carefully. Loka wasn't some high-spirited lover. He might not know that men and women sometimes teased each other, that it was possible for them to laugh and play.

He didn't trust her; she knew that. And he wasn't her lover.

"Loka?"

She didn't really expect him to answer. Still, when the silence stretched on, she experienced a moment of abject loneliness. They'd spent most of a day and a night together and he'd been in Fern Cave with her. Now they were apart, and she felt more alone than she had in her entire life. The weariness she'd been experiencing a few minutes ago no longer mattered. Nothing did except finding him.

The wilderness stretched out around her, called her to it; she had no urge to fight its pull. She made her way around rock and brush, over rises and into small gullies drawn by a powerful and undefinable force. With every step, she felt herself moving farther and farther from civilization and toward the only place she wanted to be.

With Loka.

She became aware of his presence by degrees. At first he was nothing more than a shadow beneath a scraggly evergreen, but slowly, hauntingly, shade became substance—his substance. Shaking a little now, she continued toward him. She felt the afternoon's sun beating down on her head; the summer heat filled her with energy. She'd told Fenton she would be leaving soon but now, coming closer and closer to Loka, the future meant nothing.

He looked no different from the last time she'd seen him, and yet it felt as if she were absorbing him for the first time.

She'd never known a man who took his body so much for granted. None had ever accepted near nakedness as if it were as natural as breathing. Loka did. And the way he was looking at her—not like a warrior studying his enemy but like a man watching his lover approach—did she dare believe?

"I sensed—somehow I knew you were here," she managed.

"I have been watching you. You do not look where your feet take you."

How can I? You're all that matters. Feeling as if she might splinter at any moment, she waited while he stepped out of the tree's shade and easily, effortlessly, covered the space separating them. His eyes were so intent on her that she wondered if he was trying to strip her naked. She didn't mind. Nothing mattered except that they were together again. For this moment. Finally she found her voice. "You were there earlier today, weren't you? In Fern Cave."

He nodded, the gesture allowing his ebony hair to slide forward. He pushed it out of his eyes with a practiced gesture. If they were ordinary people, she would ask him if he wanted her to cut his hair, and when he said yes—she needed him to say yes so she could touch him—she would draw out the act until taking lock after lock of hair between her fingers became part of the act of lovemaking. "How did you get in there?" she thought to ask. "There's only the one entrance, the one Fenton and I used."

"You do not understand." He'd stopped just out of her reach. She wondered if that was because he didn't trust her, or didn't trust himself around her. "No one but a Maklaks can."

"No." She felt as if she were starving, sustenance just out of reach. "I can't believe that. You took me up Spirit Mountain. I saw Eagle. Impossible as it is, I believe in Eagle, and in Wolf. I want to know everything, Loka. Everything about you and your world."

For the briefest fraction of time, she knew he wanted to give her what she'd just asked for. But then, all too soon, the

window between them closed, and he was again a warrior
testing his world for safety.

"I heard," he said. "I listened and I heard. The man you
were with seeks to dishonor a holy place."

"I—yes."

"I will kill him."

"No! Loka, you can't!"

"What would you have me do? Allow him to bring uncounted numbers of the enemy to where my people spoke
with the ancients?"

"Spoke with the ancients? I, ah..."

His eyes narrowed. Much as she hated it, she understood
he was questioning the wisdom of saying anything more to
her. She didn't blame him. Given what had happened to him
and his people, would he trust anyone, even her? "Loka,"
she said softly. Tears crowded her throat. "Fern Cave was
a sacred place for the Modocs, wasn't it?" She took a deep
breath, not because she needed to, but to give herself time
to consider what she might say next. In the end, only the
truth mattered. "Sacred because that's where the spirits of
your ancestors dwelled. At least where everyone believed
they'd once been."

He didn't move so much as a single muscle, and yet she
felt his intensity. Whether he believed she had no right being privy to what had been his secret she couldn't say, but
then it didn't matter because she'd spoken with every ounce
of honesty in her. "Loka, I felt something that first day out
at Captain Jack's Stronghold. I told myself I was simply
reacting to standing where the Modocs once had, but maybe
it was more than that. Maybe—oh, I don't know what I'm
saying."

He shrugged, the gesture slow and studied. If he'd thrown
a thousand words at her, the impact couldn't have been
greater. Heedless of any danger, she stepped closer and
touched the back of his hand. He looked down at what she'd
done, still motionless, still as much a part of his surroundings as any wild animal. She would never say there was a
vulnerability to him, but something—maybe it was the

loneliness he'd endured since awakening—was etched on every line of his body. He had his memory of his son, Eagle and Wolf, the essence of his people still living in the air around him, but she was the first human being who'd touched him in six months—no, in over a hundred years.

Thinking of nothing except putting an end to that, she slipped closer. She could plainly see his chest rising and falling and focused on that. The wilderness-scented air seeped into her lungs, into her pores and memory even. She saw nothing except brush and trees and rock, heard only the beating of her own heart and the faint call of some unseen bird. All hesitation fled, leaving her with nothing except longing.

He continued to watch her, his beautiful eyes seeing things in her she knew no other human being ever had. *I've been alone, too,* she said with her heart. *I know what you're feeling. Not everything, but enough. Please believe me. Enough.*

His powerful fingers closed over her wrist, laid a molten trail up her arm, heated her shoulder, covered the back of her neck. He drew her close, closer, gentle despite his strength. Her heart now pounded; she could barely remember how to breathe. Silence still coated the air between them, and yet, because his eyes no longer kept anything from her, she knew. He wanted her. Nothing else mattered. He wanted her.

Could she give herself to a warrior, to a man who had killed?

Could she not surrender to the only human being in her world?

Don't think, she warned herself. *Just take, and give.*

Chapter 13

The sun loved his hair. Although it was black as the darkest
night, today, red highlights ran through it. His jaw, squared
and hardened by nature and what he'd endured, called to
her. Keeping to her vow to let no outside thought filter in,
she stood on tiptoe and touched his jaw lightly with her lips.
When he ran his fingers up the hair at the back of her head,
she followed her first kiss with another.

Her body seemed to be losing form. It flowed warm and
liquid around her, and she drank hungrily from what she
found of his essence. Growing bolder, she rested her hands
on his shoulders, feeling the hint of velvet on his flesh.

She tried to remain calm, struggled to stay in control of
her emotions, but the feeling that she might never return to
what she'd once been continued to grow. Afraid of and yet
craving him, she ran her lips over his throat, his cheeks, the
tip of his nose. He flattened his free hand against the small
of her back, guided her to him.

Her belly was now pressed against him, increasing her
awareness of him, her knowledge that they'd stepped over
a line from which they could never retreat. Her face felt

flushed; surely he knew what was happening to her. But maybe, maybe his own body and emotions overwhelmed him. If they did... Breathing. Feeling. Need. Nothing except that.

When it was the last thing she wanted, he gripped her waist and drew her away from him. She continued to cling to his shoulders, her mouth slack, breathing quick and honest.

"You want this?" he whispered. "I must know. You want this?"

No! If I give myself to you, I'll never be the same. "I don't know how to answer." She should look around and assure herself that they were alone and he safe, but she couldn't take her eyes off him, might never have enough of looking at him. "I don't..." She'd been about to tell him she wasn't the kind of woman who jumped into bed with a man she'd just met, but in his world maybe something like that didn't matter. She tried to remember what male/female Modoc relationships had been like, but the sun still colored his hair with life and his eyes were dark and his lips waited for her.

"I have watched," he said. "Watched men and women who think they are alone. Something happens between them which I know little about."

"You've seen them making love?"

He nodded with no hint of embarrassment, with nothing except loneliness in his eyes. He'd been alone, had wanted it that way. But he'd still needed to know what it could be like for others. Not sure how much longer she could put off experiencing him—all of him—she pressed her hand against his chest. She should be able to say something, anything, shouldn't she?

"Making love," he said. "I do not understand what that means."

"You don't?"

"They were filling their need. Copulating. What is this making love?"

How could she ever explain romance to a man who thought of sex as simply that and no more? "When people care for each other," she began, "when they want to be with each other and no one else, when they're ready to take certain emotional risks...." The words died inside her, unmourned because maybe they weren't needed at all.

Leaning forward, she kissed first one hard breast and then the other. She sensed him sucking in his belly, had no doubt that he was physically ready for her. In that private and uncivilized part of her that she'd always kept at bay, the wanton woman she could be struggled for freedom. Lovemaking didn't matter. She would take sex, raw and wonderful.

But if that happened between them, he would never really know her and she would never know the man she believed he could be. Reining in what she could of her need, she gripped his hands, which were now cupped over her buttocks, and placed them firmly by his side.

"I don't know what it was like between you and your wife, Loka, but I'm not that woman. I need—I need..." She swallowed, but that did nothing to help recapture her failing self-confidence. "I don't know if I'm going to say this right. All I can do is try. I want you—never think otherwise." He started to reach for her again, but she stopped him, firmly placing his arms back by his side. He was so damnable powerful, so male. Not thinking about that was impossible. Not responding took every bit of self-control she had in her.

"When you got married, it was because your parents had arranged it, wasn't it?"

"Yes."

"Your wife—the first time you slept with her, what was it like?"

"She had been married before—her first husband died. She knew what was expected of her."

Expected. "Did you want to sleep with her?"

"Want? I had needs. It was her role to satisfy them."

Role. "I understand. But beyond that?"

"Beyond?"

Why had she started this? It would have been easier to simply surrender to the needs he'd spoken about. But, she believed, he'd watched lovers not because he was a voyeur, but because he realized they were experiencing something he desperately needed. "Did you love her?"

He lifted his hand as if to push away her question. "No."

"But you lived together. You had a child together. Surely you cared—"

"It was not right for either of us to live alone. The tribe was strengthened by our marriage."

"I understand," she said, wondering if she ever truly could. The hot hunger she'd experienced at his touch had cooled a little, but if she didn't guard herself against him, it might take no more than a single word. The slightest touch.

"Loka, it's no longer like that. These days, when people marry, when they live together, it's because they want to, not because their families or chiefs have told them they must."

"Want to?"

"Because—" She swallowed in an attempt to free her dry throat. "Because they're in love, or think they are. There's physical need—that hasn't changed. But it's the emotional component that..." Damn it, she sounded like a psychiatrist when a studied and stilted explanation meant nothing to him. "When you were with your wife, did you feel as if you wanted to spend the rest of your life with her?"

He tried to keep his features immobile. Hurting for him, she concentrated on the effort and understood a great deal about him, knowledge that found a home deep within her heart. "We did not want the same things out of life," he said. "Our hearts did not sing the same songs."

This was a primitive man, a man ruled by nothing more than the need to stay alive? Looking into his eyes, she joyously answered her question. Yes, concerns and hardships she couldn't imagine had consumed his days, but he'd stared into night skies and listened to the wind and felt the same stirring in his soul that she did.

His heart needed the same things hers did.

"Did—did you ever look for someone who thought and felt like you?"

"Once."

"Once?"

"Before I was married, before we were forced onto the reservation with the Klamaths. It was a long time ago."

"I want to hear about it."

He blinked, sighed. "We laughed together, shared our bodies, watched a mother rabbit with her young and spoke of children. But she was promised to another, and I did what I had to and forgot her."

Except he hadn't. She didn't resent the woman from his past. Instead, she sent up a prayer of thankfulness that he'd experienced the most precious of emotions—love. "That— that's what it's like, what everyone looks for these days. People marry for love. They sleep together because they love each other." It wasn't always like that. He must know that as well as she did, but standing in front of him with his life force flowing around her, nothing except him and her and the two of them mattered.

"I want you."

His hard words shocked her. It wasn't until she forced herself to study him that she understood. He didn't know what to do with what she'd told him, didn't know how to handle his reaction to both her and the dawning understanding that there could be something precious between a man and a woman. As a consequence, he was reverting back to what his people had expected him to be—a stoic and fearless warrior. Proud and defiant, he was using words to protect himself from her.

"Take me, then."

That made him blink. But instead of saying anything, doing anything, he simply stood, arms tense at his sides, hands fisted. He seemed to have pulled into himself. She guessed he was weighing, not what he could do with her offer, but what might happen between them if nothing except physical need drove him.

"I won't fight you, Loka. It won't be love, but it won't be rape, either. Do you know what I'm saying?"

"Many of our women were raped by soldiers."

"I know." It was as if she could hear the women's cries and feel their men's helpless anger. "That still happens," she was forced to tell him. "But it's not part of lovemaking." *Not part of what I need from you.*

"I will not be like the soldiers."

She'd been fighting instinct too long. She had to touch him, to feel his warmth against hers. He shuddered slightly when her fingers brushed his waist. For an instant she saw the depths of this man who had slept alone too long.

I want you to feel alive again, whole. To be the woman you turn to at night. Forever.

Of course it was insane. Forever wasn't for them, not with worlds and generations separating them. But they had today. She would cling to today.

"You weaken me," he whispered when he held her in his arms. "I think of you and I forget everything else."

"You're all that matters to me," she said from the shelter, the mountain of his chest. She heard him suck in a long and unsteady breath, but it gave her no feeling of control over him. What was it he'd said? That she weakened him? Did he have any idea how helpless, how molten she felt at this moment? She needed to tell him she was nothing without him, but if she did, she would have to think about tomorrow, and she couldn't.

She wouldn't.

His hands that had fought her great-great-grandfather's army slid over her arms and back, her neck and hips, less insistent this time, more as if she were a precious jewel that had somehow come into his possession.

She felt safe with this man, and yet her heart continued to beat out of time. Her body belonged, not to her, but to him, to what he was doing to her. To the world he was taking her into. Because he already wore next to nothing, nothing stood in the way of her exploration of him, and yet she held back. She had kissed his lips and chin, wrapped her arms around his neck and held on to his powerful arm, but if she gave in to the need to trail her fingers over his hips, to stroke his thighs, to hold his weight in the palm of her hand, she might lose herself.

She was already lost, she admitted with something that might have been laughter but was probably a silent sob. Loka, who knew nothing of the nuances of lovemaking, obviously thought nothing of claiming her breasts, her belly, of drawing her leg up and around him. If he'd been anyone except who he was, she would have warned him he was going too fast, taking too many liberties. But she'd entered his world and what he wanted was right. Anything he wanted.

He managed to unbutton her jeans but knew nothing about how a zipper worked. After kicking out of her shoes, she showed him, not just because she didn't want to see him frustrated, but because she needed to be wearing no more than he did. When he pulled her jeans down over her hips, she clung to him, moving with his hands until she stepped out of the garment. He slid his hands under her blouse and began to push it upward but stopped when his fingers grazed her belly. Leaning back, he narrowed his gaze on her underpants. She told him what they were but could only imagine what he was thinking.

"They are useless."

"Useless?"

"Do they keep you warm in winter? Do they protect you from injury?"

"No." She smiled, shivered, when he slid his hand under the waistband and tested it. "But it's no longer that kind of a world, Loka. Protection and warmth—most people take that for granted."

"They do not fell trees and split logs for heat?"

"No," she said, trying to imagine what it had been like for him and his people as they huddled in unheated caves. Shadows settled in his eyes and told her he was thinking the same thing. "Don't live in the past," she begged. "Please. If I could change it for you, I would, but it's behind us now. There's only today. And the future."

"The future?" His hold on her increased, became an unspoken demand. "Tell me about my future, Tory."

She wouldn't, couldn't do that, not just because she feared what tomorrow might bring for him, but because her body was interested only in today. This moment. Him. Telling him that, not with words but with gestures, she covered his bronze breasts with her paler hands.

He looked down at her, sunlight slowly returning to his eyes. She'd never thought of herself as a particularly feminine woman. True, her body had been designed with a gentle hand, but she'd always been more interested in her brain than the physical package. Today she felt new and alive, prayed that her body would please this man, trembled at the thought of what their coming together would be like.

"You are so small," he whispered. The top button of her blouse came free under his fingers. "Like a bird."

"You make me think of a cougar." She wanted to go on touching him, giving him pleasure, but soon she would be naked. She couldn't think beyond that.

Another button. "A bird and a cougar? No, we are not that."

"It—it's a lovely thought." Button number three.

"Lovely? I do not know the meaning of the word."

"Then I'll teach you," she told him before her throat closed. The final button had been released. She sagged forward slightly as if protecting herself from his gaze, from his fingers. But when he touched the base of her throat and trailed his fingers downward, she straightened. Gave him permission to do what he wanted with her.

The same quizzical expression that had touched his features at the sight of her panties returned. "I have seen this garment." He indicated her bra. "But I do not understand. Why are white women afraid of their breasts?"

"Afraid? No, it's not that. It's—it's the way things are done now."

He chuckled, then pulled a strap off her shoulder. A warm breeze skittered over her newly exposed flesh, but that wasn't why she trembled. Although she knew he was frustrated with the workings of her bra, several minutes passed before she showed him how to release it. It shouldn't matter; they'd gone too far to stop now. But once she was naked, nothing would remain of the woman she'd been only a few minutes ago. The lines between them would be erased, all barriers gone.

Was she ready to expose her body and heart to him? To herself?

He ran his hands down her unbelievably sensitive back. If she hadn't been so eager for him, she might have found his fingers too rough, but she was beyond such concerns, needed his touch too much. His flesh felt warmer than it had before. It might be the sun; it might be his reaction to her. If that was it, she was happy, and if earlier he managed to keep some of himself locked off from her, she didn't want to think about that.

Didn't want to know.

"You are a bird. Your bones are so small."

"No," she protested from the void that was her mind. "I'm not—"

"I do not want to hurt you."

Now that she understood his concern, she wanted to put his mind at ease, but how could she when he'd taken hold of her—all of her? He seemed to be everywhere at once, his hands roaming her body as if he couldn't get his fill of her. Somehow they'd sunk to their knees, not on hard earth, but on a mat of fallen leaves and thick grass. Their knees and thighs touched. She fastened her arms around his neck and kissed him frantically, deeply, unable to do anything except respond to hands running over her belly and hips. A whimper came to life deep in her throat. She followed its upward trail, cared not at all when it escaped her.

He pulled her hands off him and pushed her away from him, staring at her with an intensity that rocked her. "You cry?"

"No. Not cry. I..." *I want you so much.* Although he continued to look at her, his eyes filled with passion and concern, she couldn't make herself say the words that would

expose her deepest emotions. "It's all right," she said when,
finally, she realized he was determined to outwait her silence. "I'm all right."

"You are afraid of me."

"No." She started to shake her head, but the gesture made
her dizzy. *I'll never be afraid of you,* she nearly said, but
because that might not be the truth, she stopped herself in
time. "Loka, please, can't we just—all I want is—please,
make love to me."

"Make love?"

"Sex!" she blurted out in desperation. "I want to have
sex with you."

She was terrified he'd want a further explanation when it
was all she could do to keep herself from flying apart. In an
attempt to keep him silent, she lunged toward him and covered her mouth with his. His grunt of surprise nearly
stripped her of her courage, but she hung on with a will she
thought she'd lost, and gradually, too gradually, she sensed
question and doubt seep out of him.

It was impossible. Surely she didn't have the strength to
mold this warrior to her will, but maybe—yes—he had to
want this thing they were doing as much as she did.

Sex, lovemaking—what did the words matter? There was
only need and hunger exploding inside her, her hands restless again, his hands bold and indiscriminate on her body.
Falling onto her back beneath him, looking through glazed
eyes at his muscled form covering hers, arching herself toward him, telling him she was ready for him.

Perched over her, his body hard and shaking, he held
himself suspended until she thought she would scream.
"Wha—"

"*Sloa.*"

"What?"

"You are *Sloa.* Wildcat."

"No. No."

"Wildcat."

Maybe she was. "I can't help what I am, Loka." *Loka.
How beautiful his name sounded as it echoed inside her.*

"*Kiuka,*" he whispered. She felt his manhood graze the inside of her thigh, arched toward him even more. "You are *Kiuka.*"

It didn't matter. Nothing did except that he'd found her center, that she was moist and hot. Flying into countless pieces. Accepting him. Drawing him deep inside her. Feeling him push himself even farther, filling her, taking her— taking her away from herself.

It had happened too fast.

Careful not to let too many thoughts in at once, Tory opened her eyes just enough to assure herself that Loka hadn't left her. He lay on his side, his slickened body quiet and magnificent. She wanted it to be like that forever, but even in the halfway world she clung to, she knew that wasn't possible. For these precious moments he was her lover, even if he didn't understand everything that went with the word.

Lover.

Lover.

Only when she tried to say it for the third time did she force herself to face the truth. They'd had sex, quick and hot and urgent. There'd been nothing gentle or loving about their joining, although neither of them had hurt or been hurt. While caught in the moment's onslaught, she hadn't wanted anything else. Or maybe the truth was there hadn't been enough of her left over to care about anything except the volcano consuming her.

He'd satisfied her, spent his own need.

And it had happened too fast.

Shutting her eyes, she tried to turn her mind to what he looked like, the rawhide muscles, midnight eyes and sun-loving hair. She wanted to see where he lived. If she asked him, would he take her there? She knew nothing about how he obtained the food that kept him alive. Would he let her accompany him while he hunted? If she asked him, would he show her how to gather the plants that had sustained his people?

She ran with that thought, imagined herself dressed in the softest of doeskin while she picked berries to dry for winter use. He would have been off hunting, and as the day ended, he'd step into their home and take her into his arms and—

"Loka," she heard herself say. She opened her eyes and looked over at him, started to shake all over again. "Loka."

For several seconds, he stared at her, his expression unreadable. "You regret what we did."

"Not regret. Never that. But . . ."

"Say it, Tory. I cannot see what is in your heart."

"What we did was because we were so hungry for each other. I—I'm not ashamed. I take full responsibility for the way I acted." *How? You nearly lost your mind.* "And you've been alone so long."

"Yes."

Yes. Such a simple word to explain what he'd had to endure.

"It could be different," she said, forcing herself not to drop her gaze. "Sweet and gentle."

"And you want that?"

"Yes. Don't you?"

Chapter 14

Loka rolled away from her and stood, oblivious to the fact that he was naked. She tried to hold on to what she'd just asked him, but the sight of him nearly turned her into a liar. She'd told him she wanted sweet and gentle lovemaking, but if he turned toward her with hunger and urgency in his eyes, his body hard and healthy and ready, she would respond. Simply respond.

"When we were at Spirit Mountain, it seemed that the night would never end," he said. "I wanted to return to you, to bury myself in you. But I was afraid of the man in me. And I did not know whether I could trust you."

"Afraid of yourself?" she whispered. She didn't want to know what he meant by not being able to trust her, or whether that had changed.

"Of my need. It was a winter storm inside me."

She hadn't known that. How could she when he'd slept apart from her? "Is that why you were so quiet?"

He nodded. "That, and Owl's message."

She almost asked him what he was talking about before she remembered his superstition that an owl's call foretold death or danger. Who was she to belittle anything he believed in? After all, his existence was proof that some extraordinary force was at work. "Just because an owl hoots doesn't mean there's danger out there."

He remained silent. Her mind whirled with what she might say to put his concerns to rest, to remind him that owls were nothing more than night creatures. She wanted to tell him he was a miracle, the only living link with his people's heritage, but if she did, she might say the rest—that he couldn't keep his wisdom locked within him. The wrong words and he would turn from her as he'd done before, and she couldn't stand the thought of not seeing him again.

Not making love to him again.

Ignoring her own state of undress, she stood on less-than-steady legs and walked over to him. They were alone in the solitude of his world. Funny, she'd given it no thought earlier. She took his hand and brought it to her breast. He gave her a quizzical look but didn't draw away. She spread his fingers over the sensitive mound, showing him with gestures and smiles and silence that she was placing herself in his hands and in return wanted him only to be gentle with her.

"Think of me as a flower," she whispered. "A fragile flower."

"A flower does not feel."

"No," she admitted. "And I do. Believe me, I do."

Their exploration became hands and lips again, touch and retreat, tease and urgency, whispered encouragement, quiet reminders, a slow building of emotion and sensitivity. And always the awe of being with him, believing in him. Maybe loving him.

Fighting her own urgent body, she trailed her fingers lightly over his arms and ribs, surrendered to his embrace and then pulled back. Not once did she stop touching him; he did the same, smiling as he learned what pleased her. Not as hungry as the first time, she drew out the foreplay, explored and retreated, challenged before backing off until she felt in control again.

When she stopped being the teacher and simply began sharing, she couldn't say. It might have been when his tongue invaded her mouth for the first time. Maybe it was when he turned her around so her back was against him and he ran his hands firmly, possessively from the base of her throat to the apex of her legs.

She began moaning when he did that, couldn't stop. Head thrown back, she gulped in needed air. That only increased his access to her. She tried to stop him, but his power over her and her helplessness—her wanting—was so great that after a few seconds, her hands dropped uselessly by her side. No longer caring, she listened to herself whimper, knew nothing except his strong fingers invading her most private parts.

He guided her so that she faced him once more, careful to keep his hands on her so she wouldn't collapse. He was smiling; despite the red film curtaining her vision, she could see the beautiful and knowing gesture.

"A flower?" he asked. He forced her to stand in front of him, arms still limp, while he ducked his head and flicked his tongue over her taut nipples. "I think not. A flower is easily crushed. You only blossom more."

He was right, right as only a man who knows what pleases a woman can be.

As had happened the first time, she suddenly found herself no longer standing. This time she wasn't on her knees but already on her back, reaching for him, reaching and whimpering again. He knelt with one leg on either side of her hips, growling deep in his throat when she ground the heels of her hands against his chest. She tried to open herself for him, but he held her trapped under him. Fear flickered but died when she saw the passion she felt etched on his features. He wanted this—this lovemaking—as much as she did. The evidence of that was clear. But he'd learned, or maybe he'd already known, that ecstasy long anticipated becomes all the richer.

When he slid to one side of her and slowly, gently, firmly, slipped his hands between her legs, asked permission, she fastened her hands in his hair and pulled him down to her for one last passionate kiss before—

Before lovemaking.

"Gew'ks."

Tory struggled to pull herself out of the dark cave she'd fallen into, but it wasn't until Loka repeated himself that she managed to focus. He was sitting up, one hand clutching a rock, his attention fixed on a tall, thin pine tree some fifty feet away. At the top perched an owl large enough that it made the spindly branch sag.

"Gew'ks? Owl? Loka, he's just—"

The owl stretched its neck; its long, mournful hoot stopped her in midsentence. Instantly, what Loka had said about an owl warning of death came back to her. She stared at Loka, trying to think of something to say that would make him see nothing more than a bird, but he'd been conditioned by a lifetime of legends and spiritual belief.

Besides, what if he was right?

"Loka." She scrambled to her feet but stopped before reaching him. Even while he tied his loincloth back into place, his eyes never left the owl who again shattered the quiet with his haunting call.

"Gew'ks."

"He belongs here, Loka. He's hunting. That's all just hunting."

"Your heart is not Maklaks. You do not know."

No, she didn't. "Tell me, please. Why..."

"Gew'ks speaks. I listen."

"What about me?" She hated the fear, the loneliness in her voice, but couldn't kill it. "Won't you listen to me?"

"Gew'ks is born of Kumookumts. Kumookumts created all Maklaks."

And she wasn't Maklaks. "They're gone, Loka. You said so yourself. Please turn your back on the past. Walk—walk into the present."

"I do not know what is my present, Tory. I search and ask and pray. I know restlessness that threatens to tear me apart. I want—I want to belong somewhere. But—"

"You belong with me!"

"Do I? And is it enough? Tory, the past claims me. It is all I know. I do not want to leave it behind. I do not want my heritage to become dust. Who except for me will keep it whole?"

Without looking at her, he strode off into the wilderness.

Was she ever going to sleep again?

Despite the exhaustion etched deep inside her, Tory sat up and slipped out of bed. Not bothering to look for shoes, she walked over to the nearest window and took in her surroundings. Morning was little more than a faint cast in the night-dark sky, but she remembered what dawn had looked like from the top of Spirit Mountain—when she stood beside Loka and he told her about the untold generations of Modocs who'd believed that the world began and ended with what they could see from up there.

They'd been right, she acknowledged. At least back then, what existed beyond where the Modocs ranged hadn't mattered. Loka had a growing grasp of today's world, but he'd never seen a city, and no matter what he'd read or heard, he would have only a rudimentary understanding of what one was like. His world had ended before the invention of the telephone. How could he comprehend computers and fax machines?

She tried to tell herself it didn't matter because he still lived on the land that had nourished him and his people, but the attempt at self-delusion didn't last long. He might carry an ancient knife and put his faith in messages brought to him by wild animals and birds, but The Smiles Of God was no longer his domain, and he knew it. It had been invaded by those he considered his enemies, and unless he spent the rest of his life isolating himself from them—which in his heart he didn't want to do—eventually they would learn of his existence, and he would have to learn how to coexist with them.

We can do it, Loka. Together. If you'd just trust me, share your wisdom and spiritual richness with the rest of the world...

In an attempt to ward off the headache building behind her temples, she dug through her meager supply of groceries. She came up with some fruit and a bagel and washed breakfast down with cool, sweet water. She'd brought enough food with her to last a couple of days; most of that was gone, which meant she would have to drive into the nearest town to restock.

She walked into what passed for a bathroom and splashed water on her face. Only then did she look into the small mirror and face the decision she'd made.

She couldn't leave.

Couldn't because Loka had crawled under her skin and she couldn't walk away from him and go on living.

He doesn't want you. He left you yesterday, remember.

He left because an owl warned him of danger.

Danger from you?

''Enough!'' she blurted, shaken by the realization that she'd spoken aloud. But although she turned from the mirror so she wouldn't have to stare at her hollowed-out eyes, she couldn't hide from her thoughts.

She'd made love to Loka. Maybe fallen in love with him. The last thing she'd ever do was endanger his existence.

But was it possible that she had by coming here?

No, damn it, no!

Maybe.

Groaning, she pressed her hand against her forehead. What she needed was her very own Eagle. If she had a spirit, she could call on it for the answers to questions that threatened to drive her crazy.

Well, she didn't have one. The only alternative was to get out of this blasted cabin so maybe her thoughts would stop ricocheting off the walls. Heartened by the thought that she had a plan of action, she dressed and walked outside. She'd covered most of the distance separating the cabin from park headquarters before she admitted that she'd spent the time looking for some sign of Loka.

He wasn't here; if he'd been, she would have known. Her body, so sensitive to him, would have told her.

Maybe he was still sleeping, alone, dreamless. Maybe he was awake and thinking about what he perceived to be Owl's warning.

And maybe—

She stopped in midstride as an unwanted thought hit her. Loka had been adamantly opposed to Fenton's plans to exploit Fern Cave. She'd tried to tell him that opposition by any number of environmental groups would put an end to that insanity, but had he believed her? Was it possible that he'd decided to stop Fenton in the only way he knew?

Stomach knotted, she was forced to ask herself if Loka might risk his life protecting what his people had held sacred.

Of course he would.

Hurrying now, she tried to come up with a plan. First, she'd call Dr. Grossnickle and tell him she didn't know when, if ever, she'd be rejoining him. He deserved as much of the truth as she could give him, which, in order to protect Loka, wouldn't be much. She could tell Dr. Grossnickle that she'd discovered a risk to an historically sensitive site and didn't dare leave until she could be sure that it was safe. He'd argue that what he was trying to accomplish was more important, but she'd hold firm. If he told her she no longer had a job—

What did a job matter? Owl had cried of death yesterday.

"You're still here?"

Tory winced, then admitted that she'd known her chance of getting in and out of park headquarters without Fenton spotting her had been slim. At least she'd managed to make her phone call. Turning her thoughts from Dr. Grossnickle's terse command that she either wind things up here or he'd be forced to look for a replacement, she faced Fenton, who looked inordinately proud of himself this morning.

"Actually," Fenton said as he joined her, "I'm glad I caught you. You're the first to know this. The senator's coming here next week."

"He's what?"

"I caught him in a weak moment. Actually, I made my uncle an offer he couldn't refuse. He's getting a lot of flak about not getting out enough. I told him he could fly here and take a tour, with photographers around to record his concern for an historic landmark, of course. Once the public show's over, he can get in a little bird hunting."

Thinking of the vast wetlands that had been preserved to protect the large number of birds that made their home in this part of the country, she couldn't believe the senator would want to be seen hunting. However, when Fenton explained that he'd arranged to get his uncle onto on private land far from prying eyes, she understood. "You bribed him."

"You might say that. Hey, as long as he comes out as being concerned for the lava beds' future, what do people around here care? They'll see him, hear him and think there's going to be money following in his wake—money I've laid the groundwork for."

She didn't want to hear any more, but if she didn't pretend to be fascinated by Fenton's latest plans, she wouldn't know how all this might impact Loka.

Loka, who would perceive a self-important politician and the press as a threat to his sacred land—to the only thing he had left in life.

"Next week, you say?" She made herself ask. "How did you manage to pull it together so fast?"

"Brief congressional recess. Pheasant and duck season. The timing couldn't be better."

"No. I guess it couldn't."

Fenton studied her for a minute, making her all too aware of what she must look like. She'd made love to Loka twice yesterday—abandoned and unashamed lovemaking. Her lips still felt swollen. She'd brushed her hair but had been unable to do much to restore bounce to it. And her eyes—her eyes had *that* look this morning. "I take it you're going to show the senator Fern Cave," she said in a desperate attempt to take his thoughts off her.

"You bet." Fenton gave her a self-satisfied grin. "It's going to take some stretching of the rules, but one way or the other, I'm going to get him down there with the press. Can't you just imagine it? Shots in newspapers all over the country of Senator Baldwin studying the petroglyphs, crouching over the ferns. If that doesn't increase interest in this area, I don't know what will. In fact—what do you think of this? I've been mulling it over half the night. If he's favorably disposed—and why wouldn't he be if he gets in some good hunting and even better press?—he'll spread the word among his colleagues. I'll work through him, let them know I'm their contact man when and if they come here. Get enough of them interested in this chunk of Northern California so that when it comes budget time, they'll vote to increase the allocation for the lava beds."

"That's—that's pretty ambitious."

"I'm just getting started." When he smirked, it was all she could do not to wipe it off his face. "I'm sure you heard about the restoration they did to the lodge at Crater Lake, how hard it was to get the money allocated. In the end it happened, and that's what matters. Well, the lava beds haven't begun to tap their potential. I mean, look at what they've got, nothing but a couple of cabins like yours and that dinky camping setup. But a lodge—I can just see it! I wonder how big they could make it? What do you think, at least a hundred rooms? There's sure as hell enough land to build it on. Of course they'd have to put in a parking lot and maybe a few more roads, particularly one out to the Thomas-Wright Battlefield. Having to walk out there the way people do now just isn't cutting it. Getting my uncle revved up, that's the first step. And I'm the one to do it."

Feeling as if she'd been plunged into ice water, Tory could only stare openmouthed as Fenton went on and on about his plans for the lava beds. She nearly interrupted to remind him that just a few days ago he'd seen the lava beds as nothing more than a brief stop in his career. Now, if he had his way, this beautifully wild and serene area would become an overcrowded tourist trap. She had a horrible image of fast-food restaurants and gift shops springing up like weeds.

"I know, I know," Fenton said at last. "All of this is in the future, but it's got to start somewhere, and I'm the man to get it done." He swiped at a bee. "I can't believe you're still here. The appeals court has set a date to hear the Indians' objection to what Dr. Grossnickle and the university is planning, you know. I thought you'd have burned rubber getting back to him."

She hadn't known that—she hadn't talked to Dr. Grossnickle any longer than absolutely necessary this morning. She was about to tell Fenton that she still hadn't completed her exploration of the area when she realized he would never believe that, would see through the lie. Feeling trapped, she said the only thing that might satisfy him.

"Yes, I know I should be leaving, but, well, the truth is, General Canby was my great-great-grandfather. I don't know when I'll have another opportunity to see what his world was like."

"You're what? No kidding? Why didn't you say something before?"

"Because my coming here is for me," she said firmly.

"General Canby's great-great-granddaughter." His eyes took on a speculative look, and she guessed he was trying to think of a way to exploit what he'd just learned. "You can prove that? Not that I don't believe you, but it'd have a lot more impact if it was documented."

"I just told you, my trip is a personal thing. I want to touch base with what he experienced, try to understand it, have something to tell my children someday. It's no one else's business."

"You're wrong. Wrong. Wait a minute! Does Dr. Grossnickle know?"

"No."

"In other words, he doesn't know the real reason you haven't hotfooted it to his side?"

Convinced she was walking into a trap, she could only stare at him. Instead of challenging her, he simply nodded, his eyes speculative, questioning. He glanced at his watch. "Black is going to be here any minute. He called last night, wouldn't say why he wanted to talk to me, just that I'd better not try to dodge him. I figure he'd already heard about the senator coming. Of course he's going to object—I don't have to be hit over the head to know that. But there's nothing he can do about it. It's a free country. I can invite anyone I want. I don't get it, Tory. Why wouldn't you want anyone to know who you are? If you did, I'm sure everyone here would go out of their way to tell you everything they can about General Canby."

She couldn't tell him that since the first time she'd looked at Loka, she'd been unable to put her mind to anything else. "Maybe I should have," she said weakly.

"I sure would have. And if I had to cover my tail with my employer, I'd have told him the truth. If that's the truth."

Wary, she waited Fenton out.

"I'm not saying you aren't who you say you are. However, you've been here for days now, and from what I've seen, you haven't spent a whole lot of time trying to learn more about the general."

"You've been watching me that closely?"

"You know what I mean. Like I said, if I was you, I'd be digging through old military records, asking for anything and everything the general might have written while he was here. Instead, when I took you into the archives room, all you were interested in was what we had on the Modocs."

Stomach knotted, she frantically asked herself if there was any way Fenton could know she'd been with Loka. But only she had proof of Loka's existence, didn't she? With a sinking feeling, she remembered her first conversation with Fenton, when he'd waxed eloquent about the possibilities for exploiting rumors of a ghost warrior. Did he suspect, or know, that they weren't rumors? Had he actually seen Loka—with her?

Belatedly she forced herself to concentrate on what Fenton had just said. She told him that as an anthropologist, of course she was interested in Modoc culture and after seeing the caves where the Indians had been forced to live, her curiosity had only grown. Not once did he take his eyes off her, and she had the sinking feeling she was rattling on, protesting too much. "You're right," she finally wound up. "I do want to see what's in storage that pertains directly to General Canby. I hope to do that today."

"Hmm. By the way, you were at your place yesterday, weren't you? Alone."

Alone. "What are you talking about?"

"I looked out that way a couple of times. I knew you hadn't left because your car was still here. I kept trying to find time to come out, but yesterday was insane."

"I imagine it was," she said despite her dry throat.

"The thing was, I swore I saw someone out there."

"What?" Hoping to make a point, she glanced back at the cabin. It wasn't visible from here. "How could you—"

"Binoculars."

The way he said the word, smug and not at all ashamed of what he'd done, she didn't know whether to beg him not to say anything about what he might or might not have seen or pull a bluff. "You couldn't have been as busy as you said you were if you had time for that. What were you doing, spying on me?"

Smiling a little, he shrugged. "I make it my business to know everything that's going on here, especially if I think there's a way I can use something to enhance the park's resources, and my career."

What did he mean by that? She debated demanding he explain himself, but decided she didn't want to tip her hand by appearing to be too interested in his innuendos. "I'm glad you told me that," she said instead. "It gives me the opportunity to tell you as clearly as I can that I have no intention of trading on my relationship with General Canby, and I expect you to do the same."

"Is that so?" He leaned forward, his smile friendly, his manner intimidating. "Somehow I don't believe you, Tory. You're an ambitious young woman. You wouldn't have gotten where you are in your career if you weren't. Something's got your interest here—something maybe we both know about."

Don't say a word. Don't give anything away. "Something?" she asked, hating herself the moment the word was out.

To her frustration and concern, he merely gave her another of his noncommittal shrugs. She might be imagining it. Given her emotional state, she couldn't trust her reaction to anything he said or did, but it seemed as if his gaze had become more knowing, more superior. As if he knew something but wasn't willing to tip his hand, yet.

Loka, be careful!

"So," he said after too long a silence, "when are you going to start looking at what of General Canby's has been preserved? Or maybe you have other things to do, other places to go today."

"What do—" As a rough and yet familiar sound reached her, she stopped in midsentence. Looking down the road, she recognized Black Schonchin's old pickup and let out a silent sigh of gratitude. The old Modoc man would keep Fenton occupied for a while, hopefully long enough for her to decide what she had to do—and how much danger Loka might be in.

"Black," Fenton called out as the Modoc got out of his truck. "You remember Tory Kent, don't you? The anthropologist?"

Black nodded but said nothing. He walked toward them, his gait slow and dignified. Despite her suspicion that Fenton had something up his sleeve, she couldn't help imagining what it would be like if Black Schonchin and Loka could meet. Somehow, damn it, she had to make Loka realize that he could trust. That he could share his vast treasure of knowledge with someone.

Like her? But because of her, his freedom might be in jeopardy.

Fenton said something to Black about wanting to keep the Modoc council apprised of everything that was being planned for while the senator was here. He certainly hadn't intended to exclude the Indians; he just hadn't seen this brief visit as something that would interest them.

"I'm not a fool," Black cut in. "If you can possibly turn the lava beds into your own private triumph, you will. I spent last night on the phone with the council's attorney. He's looking into the park's bylaws and standards to ascertain whether we can block you from turning this visit into a media circus."

Tory wanted to applaud Black for his direct, no-nonsense approach. Although he gave the impression of being a quiet and somewhat backward man, obviously he was anything but. And Fenton was getting that message loud and clear.

Glaring, Fenton sputtered that he didn't appreciate having the Modocs question his motives when he was working day and night to assure that park funding was maintained.

"The only thing you're interested in is what you get out of it," Black interrupted. Holding up his hand to keep Fenton quiet, he swept his gaze over the horizon. "The spirits of our ancestors have been disturbed. They sense danger to our land. Owl warns of death, as does Coyote."

"What are you talking about?" Fenton asked, his attention not on Black but on Tory.

"Whites call it a mirage, a trick. But we Modocs know different. *He* is here."

"He?" Tory managed.

Black barely glanced her way and didn't answer her question. She knew all too well what he thought of her profession. Still, she couldn't pretend the conversation didn't concern her. "You said something about this—this—warrior the other day." Again she struggled for a calm tone. "Are you saying you actually saw him this morning? Or

thought you did?'' she amended, belatedly putting doubt in
her voice.

"*He* was watching me this morning. I looked over at
Captain Jack's Stronghold as I drove by and saw him. He
was waiting for me."

Emotion rolled through her, briefly making it impossible
for her to speak. Loka must have heard Black's truck approaching and deliberately revealed himself. She could only
guess at Loka's reason for reaching out to the old Modoc.
Maybe her argument had been responsible. Maybe he had
decided on his own to risk crossing the bridge from past to
present.

"What are you trying to pull, Chief?" Fenton asked.
Sarcasm fairly dripped from him. "Wait a minute. I get it.
You're going to turn this spirit-warrior business into a big
joke, aren't you? Or maybe—" His gaze narrowed. "It's
been your people all along. Is that it? You've got some of
your men parading around like savages to stir up the visitors? No." He turned toward Tory, looking confused now.
"No, that doesn't make sense. The last thing you'd want is
some cheap tabloid showing up."

The way he was looking at her made her blood run cold.
"All this mumbo jumbo is giving me a royal pain," Fenton
said. "Until you've got something concrete, I'll thank you
to stop trying to throw your weight around. Wanting Spirit
Mountain closed off because it was once considered sacred—you're going to have to give me a lot more than some
babbling about seeing a Modoc ghost on it, or anywhere
else, before that's going to happen. Wait a minute. Wait just
a damn minute. I've got it!" He laughed harshly. "Miss
Kent is more than an anthropologist taking a busman's holiday. A hell of a lot more. Go on, Tory. Tell him who you
are."

Knowing what he was going to say, she could only wait.
It didn't take Fenton long. "This young lady's related to
General Canby. In fact, he was her great-great-grandfather.
Maybe there *is* a ghost around because her ancestor killed
him." He laughed again. "What do you think of that?"

Chapter 15

Eyes not at all dimmed by age bored into her. She'd thought that only Loka's eyes had the power to turn her inside out, but maybe Indian eyes, no matter whose they were, would always touch her like that.

"You carry the general's blood in your veins?"

The softly asked question rocked her because Black's words so closely paralleled what Loka had asked. Did Black live in two worlds, one of attorneys and legality, the other primitive and basic, and maybe enduring? She started to nod, then decided to give him a more honest answer. "Maybe that's why I feel so drawn to the lava beds. The first time I came here, it was as if I'd waited all my life to see this country."

"The first time?"

"Last winter. It was just for a day, but it whetted my appetite for—"

"Last winter?"

"Yes," she said, wondering why that mattered. "I really didn't have the time. It was pushing it to come at all, but—"

"Tell me," Black insisted. "When you came, what did you feel?"

Not what did she see, but how her emotions had been touched. Beginning to understand, she answered as honestly as she could, because on this quiet morning nothing mattered as much as learning the truth. Being part of the truth. "I'd bought some Indian flute music in Klamath Falls. I listened to it all the way out here, so I was feeling pretty tuned in to the whole Native American experience. It was cold. I remember a brisk wind and wondering how long it would be before it started to snow. There weren't that many other people around. A tour bus, I remember seeing that."

Black was watching her so intently that she felt as if she were being scraped raw by him, but the past had her in its grip and she couldn't temper her words.

"I was going to go right to the headquarters so I could get oriented, but the sky was so incredible, clouds building on the horizon, the wind flattening grass and bushes. I wanted to know what it sounded and smelled like so I got out of my car." She scanned her surroundings, seeing, not today's clear sky, but last year's clouds. It had been a feeling, something she might never have words for. All she knew was that she'd felt empty and had somehow known the feeling would go away only if she experienced, really experienced her surroundings.

"I heard birds, thousands of them. They were in and around the lake. I wondered if it had been like this back during the war. I hoped so, because the birds gave me a feeling of contentment, and I wanted the Modocs to have felt the same way. The air—" Tears gathered inside her, but she was helpless to fight what she was feeling. "I've never smelled anything so clean, so pure. Once the tour bus was gone, there were absolutely no sounds of civilization."

Black hadn't once taken his eyes off her. She spoke to him, her heart exposed. "I turned so I didn't have to look at my car. It was so easy to pretend that I'd stepped back in time. I—I know it sounds crazy, but I reached out with my mind looking for something, anything that might remain of my ancestor. Some sense of what he'd experienced and felt. I didn't find that."

"What then?"

Black's question was gentle. It gave her the courage to continue. "Something. An essence, a presence. Later I told myself it was because I was standing where Modocs had stood for thousands of years and my imagination had gotten away from me. But for a little while... I felt as if I wasn't alone. That someone was watching me."

Exhausted, she fell silent. She still couldn't take her eyes off the elderly Modoc, but she wasn't trying to connect with him. Instead, she faced herself and something she'd denied for the past six months.

For as long as she'd been at the lava beds, she'd felt part of a force greater than herself. Ancient and powerful. Living.

"You," Black said. "You brought *him* back."

"*Him?*" Fenton spat the word. "What the hell are you talking about?"

Black jabbed a gnarled but still powerful finger at her. "She knows."

Tory was standing near the barred entrance to Fern Cave before she forced herself to go back over what had happened. Even though it had been a good two hours ago, she still shook from the impact of what Black had said. No matter how much Fenton had pushed, the Modoc had refused to explain himself. Not that she'd needed him to.

Yes, she could admit now, she did know.

That's why she'd come here, not just because she felt closer to Loka, but because she now knew she *was* responsible for his awakening.

"You don't know how to reach out to anyone," she whispered. "You want to. You know your heritage is too rich to remain in the past, but who can you trust? So far there's only me because—because, maybe because we were destined to find each other."

She shied a little from the word *destined,* but she didn't have to justify it to anyone, and in the end let it go. When she'd been inside Fern Cave earlier and had looked at what had been left behind by Loka's ancestors, she'd told herself he wasn't really, totally alone because he had history to sustain him. But that had been before they'd become lovers, before they'd both discovered the wonder of truly being part of another human being.

She still lived in the world of people. She could pick up a phone and call her parents. She had a job to go to, people she considered friends.

All Loka had was antiquity.

And memories of making love to the woman who'd taken him from there.

"I'm sorry," she whispered. "I wish I'd never come here. Never brought you back because maybe you don't belong here—because you won't let yourself belong."

"Maybe I do not dare."

Although she jumped, on a subconscious level, she'd been waiting for Loka to speak. Straightening, she watched him stride toward her. Someday, if she lived long enough, she might no longer feel as if she were coming to life simply because he was near, but that time hadn't yet come.

He looked different from yesterday, different and yet achingly familiar. She couldn't put her finger on what had changed about him. Maybe it was only that she now knew him in the most intimate of ways. And maybe...

"You were right to reach out to that Modoc," she said, reluctantly concentrating on what he'd said. "I talked to him this morning. Black Schonchin. He cares about this land. He's going to do everything he can to keep it from being exploited any more than it already has been. Loka." She stepped toward him, stopping just out of reach because she might fly apart if he touched her. "He believes in you."

An emotion she didn't understand settled in his eyes. She wanted to ask him why he'd shown himself to Black this morning but couldn't hold on to the question. She'd been so lonely without him beside her, had hurt so deep, she couldn't begin to tap its source. It was as if she'd lost part of herself while they were apart, and although it terrified her to realize how deeply he'd impacted her being, at the same time she never wanted that to change.

"I—there's something you need to know. Fenton James, the man you saw me with in Fern Cave, he might have seen us yesterday."

Loka shifted his weight, drawing her attention to a dark length of naked thigh with his obsidian knife resting against it. She imagined her fingers on his flesh, looking into his eyes for his reaction, feeling it through her own flesh.

"I know," he said.

"You—you were aware we weren't alone? Why didn't you say something?"

"It was too late."

Because Fenton had already caught them in his binoculars or because Loka had been incapable of tearing himself from her? "You should have told me. The way he talked, I don't think he's sure of what he saw. If I'd known, I wouldn't have been so surprised when he said what he did."

"What did you tell him?"

Loka didn't trust her. Damn it, considering what they were to each other, she deserved better. Didn't she? "Nothing. Absolutely nothing." Was that true?

He folded his arms across his chest. Although she'd seen him do that before, her reaction was as total as it had been the first time. Nothing could harm this man. He was timeless, endless. Proud and powerful. Mist and substance.

"I dreamed of Grizzly last night."

"Grizzly?" she repeated stupidly.

"Grizzly knows when a Maklaks has an enemy. He comes to him in the night and warns of danger."

"Danger? Loka . . ." She couldn't tell him that he wasn't making any sense, that there couldn't possibly be anything to a simple dream, because everyone who knew of him or suspected he existed might constitute a threat. "Did you ask Eagle for guidance?"

"Not yet. I came to you first."

He put her before his guardian spirit? Feeling weak, she spread her fingers over his forearm. Although his flesh felt cool, she took warmth and strength from him, nearly lost herself in memories of when he'd taken her into his arms and more. "Why? To tell me of your dream?"

He didn't answer her. Instead, he briefly studied a bee, which was drawing nectar from a nearby bitterbrush flower. "At dawn I went to the mother lake. While I crouched there drinking, a water snake wrapped itself around my leg."

"A snake?" Her attention flickered to his bare leg.

"When one does that, it means a Maklaks will have a long life."

"It does?" Loka didn't seem aware that she was touching him. Feeling as if she'd somehow invaded his privacy, she drew back. "You have an enemy, but you will have a long life? I don't understand."

"I must find my enemy. End him."

Kill him, he meant. "No! Loka, you'll be treated like a murderer. If you're caught, they'll throw you in jail."

She wasn't sure if he knew what jail meant, but when his eyes narrowed, she had her answer. "A warrior does not run from his enemy. A warrior is like Grizzly."

"I know." Looking at him, she believed that with all her heart. Thinking to remind him of the snake's promise of a long life, she again reached for him, but before she could say anything, an undeniable fact struck her. He had already lived longer than any other human being.

"Loka, I don't want anything to happen to you. The thought of you being hurt or killed…" Forcing her fear into submission, she went on. "Things can't go on the way they are. More and more people suspect you exist. And now that you've shown yourself to Black, he'll no longer have any doubt. Fenton told him who I am. He believes that my presence here woke you. Do you understand? He believes the same as you do, that something in my genes or blood, or something, reached you. Loka, why did you let him see you?"

"I do not know."

"I think you do. No matter what you say, no matter how he dresses and talks, he's a Modoc."

The muscles in Loka's shoulders contracted, making her aware all over again of his strength. She'd bumped over a barely used road to get here. Because there was a fair amount of earth in with the lava in this particular place, the shrubbery was tall enough that it hid them from anyone who didn't know how to get back in here. Earlier today she'd told Black what it had been like that first day when she felt as if she'd stepped back in time. Except for the heavy metal grate over the cave opening, civilization hadn't made an impact. Not sure what to do with herself, she stepped back from Loka's impact. Her gaze fell on what she could see of Fern Cave beneath the grate.

"How did you get down there?" she asked. "You don't have a key."

"No."

"Then how?"

He gifted her with one of his rare smiles, then sobered. "It is not a thing for the enemy to know."

"The enemy? Is that what you're saying I am?"

"I do not know."

"Don't you?" She felt like screaming, like beating her fists against his chest until he understood, until he admitted that something rare existed between them. "We made love. We wouldn't have if we didn't trust each other."

"Trust?"

"Yes," she insisted. "If I believed you were a savage, I would have never gone up Spirit Mountain with you. Never spent the night with you." She said the last without any hint of embarrassment. "But I did because..." Because what? If she told him she'd been ruled by nothing more than a physical need for him, that would be a lie, but could she tell him she'd fallen in love with him? Had she?

"Loka, I've tried to talk to you about this before. I know how you feel about entrusting your knowledge of your people's tradition to someone. I understand. If I was in your place, I wouldn't want anything to do with those responsi-

ble for changing my world. But, Loka..." She couldn't stay
where she was, not with him looking at her that way. Still,
erasing the distance separating them took even more courage than it had the first time. She stood within reach and
waited for his reaction. When he didn't move so much as a
muscle, she went on.

"I want to know everything about who and what you are.
For myself, not because I'm an anthropologist."

"For yourself?"

"Yes. Loka, something is happening between us."

That made him nod. After a moment he unfolded his
arms, a thumb briefly grazing his knife before sliding toward her. When he took her hand in his, she thought she
sensed a struggle within him and could only wonder at its
cause. His hand slid up to cup her chin. He tilted her head
so she was ready to receive his kiss. Their lips met, gentle as
a butterfly's touch. She clung to the sensation, thinking of
nothing except being with him, tasting the promise of more,
living in the moment.

"I do not understand," he whispered with his lips still on
hers. "When I think of you, I do not know who I am."

That's love, she wanted to tell him, but the emotion felt
too new and fragile for her to risk more. "I can't make myself leave," she told him. "I have a job. I should already be
there. But I can't walk away from you."

"What you feel, does it make you strong?"

"Strong? No. Anything but."

He groaned and then kissed her again, the coming together more challenging than before. She should be used to
his economy of words, but she needed more from him.

Or did she?

His body spoke of a man who was learning things about
himself he'd never expected. He might not yet be able to
make sense of it, but he was willing to risk the journey, and
she was part of that journey—maybe all of it.

She understood because the same thing was happening to
her.

Trusting Loka's keen hearing to warn them of anyone coming, she lost herself in him inch by inch. She'd always been proud of her brain, her intellect, but today those things meant nothing. Sensuality was everything. That and energy and a need as strong as it had been the first time they'd made love. She couldn't stop her exploration of his body and felt as if she might explode each time his fingers touched some new spot. She sensed his urgency and matched it with a like response. Although she was still dressed, he seemed capable of reaching beyond fabric for flesh that couldn't get enough of him. Moving, always moving, they danced discovery's dance until she felt as if she were on fire.

A word, a touch, that's all it would take and she would give him everything. Telegraphing her need, she ran a hand down the inside of his thigh. Sweat slicked the sides of her neck and throat, and she couldn't breathe deeply enough. His breathing was just as ragged, his body just as hungry and yet—

And yet he didn't make love to her, held her apart from him, his eyes smoky. "I do not trust myself."

"Don't trust?"

"I stand at the edge of a cliff. A single step and I might step off it. You are that cliff."

She didn't understand and yet she did because she felt the same way. Although her body continued to quiver and burn, she didn't attempt to get close to him again. After taking in several great gulps of air, she felt calm enough to speak. "I know so little about you. I don't know where you live, whether you've kept anything of your former life with you." She nearly bolstered her comment by telling him that he knew everything about her, but that wasn't the truth and they both knew it.

By the way he held himself, she sensed he was struggling with the question of whether he wanted—dared—fulfill her request. She could tell him she might not be here tomorrow, that this wonderful and unexplainable thing between them would soon end, but this had to be his decision.

"You will tell no one what you see?"

"I—"

"Whatever you answer, I will believe you speak the truth."

He trusted her when hard lessons had taught him otherwise.

Feeling both blessed and trapped, she nodded. "You know what you're asking, don't you?" she said. "If I see something that no one else knows about, I'm going to want the world to know."

"If that happens, maybe they will destroy it. Tory, this is for you alone."

He turned and took a step back the way he'd come, then looked at her over his shoulder. Every line of his body gave out a single and unescapable message. Her next move would determine the life or death of their relationship.

Leading the way, Loka headed toward where he'd stood the day he first saw her. The lonely land called to him to return to the isolation and safety he knew, but with Tory behind him, the entreaty was a faint whisper.

He'd told her only a little about his dream of Grizzly, not because it mattered to him whether she believed him or not, but because the dream still clung to him with sharp claws.

Grizzly had been massive, its great teeth exposed as it emerged from the trees. A fawn had fled; a rabbit had frozen in fear. Ignoring the lesser creatures, the bear had lumbered toward him. Although he'd been awed by Grizzly's magnificence, he hadn't feared the beast because he'd known Grizzly had come to warn of danger, wasn't the danger itself.

Owl, Coyote and now Grizzly, all sending messages that made him clutch his knife with taut fingers.

His heart's cadence put him in mind of a drum being beaten by a powerful man. He didn't look back at Tory, told himself he would not allow the sight of her to distract him from questions asked and answers sought, but it was already too late. She'd weakened him as a warrior, crawled under his skin and into his thoughts until he couldn't remember the solitary man he'd once been.

He'd approached her this morning because, he'd told himself, he'd wanted to study her eyes and body to see if she spoke the truth. Only then would he know whether she was the enemy Grizzly had warned him of.

But then she'd asked him to show her his world, and he'd been unable to refuse. Had wanted to give her this gift as he'd once brought a fox kit to his son.

She turned him around, took him far from the only truth he'd ever known, left him incapable of thinking about anything except her.

If she was a lie, if he learned that she was using her woman's power to weaken him, he would kill her.

"Here."

Tory looked where Loka pointed. At first she saw nothing different from what she'd been looking at all day. Then she realized that what she'd thought was a dead bush was instead a pile of dry branches. Obviously, it had been put there to hide whatever was under it.

"That's where you live? Down there?"

"Not there, but this is how I reach Wa'hash."

"Wa'hash?"

"The sacred place. My home."

She couldn't imagine anyone willingly going down there, let alone making that their home, but Loka's people had lived like that when they were hiding from the soldiers. Even now, long after the war, he believed no one should know of his existence. Wa'hash was sacred, a link with his time and people.

"Will you show me?" she asked.

He hesitated, but then, she'd expected him to. She could only wait him out, wondering whether he'd changed his mind about trusting her. If he had . . .

Instead of answering, he moved the brush aside and lowered himself into the hole he'd uncovered. When he disappeared, she looked down and discovered a pole-and-rope

ladder. He stood at the bottom of the ladder looking up at
her. Despite her apprehension at going into such a small,
dark place, she planted her feet on the top rung and began
a slow descent. When she felt his hands on her ankles, she
let him guide her the rest of the way. Stepping away from the
ladder, she looked around. It was cool but not cold down
here. The air lacked freshness, but it didn't bother her that
much. After a few moments, her eyes became accustomed
to the gloom, and she realized she was in the middle of a
tunnel. When he reached down, picked up a flashlight and
handed it to her, she didn't ask where he'd gotten it. She
turned it on.

Loka pointed. "This way leads to Fern Cave."

Remembering that she'd seen him in the cave when it
should have been impossible, she took a few steps in that
direction. Then she turned back around. Loka hadn't
moved. He pointed down the other corridor. "Wa'hash,"
he said.

Wa'hash. A place of mystery and wonder, of proof that
Loka had created a home for himself. Thinking about that,
it was easier to tell him she first wanted to see how he'd gotten into Fern Cave. If he trusted her with that, it might make
the rest easier—for both of them. Trying to keep her tone
calm, she told him she wanted to experience Fern Cave
through his eyes. Nodding, he slipped around her in the
narrow space. As he did, their bodies brushed. Much as she
wanted to feel his arms around her, her sense of urgency was
stronger. Their moments together were so precious, so limited. She *had* to have everything she could of him.

The tunnel wandered in one direction and then another.
A few times she had to crouch low to keep from hitting her
head, but most of the time the opening was high enough that
even Loka could stand upright. Occasionally she held her
arms in front of her to keep from scraping them on the
sides. Twice the tunnel widened out so that it was almost like
being in a room. She'd studied the map the park personnel
had done of every known cave and tunnel at the lava beds.
This one hadn't been discovered. Considering that there was

only that small access hole out in the middle of nowhere and that Loka had concealed it, she wasn't surprised.

When Loka stopped, she saw he'd reached a large boulder, which blocked their way. He placed his hands on it, muttered something which made no sense to her, then pushed it effortlessly forward and to the side. Her flashlight revealed the far reaches of Fern Cave.

"That—that's how you—but..." She set her shoulder against the boulder and shoved, but it refused to move a fraction of an inch. "Loka, what—"

"Cho-ocks."

"Cho-ocks?"

"When the army men came, the shaman placed the rock here so the enemy would not know that this tunnel leads to Wa'hash."

"Placed it here?" Again she tried to move it. Her second attempt was no more successful than the first. "Loka, that's impossible."

"I told you, Cho-ocks's medicine was strong. He blessed the rock so that only a Maklaks can move it."

Cho-ocks was the shaman who'd given Loka the sleeping medicine. Knowing he could keep life suspended, why couldn't she believe that he could render a mass of granite weightless, at least to a Modoc? Unnerved by the realization of how little her generation would ever know about an Indian medicine man's power, she peered at Fern Cave. It was open to exploration only once a week and under strictly controlled conditions. That would change if Fenton had his way, but for now, it remained serene and yet haunted.

Haunted? Would Modoc spirits leave this special place if too many of the enemy invaded it? Not wanting to disturb essences she'd come to believe in, she backed away. "I've seen enough," she explained in response to Loka's puzzled look.

He again placed his hands on the rock, his chant echoing against the rock walls and sides. Then, while she watched in disbelief and shock, he clutched a couple of projections on the boulder and pulled it back into place.

Chapter 16

They were back at the cave opening before Tory could bring herself to speak. Down here, with him, she felt cut off from the rest of the world. She'd had the same reaction while they were on Spirit Mountain, but up there she'd been aware of sights and sounds, vast space. Being in the dark was a form of sensory deprivation with the result that her entire being was forced to focus on the only other living creature within reach.

Loka wasn't just a man. Knowing who and what he was, she couldn't put such a simple label on him. Watching him move a boulder had brought that fact home to her. It was so simple. He believed in his shaman's magic. Because he did, he was capable of rendering tons of rock weightless.

"Wa'hash," she whispered.

"Wa'hash." He stood with his hand on the ladder, his attention on the small amount of sky they could see. His body language gave away everything of his struggle. It had been hard enough for him to show her the Modoc entrance to Fern Cave, but the enemy had long invaded that place and it was no longer wholly his. Wa'hash was different.

Whatever it was, it belonged to him alone—unless he shared it with her.

Unless he trusted her enough.

Pulling his hand off the ladder, she spread it over her throat. "You hold the power of life and death over me," she told him. "If you think I can't be trusted, you know how to keep me silent."

She prayed he would draw away. Instead, his touch remained until she felt completely under his power. "You do not fear death?"

Didn't she? She couldn't put her mind to the question. "I'm not afraid of you."

"Maybe you should be."

Maybe, but with him towering over her and his world surrounding her, those things were her only reality.

Eagle. Hear me. Answer. Did you send Grizzly to warn me of her?

Stopping, Loka strained to hear. Eagle would never come down here, because his great wings were made for flying, but if he'd heard his prayer, maybe the sound of his fierce scream would penetrate. There was only silence.

Tory waited behind him, but he couldn't tell her he was asking his spirit if he'd jeopardized everything by heeding her plea instead of the warning that had come to him in the night.

Eagle. She tempts my body. Makes me forget my vow to safeguard my heritage. She lives; everything else is dead. Tell me, can I trust her? Can I walk in today?

Silence pressed around him. It was broken by his heart's beating, nothing else. He tried to imagine what Eagle's heart sounded like, but how could he when Tory stood so near?

Eagle. Do not desert me.

"Loka? What is it?"

He ignored her, but her question was enough of a distraction that he could no longer bury himself in prayer. Making his way instinctively, he thought about the world above him. Rabbits and deer, lizards and birds, maybe even a lone coyote would be about. Even if the enemy ventured close, the creatures who belonged here would simply wait until the intruders had left. He had tried to use their wisdom for himself, but because he was a man, he knew anger—anger at those who had destroyed everything.

Anger, he'd learned during the lonely months of his new life, ate at his soul, but he was only one man. He could not chase the intruders from where they didn't belong. All he could do was protect and shelter all that was left of the Maklaks, ask himself if past and present could ever unite.

Today he was bringing one of the enemy to what was most sacred.

Eagle! Who was Grizzly warning me of? My heart will not believe she is evil. My body needs to join with hers. My head—my head is silent.

Unable to deny the truth, he closed his ears to the sound his heart made and again took his thoughts to the land above him. In his mind he saw the endless sky, but no matter how intently he swept his eyes over the horizon, he found no sign of Eagle. Heard no cry. When, exhausted by the effort, he returned to where he walked, he became aware, not of his heart again, but of the essence of the woman behind him.

The first time he'd seen her, he'd thought she was so thin that she wouldn't survive a winter here. That was before he'd discovered the strength in her arms and legs, the soft challenge of her breasts and belly and thighs. His wife had never reached for him in joy and need, and he barely remembered that other time when he'd lain with a woman because he wanted to, not because it was expected of him.

Tory brought him to life. With her under him, he felt strong. With her, he no longer asked himself why he'd been forced into this world not of his making. With her, he had a reason for being.

Eagle! I cannot reach you. There is only her, blinding me to everything except her.

* * *

A sliver of unexpected sunlight ahead caught Tory's attention and pulled her out of the mist she'd been wrapped in. Looking around Loka's shoulders, she spotted a long, thin slit in the rock ceiling. They were entering a room, smaller than Fern Cave but larger than the wide places in the tunnel. Barely aware of what she was doing, she aimed the flashlight at the floor so she could see the room in its natural light. She couldn't make out any details beyond what must be his bed placed a couple of feet to the right of the slit. Staring at the bed, she realized it consisted of dark fur. It was so large, she couldn't imagine it having come from anything except a bear. A bear pelt for sleeping when she'd always had a mattress and blankets.

"This is it?" she asked. Her voice was the barest whisper. "Wa'hash?"

Disappointment slammed into her. She'd expected where he lived to look more dramatic, although what she meant by dramatic she couldn't say. From what she could see, there weren't any artifacts, nothing that hinted at the people who had considered it sacred. Still, there might be something in the corners.

When she stepped into the room, Loka remained where he was. Taking that as his cue that he didn't care what she did, she aimed the flashlight into one of the corners. She instantly recognized a number of spears, several bows and more arrows than she could count piled together. A sense of discovery began to grow in her. If Loka had preserved the weapons his people had discarded once they had access to rifles, what else had he kept?

Tule rush baskets.

Tule moccasins and mats, even clothing made from bulrush.

Two-horned mullers for cracking wokas seeds.

Fishing nets and hooks, dip nets, long, narrow gill-net seines, harpoons.

Deerskin shirts and leggings, an incredibly ornate dress decorated with what must be pounds of shells. Snowshoes.

Hairbrushes made from a porcupine tail.

An infant's bed created out of soft tule, several board cradles.

Her gaze fixed on the bed. Although she was in awe of everything she'd seen and things she'd just begun to be aware of, that small bundle made the most impact. The Modocs were known as the tribe that went to war against the United States and murdered a general. In all that history, factual and otherwise, the simple fact had been lost that they were also men, women and children—families.

She knelt near the basket and ran the back of her hand lightly over the fragile creation. Loka might have brought it here because it was what his son had used, but even if it had belonged to another child, the fact remained that someone had gone to the effort of gathering and working the tule plant so their newborn would have something to snuggle in. Tears stung her eyes. She blinked several times in an attempt to clear her vision. Although she wanted to ask Loka about the basket, she didn't yet feel strong enough to face him. Instead, she focused on the nearest wall.

It was covered with drawings.

Picking up the flashlight again, she trained it on the drawings. Their richness and clarity, their unbelievable abundance took her breath away. Trembling a little, she stood and moved a few feet to her left. No matter where she looked, there wasn't a stone surface that hadn't been etched or painted.

She saw stick figures of hunters going after a herd of deer, more figures seated in a tight circle with a costumed figure in the middle. There was a depiction of a large village complete with fish-drying racks, canoes, even children playing in front of a sturdy-looking wickiup.

Crouching a little, she studied twelve separate and yet interrelated scenes. In one a man was standing under a tree while what must be leaves fell around him. In the next, a heavily bundled figure looked up at snow. Others showed women standing in hip-deep water while they gathered tule. Twelve scenes, all of them showing people involved in their environment and the weather. Could this be the Modoc calendar?

Her shaking increased. Still, she managed to face Loka. No matter what she started to say, they all seemed like the words of an idiot. No, not an idiot. A woman who has discovered the heritage, the tradition, the past of an entire people.

"Loka. This—this is what has kept you going, isn't it?"

By way of an answer, he walked over to the nearest wall and pointed at something. She joined him. He'd drawn her attention to a petroglyph of an eagle with its wings spread over a man wearing a fierce-looking mask. "The first Kiuka."

The first medicine man. Feeling hot and cold at the same time, she tentatively touched the rock. Instead of the cool she expected, she felt warmth—the same warmth she thought she'd sensed when she touched the drawings in Fern Cave. Unable to accept the impossible, she briefly withdrew her hand, then brushed her fingertips over it again.

Warmth? Heat?

Her mind stumbled over possibilities, all of them more incredible than the last. She knew firsthand how unbelievably powerful Cho-ocks had been. Somehow the Modocs had been able to keep their shaman's skills from whites, but this drawing clearly showed Kiuka controlling an eagle.

It wasn't simply a drawing. The bird, she realized, wasn't just any eagle. It *had* to be the one the Modocs credited with naming all other animals. Until this moment, she'd believed it to be yet another part of Modoc legend and superstition, an interesting story, nothing more than that.

She no longer did.

"Kiuka?" she whispered. "Please tell me about him."

Loka's gaze slid from her to the petroglyph. "You want this?"

"Yes. Yes. Please."

His shadowed features contorted. She felt his inner struggle, could only wait. "Kiuka lived in the time of Kumookumts," he said after a long silence. "He lived more

than a hundred winters. Part of him still exists—here." He
indicated the drawing. "And at Fern Cave, on Spirit
Mountain, wherever he once walked."

I believe you.

"Kumookumts entrusted him with great knowledge,
warned him that he must safeguard that knowledge and
share it only with those who are worthy."

"Like Cho-ocks?"

To her surprise, Loka shook his head. "Cho-ocks did not
have Kiuka's wisdom. He had walked too long in the white
man's world, ate his food, used his weapons. He answered
when the army men called him Curly Headed Doctor. His
heart forgot how to beat as a Maklaks."

"But Cho-ocks kept you from dying. He did—he did
something to that boulder."

"Yes."

A simple yes wasn't enough, but she wanted the explanation to come from him willingly and not because she
begged for more. Waiting for him, she gave the eagle figure
a closer look but didn't touch it or the one of Kiuka again.
Many of the drawings were crude; these two had been done
by a craftsman. Even the eagle's feathers were clearly de-
tailed and something had been done to his eyes to make
them shine. Kiuka's eyes, too, looked alive.

"Cho-ocks told me something," Loka went on. "I asked
why he did not take the sleeping herbs himself. He said there
was only enough for one warrior. Kiuka had come to him in
a dream and told him he had to die a human's death so the
enemy would not know of ancient truths. Kiuka chose me
because Eagle and I shared the same heart. Because my love
for my son was so strong."

This was too much for her to absorb. Needing distance
from him, she began a systematic examination of the petroglyphs. It was more than a random selection of scenes,
drawings that had been put here simply because they satisfied someone's whimsy.

"This is incredible," she whispered. She didn't care that
she must have already said the same thing a good dozen

times. No other words could possibly express what she was feeling; she couldn't keep her reaction to herself. "Absolutely incredible."

"It is Wa'hash."

Wa'hash. His people's legacy. How right he was!

"I had no idea." She went back to the drawings of those brave Indians who'd been the forerunners of the Modocs. "No one does."

"I know."

His voice held a warning note, but she was so overwhelmed by the richness that surrounded her that she couldn't concentrate on it. Nearly everything of what the Modocs had been before outsiders arrived had been lost to history. Only, it was all here. She now understood an incredible amount about their religious structure, their belief system. More than that, she knew beyond any doubt that Kumookumts wasn't simply a folk figure. He had once existed for the Maklaks. He *had* left his massive footprints in the earth. Even more incredible, he'd empowered the first shaman, not with useless bags of bones and feathers, but the knowledge of how to take herbs and plants and other native materials and turn them into something capable of keeping a human being in a state of suspended animation.

Loka was the living proof of that.

Shaking her head again at the wonder of it all, she moved over to a series of petroglyphs that showed various domestic scenes. When she had time to study this in more detail, she would better understand ancient Modoc family structure—something else that had been lost to so-called progress. She wanted to ask Loka to explain what the women were doing. Obviously they were preparing food, but the figures were so small that she couldn't make out what they were working on.

Later. Right now—

Yet another drawing caught her attention. This one was situated so that a little of the sunlight coming in through the slit in the ceiling touched it. Looking at it, she made out an elaborately decorated figure—obviously a shaman—standing over a prone figure. The shaman held two objects over the figure's body. The patient, if that was who he was, seemed to be opening his eyes. "The shaman is healing him, isn't he?" she asked when she realized Loka had joined her. "At least he's trying to."

Loka pointed at the two objects. "Sacred Eagle feathers."

"Did they work?"

"Yes, if the patient was a believer."

Loka was a believer. She heard that in his voice, only had to look at him to understand that.

"Oh, Loka! This is—" Words failed her. Overwhelmed, she gripped his shoulders and gazed up at him. His face was cast in shadows, but she could still see life dancing in his eyes. That and something else. "Thank you. Thank you. It's here—all of it. History. Richness. More—more than we've ever known about any Indian tribe. To know for certain that they lived their lives in certain ways, that their religious beliefs ran through the entire fabric of their existence, to understand the truth about Kumookumts and the first shaman..." Feeling as if she might fly off into a thousand pieces, she held on to Loka even more firmly than she had earlier. "This changes everything. Turns theory and speculation into, into..."

"Changes?"

"Yes. Once people understand—"

"No!"

He'd been wrong. A fool. How could he have been blind to what she was? Grizzly's warning—why hadn't he heeded him?

Tory struggled in his grip, but Loka didn't stop dragging her toward the tunnel opening. Even when she begged him to say something, he remained silent because there were no words for what he felt. What he feared.

What was that she called herself, an anthropologist? She'd told him enough that he knew it was her task to drag the past out of its resting place and expose it to the brightest lights.

"You can't keep this to yourself!" she gasped when he tried to push her up the ladder. "Loka, it isn't right. To keep everything buried under the ground—Loka, there are so many lessons in the past. So much that was good and right. Like putting one's trust in an eagle and spending your life knowing that eagle will protect you. Kiuka. Loka, I felt something of him. It—"

"Eagle is mine."

"No." She tried to wrench free. He released her because he was afraid he would hurt her if they struggled. "No, not just yours. Loka." She raked her fingers through the mass of her hair. "Eagle guards your life. I can't believe I'm saying this, only it's true. Eagle guides you. Enriches you. And Kiuka and Kumookumts...There are so many people, good people, who deserve—"

"No."

"I know. I know. I promised I wouldn't say anything about Wa'hash, but that was before I saw. The richness—I can't keep this to myself. I can't."

He couldn't listen to this. Maybe he was alive because he'd been entrusted with safekeeping everything the Maklaks had once been. He'd broken the most sacred of trusts because he'd allowed a woman—an enemy woman—into his world. Under his skin. The danger she represented must end today. It must! Wa'hash was his people's legacy. The past. Not hers to exploit.

Acting on instinct, he lunged. Although she tried to flee, he wrapped his arms around her, pinning her to his side. Then, mindless to her flailing arms and legs, he threw her over his shoulder and hauled both of them up to the surface. Setting her on her feet, he stepped away and drew his knife.

She stared, not at his weapon, but into his eyes. Her look weakened him, took him back to lovemaking, of having her to sleep beside. To her look of awe as she stood on the top of Spirit Mountain and looked out at his world.

She had found a home in his heart, and he couldn't silence her.

Chapter 17

Stumbling with nearly every step, Tory headed toward where she'd left her car. Although the sun beat down around her, warning of a day approaching one hundred degrees, she couldn't put her mind to the folly of staying out here without water.

The rage in Loka's eyes—no, not rage really. No matter how many times she forced herself to go over their last few moments together, she didn't understand his emotions. Or maybe the truth was, she understood them all too well and was unable to make herself face hard reality.

The Modoc warrior had been a man of violence. He'd endured a war, seen his ancestors' land torn apart by rifle-bearing strangers. He hadn't known enough of gentleness, had no reason to trust anyone. Despite his desire to find his place in the present, he didn't know how. Because of those things, he'd wanted to silence her, permanently, when she blurted that she wanted the world to know about his people's rich and beautiful past.

Something had stopped him, something that had everything to do with what they were, or had been, to each other.

Instead of plunging his knife into her and ending the threat she represented, he'd stalked away from her. Left her alone in this lonely land.

Would she ever see him again?

Did anything else matter?

Facing the awful reality that she might have killed whatever had begun between them made it impossible for her to concentrate on where she was going, and she had to trust her instinct to return her to Fern Cave. She kept looking around, hoping to see Loka, and when that didn't happen, she scanned the sky for a glimpse of Eagle. Her ears were tuned to the sound of Wolf's howl. Even if she heard an owl or coyote, she would have welcomed that, since any sign, even one that warned of danger, would have meant she was being touched by the same forces that ruled Loka's life.

This was his world, his domain. How could she have been so presumptuous to declare she had a right to share it with others?

But if no one knew of Loka's heritage, it would die with him.

The argument swirled inside her, preventing her from listening to what her heart might be trying to tell her. Whenever the possibility that she might never see Loka again intruded, she cast it away because to acknowledge it might destroy her. Instead, she placed one foot after another and struggled to find a way to blend what might be irreconcilable.

When she first felt the prickling at the base of her spine, she prayed it meant Loka had decided to return to her, but when she concentrated on her reaction, she knew it hadn't been caused by the man who'd taken her body, and heart. Someone else was watching her.

Looking around, she glimpsed a shaft of light that came from the sun glinting off something ahead of her. Cold anger mixed with a deep sense of apprehension when she realized she was looking at a man holding a pair of binoculars. How long had Fenton been watching her?

By the time she came close enough that they could carry on a conversation, she'd forced her fear to the back of her mind. Although she wanted to insist he leave her alone, she knew that would only increase his interest—as if it weren't high enough already. She and Loka had been out of range of his binoculars when they'd emerged from Wa'hash, but if Loka had inadvertently come within sight of Fenton—

Silent, she waited for Fenton to speak. It seemed incredible that she'd seen him only a few hours ago. So much had happened since then—discovery and loss.

"You do get around," Fenton said. He made no attempt to hide the fact that his binoculars had been trained on her.

"So do you."

"True." A slight smile touched his lips. "You think I had no business telling that old Modoc that you were related to Canby, don't you?"

Whatever Fenton was fishing for, she had no intention of going after the bait. Shrugging, she reached into her back pocket for her car keys. However, any hope she had of getting away from him died when he placed himself between her and her car. She realized she hadn't heard his vehicle approaching, which meant he must have come while she was too far away to have caught the sound. If he'd followed her out here today—

"I thought you had your hands full getting ready for the senator's visit."

"I'm busy enough. But not so busy that I'm unaware of other things."

What did he mean by that? But if she acted too curious, that would only feed his overactive imagination. Pretending a disinterest she was far from feeling, she wiped the back of her hand over her forehead and said something about how hot it was. Fenton agreed.

"I don't suppose you want to tell me what you're doing out here?" he said after a silence that felt laced with tension and danger.

"What are you talking about?"

"About why someone who has already been given the grand tour of Fern Cave would come out here again when she knows she can't get in on her own."

"You're letting your imagination run away with you, Fenton. Look, why don't we both lay our cards on the table? You want to wrangle an introduction to Dr. Grossnickle through me, don't you? In fact, you're thinking that knowing me might lead to working for the Alsea project in some capacity." When he didn't say anything, she planted her hands on her hips and shook her head. "I don't have that kind of pull. Neither does Dr. Grossnickle. Both of us are university employees. If you want to be part of things, you need to talk to them. I wish I could help you but—"

"Not anymore, Tory."

"What?"

"I'm no longer interested in Alsea because something much better is happening here."

Fear raced through her, numbed her to what she should say or do next. Fenton held up his binoculars, taunted her with them really. "I'm no fool, Tory. Almost from the first I didn't buy your excuses for staying here. There's something else going on."

"Is there?"

"Yeah. Something, or someone."

Her throat constricted, leaving her incapable of speaking. "Let me tell you what I saw today," Fenton went on. "I followed you. I'm not going to deny that. After some of the other things I've seen you doing, I'd be a fool not to keep my eyes and ears peeled." He held the binoculars up to his eyes and made a show of focusing on something in the distance.

"What did you see?" she asked. The time for evading and avoiding had ended. She needed to learn everything she possibly could.

"You. You weren't there for the longest time. I searched. Believe me, I stared through those damn things until I thought I was going to go blind. I almost turned around and left, but I didn't because you had to be somewhere, and I was going to find out where or die trying.''

Find out where she'd been? Just the thought of Fenton stumbling across Wa'hash made her sick. ''I hope the senator will understand why you weren't attending to business.'' She shouldn't taunt him, but the man had pushed her against a wall and striking out came instinctively.

''Oh, I think he's going to be delighted—if I decide to let him in on this. Let me tell you who I did see while I was waiting for you to appear.''

No! No!

''A naked man, nearly naked anyway. That 'ghost' that people keep talking about, the one that's got Black so stirred up. He was pretty damn far away. Even with these—'' he indicated his binoculars ''—he wasn't much more than a speck. But he was there. He was!''

No!

''You've got nothing to say, Tory?'' His superior smirk spread over his face until she itched to rip it away. ''Yeah, well, maybe you don't. What is it? Who is he?''

He didn't know, not really. Not yet. Carefully monitoring her every movement, she cocked her head slightly to one side. She could only pray he'd buy her casual stance and not sense the turmoil she felt inside. ''Not much more than a speck, did you say? Are you sure you're not letting your imagination get out of control?''

''No!'' Fenton insisted. Still, she thought she caught a little doubt in his eyes. ''There's got to be something to all these ghost rumors. There's just got to be.''

''Ghosts? Come on, Fenton.''

''Don't give me that! You've been all over this place, jeopardizing your job, acting—acting mighty strange.''

He didn't know anything for sure. She had to remember that, build on his uncertainty. But how? ''What do you mean by strange? Just because I like to spend time out here by myself? Look, I've had some pretty intense dealings with people lately. A lot of pressure. I needed some R and R.''

''I don't buy it.''

Fenton reminded her too much of a bulldog. "I can't help that." In an effort to let him know she'd grown tired of this conversation, she made a show of playing with her car keys. "What are you going to do? Tell either Dr. Grossnickle or the senator that I've been off communicating with some, some what?"

Uncertainty again flickered in Fenton's eyes. A moment later, it was gone, replaced by rigid determination and anger. "You think I'm going to make a fool of myself, don't you? At least that's what you're hoping. But how do you explain why you spent the night on Schonchin Butte—without so much as a sleeping bag or flashlight? You weren't alone. Damn it, you weren't alone!"

He doesn't know. Don't forget—he's fishing. "Wasn't I?"

"No, damn it. Something's happening around here. Something that can't be explained. But he exists. I saw him today."

"He?"

"Yeah." A frown flickered across his features. "Maybe he's some deranged joker, but I don't think so. You wouldn't be looking and acting the way you are if he was just some nut case."

"And how am I looking and acting?" she asked, although that was the last thing she wanted to do.

"Like someone who's seen a ghost. Like a woman with a lover."

The rest of the day passed in a blur. Part of it was, Tory knew, because she'd spent too much time out in the sun. But that wasn't all of it, not by a long shot. *Like someone who's seen a ghost. Like a woman with a lover.* Fenton was still trying to find the pieces of the puzzle; she didn't dare ever forget that. But his curiosity, his determination to get to the truth of things, seemed to know no bounds. Now that he'd actually glimpsed Loka, he wouldn't quit until he had proof of his existence that he could take to the press, that he could exploit.

Unless—

For the first time since she'd returned to her cabin, Tory faced up to what she was doing. Although it had taken her from late afternoon until dark to make the hard decision, she'd finally finished packing her duffel bag. She was ready to leave.

She had to. It was the only way she could ensure Loka's safety.

Heart hurting, she walked over to the nearest window and stared out at the just-emerging moon. It seemed to have been waiting for her before spreading its soft silver light over The Smiles Of God.

She loved this land. Without her knowing how it had happened, it had found a home deep inside her. Lonely and desolate to those who didn't understand its magic, it appealed to her in a way no other place ever had. In so many ways, the lava beds had never left that harsh winter of 1873. Yes, there was the park headquarters with its easy communication with the rest of the world, but as soon as she left that, the past reached out to absorb her. To enrich her.

And maybe the truth was, the spell had been cast by Loka, Eagle, Wolf, Grizzly, Kumookumts and Kiuka.

How could she leave?

Because she didn't dare stay. Because that was the only way she could hope to protect Loka.

Loka, who was more important than Wa'hash.

She tried to turn away so she wouldn't have to look at the moon and the world painted by it, but she couldn't. She loved her parents, deeply respected Dr. Grossnickle, was grateful for good friendships, had thought herself in love a few times in her life. But nothing had ever felt like this.

Loka *was* her life. Savage and primitive, wise beyond her comprehension. Part of this land, the essence of Native American spirituality.

Their hearts had touched, blended, and because of that, she'd been able to step into his world. She'd seen Eagle and heard Wolf. Sensed what of himself Kiuka had left behind.

Learned of Kumookumts's power and wisdom. Fallen in love.

And now she had to leave.

Despite her awful resolve, several more minutes passed before she forced herself to turn from the window. Spotting the two eagle feathers still on her bed, she wove them into her hair, crying a little at the memory of how they'd gotten into her possession. While she was packing, she hadn't allowed herself to think about where Loka might be tonight. Now she did. If he'd changed his mind about not putting an end to the threat she represented, he might be waiting outside right now. Still, she couldn't believe that.

For at least the fourth time, she reached for the bag that held her scant possessions. Then she looked around, trying to imagine Loka in here. He'd indicated little interest in the cabin's interior, making her guess he'd explored it while it lay empty and found little to interest him. Still, she'd like to show him some of the improvements in housing that had become commonplace since his time. The idea of taking him to a city boggled her mind. She tried to imagine him walking down a street flanked by skyscrapers, stepping into an elevator, riding in a car, but the images only made her shudder.

You belong here where the wind blows and carries the scent of sage. Where Eagle can always find you and you can reach out to him. It's lonely—oh, Loka, I know how lonely you are. But you're safe here.

Refusing to give in to the tears she knew would incapacitate her, she opened the door and stepped outside. The wilderness surrounded her. From here, she couldn't see so much as a single man-made light. The moon was full, giving her an accurate if muted view of the trail leading to civilization. She could have turned on a flashlight, but she needed this final experience—these last minutes alone in Loka's world.

I love you. I don't know how it happened, but I've fallen in love with you and everything you represent.

I will never forget you.

Both owls and coyotes were singing their ageless songs tonight. Remembering Loka's explanation that they warned of danger, she tried to find something to fear in the sound, but coyotes and owls were such a natural part of this land that she couldn't.

She was going back to the Oregon coast where what everyone concurred was the discovery of the century waited for her, but the prospect did nothing to lighten her heart. Although she would again be surrounded by the people who'd become friends as well as colleagues, she would feel more alone than she did tonight.

You have your past, your people's spirits, Eagle and Kumookumts. I have . . . nothing.

"Tory."

Although his was the only voice she might ever want to hear, she nearly turned and ran. She'd already said her silent goodbye to him, had somehow found the courage to leave the lava beds. How dare he force her to go through that agony again?

"You leave?" he asked as he emerged from the night, his voice both a shaft of lightning and the faintest touch of a downy feather.

"Yes."

She waited for him to ask why. When he didn't, she guessed he already knew. To make this easier, she tried to tell herself he must be glad, but that was before he stepped close enough to take the duffel bag out of her hand and drop it to the ground.

The moon—an artist's brush really—caught him in all his wild glory. His form spoke of endless strength, of oneness with his world, but he wasn't just a warrior who had somehow survived beyond his time.

He was also the man she'd fallen in love with.

"I have to." She hated the telltale emotion in her voice, but she couldn't hide what she felt.

"Because you must go to that other place?"

"No, not that. Not only that."

She didn't want his hand on her shoulder, his thumb tracing the sensitive side of her neck. And yet, this last touch might make the rest of her life bearable. "Tell me."

Tell you? How do I begin?

"Fenton saw you today. He isn't sure, but if I stay here, he'll keep following me. Eventually he'll know."

"Today? I did not see him."

She told him what binoculars were capable of, warning him that from now on he had to be careful of every move he made. He listened in silence, and she could only guess at his thoughts. Did he think she wanted to tell him about yet another invasion on his privacy?

"He's dangerous, Loka."

"Yes."

She expected him to tell her he wanted to kill Fenton. When he didn't, she realized he was no longer a primitive warrior. Or maybe the truth was, he'd never been a killer, merely a proud man facing danger and threat in the way he'd been taught, the only way he understood. He knew she abhorred violence, and that one violent act would invariably be followed by another.

Leaning into his hand, she took him in inch by precious inch. That she could have fallen in love with him was utterly impossible, and yet it had happened, and she didn't question the insanity or sanity of that. They—a general's great-great-granddaughter and a Maklaks warrior—had met across time. Their hearts, hers at least, had learned that his beat the same as hers. That was all that mattered.

Tonight it was everything.

She couldn't tell him more about her hard decision to leave, couldn't break the spell by asking him what he was going to do with the rest of his life.

She could only step toward him.

He'd known she was going to do that. Otherwise, he wouldn't have been ready for her, wouldn't be offering his arms and strength. Wordless, they clung together. She swayed with him, not quite a rocking motion, far from being in control. She needed the taste and feel of his lips, but that could wait. For now it was enough to absorb his essence.

Although it was night, his body still held memories of the day's warmth. Afraid to lose herself in him because she might never again find what she'd always been, she nevertheless drank from him. He seemed more than a man tonight, part and parcel of what this land had always been and what it should always remain. He was a bridge to the past, yet capable of existing intact today. If only he'd let her show him—

No. It was too late for anything except this moment.

When his hand strayed from her back to her hair, she realized he'd found the feathers. His hand, so strong and sure, felt like velvet. "You take something of Eagle with you," he whispered. "Why?"

Because I have to have something to last the rest of my life. On the brink of tears, she could only rest her hot cheek against his chest. His heart beat scant inches away; she felt as if she held it in her hands. This man, this impossible and wild man, had reached her in ways she'd never imagined. The rest of her life would forever feel empty.

"I have nothing of you," he said.

Could this leave-taking be as hard on him as it was on her? She straightened and tried to meet his eyes. The moon, behind him now, kept his features from her, but maybe it was better this way. She touched the feathers but didn't try to remove them. "What could I give you? Nothing would have the meaning these gifts from Eagle do."

Covering her hand with his, he drew it to his lips. She weakened under the gentle assault of his kisses, lost the strength to fight her tears. There was so much she needed to tell him about why she was leaving, but the words wouldn't come. Nothing did except knowing she loved him and would always love him.

"Why did you come back?" she managed. "I thought I'd never see you again."

By way of answer, he placed her hand over his heart. She waited for more, waited for the words she would carry inside her forever. Instead, he let the night speak for him. Coyotes and owls continued their haunting songs. Above and beyond and through those familiar sounds came another.

Wolf had returned.

Crying openly now, she stood in front of Loka while they both stared at the distant white light that was the moon glinting off Mount Shasta, off Yainax. Loka's body, maybe even his heart, became motionless as he absorbed the wind-brought message. She tried to match him, but her breath came in unsteady gulps.

Wolf.

Eyes on Yainax, she could almost swear she saw a single line of warriors heading upward. They carried bows and arrows, their bodies naked except for loin skins. They followed an elderly man who, despite his slow gait, showed no sign of stopping. She knew. The leader was Kiuka.

"Loka?" Her voice was little more than mist. She wanted, not for him to tell her that such a thing was impossible, but that he saw the same thing.

He bent his body toward her, and although she tried to draw his attention toward Yainax, he only looked down at her. Captured her thoughts and touched her heart again.

Wolf.

Wolf hadn't finished his song.

"You carry magic in your eyes," he whispered. "I gaze into them and forget everything except you."

"I—"

Harsh, sudden light struck her, shattered the magic Loka had just spoken of. Terrified, she whirled in the direction of the glow.

"Don't move! Don't either of you move!"

Fenton!

Chapter 18

To Tory's horror, instead of doing what Fenton had ordered, Loka started toward him. Blurting out something unintelligible, she tried to grab hold of Loka, but he was already out of reach.

"I mean it! Stay where you are."

Silent, Loka stalked closer. His right hand moved to his waist. He slipped his knife free and gripped the handle, the blade aimed at Fenton.

"Loka, no!" she sobbed.

"Stop. Don't move!"

Tory lunged for Loka. She collided with her duffel bag and tripped over it, barely catching herself in time to prevent a fall. Off-balance, she saw that Fenton, too, was armed. He held a pistol in his free hand, the barrel pointed at Loka's chest. "No!"

Neither man gave any indication that they'd heard her. She couldn't be sure, but it seemed that the pistol trembled in Fenton's grip. By contrast, there was no hesitancy in Loka's action. Oblivious to any danger, he continued to advance.

"Stop it." Her voice sounded weak and ineffective. She again started after Loka, but too much distance separated them. Fenton was obviously trying to blind Loka by keeping the flashlight aimed at his eyes. How much Loka could see she didn't know, but he seemed guided by an instinct for survival that existed beyond the need for vision. Why he didn't run she had no idea. Maybe he thought he was protecting her as well as himself.

"Loka."

Before the word was fully out of her mouth, Loka catapulted himself at Fenton. At the same instant, a blast split the air. She saw Loka continue to lunge, hoped against hope that Fenton had missed. Then, all too soon, the strength went out of the warrior's body. He sank to his knees, head still uplifted, attention still concentrated on the man who'd just shot him.

"Loka! No!"

She reached him but for a split second couldn't make herself touch him. If he'd been killed—

He hadn't. As she watched, he slowly gathered his legs under him. He managed to stand, blood running from the wound in his side. Thinking of nothing except the need to stop the flow, she started to cover the wound with her hand. He stumbled, and she offered him her body for support. He held on to her for no longer than it took him to draw in a deep breath, then pushed free and again started toward Fenton. It was then she realized he still held his knife. She grabbed for it, but he held it out of reach. Afraid she would hurt him more if she wrestled him for it, she turned her attention toward Fenton.

The flashlight now dangled from Fenton's fingers, its beam illuminating some brush off to the right. The pistol was still aimed at Loka.

"No, damn it! You've shot him! Damn you, damn you." She sounded hysterical but didn't care. For a moment she fought a terrible battle with herself. Loka needed her; she couldn't think of anything except him. But if she didn't first disarm Fenton—

"Put it down," she ordered, approaching Fenton. He was trying to split his attention between her and Loka. Despite the dark, she knew he was on the brink of losing self-control, irrationally terrified of a wounded man. A warrior with a deadly knife.

A sense of movement behind her forced her to glance back at Loka. His eyes looked wild and determined, an animal intent on only one thing—self-preservation. She would feel the same emotion, but instead of running as she would have done, Loka was walking toward his enemy.

"Stop!" Fenton bellowed. His gun stopped shaking, became deadly again. "I mean it. Stop!"

Not thinking, she flung herself at Fenton. At the same time, she made a fist of her hand and used it to hammer the weapon aside. Fenton immediately tried to raise it again. She clamped her fingers around his wrist and squeezed with all her strength. Gasping, he tried to shove her away, but she refused to let go. Locked in battle with him, she discovered she was stronger than him. Either that or Fenton was in shock over what had happened and unable to concentrate. Taking advantage of whatever was going on inside him, she grabbed the barrel with her other hand and tried to yank it out of his hand. She knew the gun might discharge, hitting her this time, but her world had narrowed down to nothing except the need to protect Loka.

For several seconds Fenton fought her. Then, suddenly, he released his grip. Off-balance, she had to struggle to keep from falling. She held the gun in her hand.

Feeling its weight, she whirled to face Loka. She couldn't see him.

"Loka! Loka! Where are you?"

"Gone." Fenton sounded hysterical. "Gone. I didn't mean—please believe me, I didn't mean—he came at me. He was going to kill me. I had to stop him."

Shutting her mind to Fenton's babbling, she hurried to where Loka had last stood. She strained to see if drops of blood indicated where he'd gone, but the night protected him and the moon wasn't bright enough.

Gone.

"Why?" she demanded of Fenton when it really didn't matter.

"I knew he'd come to you. I watched, waited. I *knew* it."

She should have been aware of that possibility. If she'd been capable of thinking beyond heartache today, she would have realized Fenton wouldn't blindly buy her contention that his imagination had gotten out of control. Now it was too late.

"You shot him." Her legs were taking her back to Fenton because Loka belonged to the night. Because she didn't know how to find him.

"I had to. He was going to stab me."

"Shot him." Her throat felt raw. Her eyes were on fire. Her heart felt as if it had been torn open. *Loka. Hurt. Gone.* "You shot him."

A sound, new and yet already a part of her, pulled her back around. Eagle, his size hiding her view of the moon, swooped down out of the sky. He hovered just about the ground, his great wings moving in a furious rhythm that stirred dirt and small rocks and leaves into a whirlpool of activity. Fenton babbled something. She didn't care. Eagle had come. "Find him!" she sobbed. "Please, find him. Take care of him."

Instead of heeding her desperate plea, Eagle continued his attack on the ground where Loka had fallen. Landing and bringing his claws into play, he raked through rocks and roots. Fenton, his voice laden with disbelief, demanded an explanation, but she ignored him. "Find him. Eagle, please!"

As quickly as he had appeared, Eagle soared upward. For a moment he was silhouetted against the sky. Then he disappeared. Silence briefly settled over the land to be broken a few seconds later by the whisper of approaching footsteps. She turned, terrified that more people meant added danger to Loka. Through blurred vision, she recognized Black Schonchin.

Hours later, Tory slipped out of her cabin. She guessed it would be morning in two or three hours, not that the time mattered. Black, his eyes locked on her, had been the first to arrive. From what little he'd said, she realized he'd seen Eagle. Why he was there she didn't know, and before either of them could say anything more, others had started arriving, drawn by the sound of gunfire.

Fenton was gone, fired.

Drawing refreshing air deep into her lungs, she tried to recreate what had happened. When park personnel demanded an explanation for why Fenton had discharged his gun, he'd told them about Loka—about being attacked by a ghost or spirit or madman or something and having shot in self-defense. Her thoughts locked on Loka, she'd been unable to think of anything that would discredit Fenton, but in the end she hadn't had to.

There'd been no proof that Fenton had shot anyone. That's what Eagle had been doing, stirring up dust and debris so not a single drop of Loka's blood remained.

Fighting exhaustion, she trained her flashlight on the ground beyond where Eagle had done his work, but if Loka had left behind signs of where he'd gone, she couldn't find them. She wished she could feel relieved because Fenton had been fired for discharging an unregistered gun on park property. Maybe she would later, but now all that mattered was that Loka was out there, wounded and alone.

Except for Eagle.

Standing, she scanned her surroundings. There'd been so many people here, all of them talking at once. Now that they were gone the silence seemed out of place. When she realized Fenton had broken a law and that his job was in jeopardy, she'd actually considered saying he'd tried to harm her to add weight to the charges against him, but in the end she'd only insisted she had no idea what had brought him here tonight.

It was a lie—if not a bold-faced fabrication, a deliberate evasion. She *had* lied when the park director asked if she'd seen the eagle Fenton kept talking about. No, she'd said, sounding vague. No bird had appeared. She certainly would have remembered if it had. Black hadn't said anything. Instead, the old Modoc had only regarded her with quiet eyes.

Spirit Mountain. Would Loka go there? The thought of him where so many of his people had gone during their vision quests filled her with a short-lived sense of peace. There was somewhere else he could go where he'd be assured of more privacy. How could she possibly find the small opening that led to Wa'hash? If he died in there—

Sick at the thought, she moved toward where she'd left her car. What she'd do once she got there she had no idea, maybe nothing except wait for morning. That and pray. When she made out the silent figure staring at her, she stopped. Waited.

Walking slowly, Black put an end to the distance that had separated them. Although, admittedly, she'd given it little thought, she'd simply assumed that the Modoc had left with the others. Looking at him now, she again asked herself what had brought him here earlier, and why he hadn't said anything about Eagle.

"He isn't here," Black said. "If he was, I would know it."

With all her heart, she wanted to trust him, to confide in him, but until she understood more she would keep what she knew to herself.

"You're going to try to find him, aren't you?"

"Him?"

"The man I saw yesterday."

Black wasn't calling Loka an illusion. His tone left no doubt that he believed in the existence of what—who—he'd glimpsed. It was possible he'd followed Fenton out here earlier tonight and had seen everything. "What are you doing here? Nothing happened. You said so yourself."

"Because the others don't need to know."

"Know what?" she asked because the time of evasion was over.

"That he exists."

He exists. The words sounded so calm. Filled with conviction. Too tired and worried to play any more games, she took in the first hint of daylight on the horizon.

"I want you to hear me out, Tory," Black said. "From the time I was old enough to care about such things, I heard my parents talk about an underground place where our people's heritage remains. As a boy, my friends and I tried to find it. I've studied the maps of the caves around here, explored. I'm not the only Modoc to have done so. It's not something we tell outsiders—non-Indians—about."

"I see."

"You're not sure how much you should say, are you? It's all right," he continued when she said nothing. "Actually, your silence tells me a great deal. You've seen it, haven't you?"

"It?"

"Wa'hash."

There was a warmth to his voice when he said the word, a caress even. Maybe it was the sleepless night and unrelenting worry for Loka that broke down the final barriers, and maybe it was simply the way that one word sounded coming from the lips of a Modoc. "It's wonderful," she managed. "Incredible. Like looking at the entire history of the Modoc people. There are things—mystical things..."

"Like Eagle?"

"Y-yes."

"And Wolf. I heard him tonight."

"Did you?"

"Don't be afraid of being honest with me, Tory," Black whispered. "I'd never betray him."

Never betray.

"Fenton—if he'd had his way, he would have put him on display. Exploited him. He—"

"I'm not Fenton. I'm Modoc—I don't want you to ever forget that. No matter what you tell me, I won't betray your confidence."

Dawn had found Black's features. She studied him. He returned her steady gaze. "I believe you."

"What's his name?"

"Loka." *Loka!*

"Ah. And you love him, don't you?"

She didn't answer; she couldn't speak.

"It's in your eyes, Tory. I saw it yesterday when I told you that I'd seen him. That's why I stayed here today. Tried to keep an eye on you. And when I saw Fenton sneak off toward your place, I knew he had the same suspicions. I didn't know what I should do. Loka knows who I am—I'm convinced that's why he revealed himself to me yesterday. And yet he chose not to do more than that. I thought—well, I'm not sure what I was thinking, except that I felt like a man on the brink of an incredible discovery, one that maybe I'd never know more about than I already did. And then I heard Wolf and followed my instinct to you."

"And to Loka. You saw?"

"Everything." He pointed in the direction of Spirit Mountain. "That's where he headed."

Knowing where to start looking for Loka drove all other thoughts from her mind. She'd already filled her backpack with her first-aid kit; nothing kept her from taking off. Nothing except for Black.

"Listen to your instincts, Tory. Them and your heart. They'll take you to him."

"I wish I could believe you. What if he dies?"

Something of what he was feeling reached her. They shared the same fear, the same desperate hope that Loka was still alive.

"Listen to me." Stepping up to her, Black placed his hand on her shoulder. "You're the only one who can possibly reach him. The only one he trusts."

"Does he? Maybe—maybe he doesn't want anything to do with me." Her shoulders sagged under the weight of what she'd just said. "Maybe he's dead."

"He can't be!" Black said fiercely. "He's the last warrior. His people need him."

The last warrior. Again and again Black's simple and yet honest words echoed inside her. Keeping her fear firmly under control, she concentrated on her goal. Black had last seen Loka heading toward Spirit Mountain; she had no doubt that was his destination because every time she looked at the solitary peak, she felt a powerful pull drawing her closer. But Loka might not have the strength to make it.

Morning was a gentle thing, pastel colors slowly washing over the night until, slowly, the world came into sharp definition. She felt light-headed and lulled by isolation. If others were about this early, they weren't in this area of the vast park. She would have known it if they were. There was only her and Loka—maybe.

"I'm here," she whispered. "Do you see me? Can you hear me?" She fell silent as she made her way around a sharp, deep lava-defined gully. Once she was back on level ground, she tried to scan the land in all directions, but a mass of bushes blocked her view. More than once she was put in mind of what it had been like for the soldiers as they made their way across what for them was alien land while the Modocs lay in wait for them.

Only, Loka wasn't stalking her. He was, if he was capable, intent on reaching sacred ground.

"Fenton's gone," she said more to keep herself alert and in control than anything else. "They fired him. He kept talking about you, you and Eagle. He insisted you'd tried to kill him and he'd only shot in self-defense, but Eagle destroyed the evidence. He sounded crazy. When Black and I lied for you, it only made things worse for him.'' She tried to conjure up some sympathy for Fenton but couldn't. The man had shot Loka.

Maybe killed the last warrior.

She had no idea how long she'd been walking and searching and talking when Eagle came to her. For a long time, the bird floated high overhead, as if learning all he possibly could about her before coming closer. She tried to keep her eyes on him, but the terrain was so uncertain that she had to keep looking at the ground. When Eagle finally caught a downward draft that brought him within twenty feet of the top of her head, she felt as if she'd passed the greatest test of her life.

''Where is he? Please, I can't let him stay out here alone.''

Eagle's screech sent a chill down her back. Looking up, she caught sight of the talons that made him such a successful bird of prey. ''Do you hate me for what happened to him?'' she asked. ''I don't blame you if you do. I should have told him to leave last night. That way, that way...''

She couldn't lie to either herself or Eagle. If she had it to do all over again, she would still open her arms to Loka. ''I'm sorry,'' she finally managed. ''So sorry. All I want is for him to live. I'll leave. That way he'll never risk his safety again. I promise, once I know he's all right, I'll leave.''

Don't.

Not daring to believe what she'd sensed inside her, she stopped so she could carefully scan her surroundings. Unfortunately, the bushes still grew so close together that she could barely find a path around and through them, let alone know what lay hidden in their midst. Eagle continued to hover over her, his wings fanning her hair and face. *I'm here, Loka. I'm here.*

I know.

''Loka! Please!''

As if her plea had been meant for him, Eagle screamed and shot forward a good hundred feet before hovering over a scraggly pine that had somehow found a foothold in the rocks. She started running. An exposed root and then a jumble of lava slowed her, but she finally reached the pine. Shading her eyes, she stared at the trunk.

Loka. Motionless.

Chapter 19

Tory didn't remember running to Loka or kneeling beside him. All that mattered was that she could touch him, speak to him—learn if he was still alive.

"Please," she whispered over and over again. The word sounded tortured, and yet she couldn't change it. She gently ran her hands over every inch of him. Although the feel of damp blood along his side made her shudder, she didn't pull back. "Loka. Loka, please, can you hear me?"

"Tory."

Hearing her name coming from his lips brought her to the brink of sanity, but she didn't dare break down. "I'm here. Eagle showed me the way."

"*Blaiwas.*"

"Yes. *Blaiwas.*" She bent over him as if covering his body with hers could heal him. It didn't seem possible that he could have traveled this far, but she should know not to judge him by ordinary men's standards. Black had called him the last warrior. How fit, how right that was.

She wanted to look up to see if Eagle—*Blaiwas*—was still here but couldn't tear her eyes off Loka. Because he was under a tree and dawn hadn't yet made its impact here, she couldn't tell whether he was clear-eyed. His voice sounded weak, but maybe that was only her fear. "I want to help you. Cho-ocks and Kiuka can't reach you. You have to rely on me. There's—you know there's no one else."

"You came." His voice held a note of wonder. When he lifted his arm so he could run his fingers over her throat and the swell of her breast, they felt familiar and strong.

"Did you think I wouldn't?"

"I did not know."

Nothing could have hurt her more. Surely he knew he meant more than anything else in her life. She couldn't leave here, couldn't go on living if he died. "You trust me that little?"

"No. You do not understand. I know what lives inside you, Tory." He pressed his hand flat against her breast to cover her heart. "Maybe I was born knowing that. But . . ." His hand slipped away to drop limply by his side.

Terrified that he'd lost consciousness, or worse, she brought the back of her hand close to his nostrils so she could feel his warm breath. "I live, Tory," he said.

Thank God. "You need help. A doctor, hospital." She stopped as she struggled to think of a way of explaining what she was talking about. The thought of bringing him to a hospital almost made her sick because once he was there, there might be no way of keeping the truth about him secret. Still she would risk it if that was the only way he would survive. "I can't get you there by myself," she explained needlessly. "But Black—he's the Modoc—I know he'd help."

"No."

"He won't betray you, Loka. He believes in you. He understands."

"No."

"Listen to me, please." She might be wearing him out by insisting on this argument, but he could have a bullet buried in him. He had to have lost a lot of blood. "He's a wonderful man. He knows about Wa'hash."

"Wa'hash?" Loka turned his head just enough that dawn bathed his features and revealed a look of wonder in his eyes.

"Yes." She fairly shouted the word. "Stories about its existence have been passed down through generations of Modocs. He says that no one else knows about it, that no Modoc has ever betrayed their heritage."

When Loka said nothing, she quickly told him that Fenton had been fired and that Eagle had made sure no evidence of his having been shot remained. "Black and I will take you to the hospital. You don't have to say anything. We'll think up something, tell them some story so no one will discover who and what you are." Even as she spoke, she searched frantically for a way of getting Black here without leaving Loka alone. Maybe Eagle—

"No hospital."

"You don't understand," she protested. "They have modern medicine men there, people who will make sure you get well."

"No hospital."

He said that with such a note of finality that she gave up. If she pressed the issue, he might leave her, and the thought of him out there alone and wounded was more than she could stand. Besides, the moment hospital personnel learned he'd been shot, the police would become involved. They'd ask questions, demand... "All right," she whispered. "We'll stay here. Maybe—we have no choice. Loka, I don't know how to treat you. If the bullet's still in there—"

"No bullet."

Instead of telling her how he knew that, he rolled over onto his good side and pushed himself into a sitting position. Much as she wanted to help him, she understood how deep his pride ran. Once he'd steadied himself, he took her hand and showed her where the bullet had exited. She hated touching him. Still, sensing that what he was letting her do said a great deal about trust, she carefully, gently examined his injury. What frightened her the most was that he continued to bleed.

"Let Black look at you, at least. Maybe he knows a Modoc with medical training. They can take you someplace safe."

"No. Tory, no."

She didn't want to look into his eyes, didn't want to see his determination and fierce pride, but she had no choice. Instead, what she found was a look of peace running through his entire body. "Listen to me," he said. "I belong here." He indicated their surroundings. "This land knows me and I know it. If I am to die, this is where it must be."

"I can't let you die," she moaned as tears heated her cheeks. "Without you—Loka, please."

She wanted to force him to continue to look at her so he would understand how desperate she was, but he turned his attention to Spirit Mountain. "I must go there," he told her with more strength than she'd heard since they began talking.

"You aren't strong enough. You tried—I know how hard you tried."

As if to make a lie of her words, he forced himself onto his knees. He tried to stand, and when he fell back, she placed his arm around her shoulder so they could get to their feet together. The tears she thought she'd never be able to stop cooled on her cheeks as she concentrated on taking the first step.

Loka was going home. Today nothing else mattered.

Two hours later, so tired that her legs trembled, Tory stared at the sunlit peak ahead of them. They'd covered more than half of the distance between where she'd found him and the mountain's base, but it had been at an awful price. Loka dripped sweat and had to stop and rest every few minutes. His deeply tanned features had bleached a frightening white. She would have given anything for more water, but he'd already drunk her canteen dry. The bandages she'd wrapped around his side had slowed the bleeding, but he'd lost a lot during the night, maybe more than he needed for survival. The thought of infection worried her nearly as much. He stumbled too many times and wouldn't have been able to continue if she hadn't been there to support him. Whenever she looked into his eyes, they seemed glazed. She wasn't sure he was aware of her presence. His gaze never left Spirit Mountain.

Loka hadn't spoken for so long that she'd almost become accustomed to the silence, except it wasn't silence because he labored with each breath and his heart beat so loudly that she was afraid it would break.

He stopped, leaned on her. Used to his need for frequent rests, she broadened her stance in an attempt to support his weight. He wasn't the only one who was played out, but she was determined to be as strong as humanly possibly for him; it might be the only thing she could give him. "Loka, please, rest for a while. I'll try to find some water."

"No water. Done."

Done. Terrified, she turned slightly so she could look up at him. Pain and exhaustion etched his features. She expected to find defeat in his eyes and struggled to steel herself for that. Instead, he looked as if he'd turned in upon himself, was trying to get in touch with a part of himself she couldn't fathom. Taking a deep and shuddering breath, he pushed away from her. Although he swayed, he managed to stand straight and tall, his arms lifted toward the sky. The sight of his injured and yet proud body took away her own breath and made her forget her thirst, even her fear for his life. Silhouetted against his world, he seemed such a part of it that she couldn't begin to separate the two.

He started chanting, and with each word his voice grew stronger. The sounds were both harsh and hypnotic. She wanted to join him in his song, but he was Maklaks and her ancestor had helped end his way of life. Maybe she'd been wrong to come to him; maybe her presence would keep who or whatever he was trying to call from coming to him.

Made sick by the thought, she forced herself to step back from him. He didn't seem aware of what she'd done. The sounds and syllables of his childhood echoed around her until she could no longer hear the birds and other creatures that shared the wilderness with them. Feeling more alone than she ever had, she could do nothing but watch.

Every few seconds a shudder coursed through his body. The rest of the time he remained motionless. He'd somehow summoned enough strength to keep his arms reaching for the sky. The lines of his body looked as strong, as magnificent as they'd always been. As long as she didn't look at his side or take note of his bloodless face, she could believe he would live forever.

That nothing, or no one, would ever touch him.

Time lost all meaning. She sensed the sun on the back of her neck. Thirst made it nearly impossible for her to swallow and yet she couldn't put her mind to that, either. She felt as if she now existed outside of her own body. Nothing mattered except him.

Alone. With a start she realized that although he'd been calling for someone or something, it was still only the two of them. Eagle had guided her to his side, but after that was done, Loka's spirit had left him. He must be calling for Eagle now. Why wouldn't the creature come?

When Loka's arms dropped by his side, she feared his thoughts paralleled hers. She wanted to walk over to him so she could offer him her love and strength, but even as she fought a terrible battle with herself, she knew her love wasn't enough. Loka wasn't an ordinary man. His life had always been guided by forces she was just beginning to understand. Without those forces, without proof that what he believed in existed, he might lose hope. And without hope, he wouldn't have the will to fight his injury.

He would die out here.

To her horror, he sank to his knees. He still looked out at
Spirit Mountain, his gaze so fixed and intent that she knew
nothing else existed for him. He continued to chant, his
voice that of a man who'd been gravely wounded. Unable
to stop herself, she stumbled over to him and dropped beside him. She tried to wrap her arms around him, but his
body remained stiff and unresponsive. She felt the words he
kept saying rumble inside him and wondered if he would
continue to chant until life seeped out of him. Head
pounding, she stared fixedly at Spirit Mountain.

Listen to him. Eagle! Kumookumts! Hear him! Help him.

His voice slowly became a whisper. One hand clutched his
knife. The other lay limp at his side. Sweat poured off him.
For a moment she thought he'd begun a rocking motion,
but that was only until she forced herself to face the truth.
He was shaking from exhaustion.

*Eagle! Kumookumts! He's the only one who still be-
lieves in you. Understands you. Without him...*

Once before she'd echoed Loka's prayers. She did it
again, not thinking about how to form the sounds. Nothing mattered except that he not die, that Eagle and Wolf and
Kumookumts and Kiuka and the others who'd been here for
him and his people heard him today. Eyes closed, holding
him, she imagined Eagle floating into view. She thought,
briefly, of the feathers in her hair, but in order to touch
them, she would have to let go of Loka, and she wouldn't do
that.

*Eagle. You gave names to all other animals, answered
Loka's prayer for a guardian spirit. He needs you, needs you
as you have never been needed. Bear, your intelligence is
that of humans. Think of him, understand him. Help him.
Wolf, you came to us before. Do not desert him now.*

She remained lost in her thoughts while her mouth and
tongue formed sounds that made no sense and yet felt as if
they lived and breathed inside her. Finally she became aware
that Loka had fallen silent.

Opening her eyes, she stared at him. His own eyes were half-closed, unfocused. His head sagged. After a moment he lifted it, but she wasn't sure whether he could see Spirit Mountain. Calling on strength she didn't know she had, she helped him lie down. Even at rest, he looked like what he was: a warrior.

Eagle. Please...

Unable to continue her thought, she bent over Loka and covered his mouth with hers. He returned her kiss but didn't lift his arms to embrace her. His breathing was no less labored.

Eagle! He needs you. We need you.

Even as she sheltered Loka's body with hers, she became aware of a presence behind her. Terrified that someone had found them and praying that Black had followed her, she straightened and turned. Her hands remained on Loka's chest.

There was no one. But the sensation of being watched continued. She concentrated on giving her surroundings a thorough look. Belatedly, she realized that the presence came not from the ground but from the air.

Eagle.

"Loka," she whispered. "He's here. Can you see him? He's..." Horror washed through her when she saw that Loka's eyes were closed. His breathing had slowed. It seemed to her that he was sinking into the earth, becoming part of it. "No! Don't die! You can't! You—"

Eagle's cry shattered the words she hadn't wanted to say. Her attention again drawn to the bird, she watched it make circle after circle above them. Mesmerized by its graceful movements, she closed her mind to everything else for as long as she could. Finally though, she was forced to ask herself if Eagle had delayed its appearance because it was incapable of miracles and hadn't wanted to see Loka die.

Die. Still staring at Eagle, she drew unwanted comparisons between its movements and that of a vulture. She'd seen them a couple of times during the past several days but hadn't given them much attention beyond acknowledging that they were a necessary part of the environment.

Not Loka! No, not Loka!

Again she bent over the warrior, her warrior, and pressed her mouth against his. Praying for some reaction from him, she nearly allowed herself to believe he'd kissed her in return, but when Eagle screamed again, she was forced to face the truth.

Loka was unconscious—maybe worse.

A need she didn't understand built inside her and forced words—sounds—from her throat. She was saying what Loka had a few minutes ago, the foreign syllables coming from a source that might be nothing more than instinct. Still, her heart had recorded them.

"Kiuka. Blaiwas. La'qi. Sloa. Kiuka."

Frightened that Eagle might leave her and Loka, she watched every movement he made. He was now no more than twenty feet above them. Although she'd seen him this close before, her awe was no less this time. His wingspan was so great that he hid her view of Spirit Mountain. When he lifted his proud head, morning light glinted off the pure white feathers. His pristine tail caught the same light and half blinded her. If she put her mind to it, she would be able to count the feathers on the tips of his wings. *"Sloa. La'qi. Tusasa's."*

Eagle dipped one wing low enough that it grazed the top of her head. A thrill shot through her at that, tempered almost immediately by her concern for Loka. Still, the despair she'd felt earlier didn't return. Either that or she'd become mesmerized by Eagle and the sounds coming from her throat. *"La'qi. Sloa."*

Again Eagle touched her. *"Kiuka,"* she whispered. *"Blaiwas. Blaiwas,* I love you. *He* needs you."

Eagle might have been doing nothing more than stretching his wing to make sure he remained airborne, but she would always believe there'd been more to the movement. As he did, two large feathers separated themselves from the others and fluttered to the ground next to her. She picked them up, feeling Eagle's body warmth in their velvet surface. She held them so that Eagle could see what she'd done, but the bird was already heading upward. Not daring to breathe, she waited for him to return, but he didn't. Instead, he flew toward Spirit Mountain until he became part of the few clouds.

She became aware of the vastness of her surroundings. A few distant birds sang. A wasp darted toward her and she brushed it away, only then remembering that she still held the feathers. She ran her fingers over the glossy black, feeling something—something beyond her comprehension. Opening her mouth, she tried to chant again, but the sounds that had come so effortlessly a minute ago now deserted her. Frightened, she looked down at Loka, thinking to ask him to help her. If he'd seen Eagle, he gave no sign. His eyes remained closed. She didn't breathe herself until she saw his chest rise and fall. Although she was able to protect his face and chest from the sun, his legs were exposed. It was still morning, but before much longer the sun would punish him with all its strength-sapping fierceness. She had to drag him into the shade and then find water and help for him.

Only, water was miles away, and he wouldn't let anyone else touch him.

"You can't die." She wanted to be strong for him because maybe then he would continue to fight, but she felt played out, frightened and sick at the thought that he might not see tomorrow. When a wasp tried to land on his chest, she waved it away with one of the two feathers.

Two feathers.

Although her eyes remained fixed on Loka, an image began forming inside her and her thoughts went back to when Loka had shown her Wa'ash. There'd been so many wall drawings that they all ran together in her mind.

Except for one.

Concentrating, she waited for the drawing to become clearer. There had been two figures, one a man lying on the

ground just as Loka was now. The other represented a shaman—Loka had told her that. In his hands, the shaman held
two eagle feathers. The patient's eyes had been opening because they were sacred feathers and the patient had believed in their power.

Loka believed.

She held the feathers in front of her. Eagle had come, not
just because she and Loka had called to him, but because he
wanted to give her a piece of himself. If she never understood another thing in life, she understood that now. She
wasn't a shaman; she would never have a shaman's knowledge. But she loved Loka, and that was all she could give
him.

Love. Placing the feathers on the ground beside Loka, she
carefully drew the other two out of her hair. She kissed one
and then the other, briefly held them up toward Spirit
Mountain. Then, acting out of an instinct older than anything except maybe the land itself, she placed them on top
of Loka's head and held them there. She closed her eyes so
she could concentrate on chanting, but after a few seconds,
the need to see Spirit Mountain and beyond that a glimpse
of Mount Shasta made her open them.

*His life is in your hands. He can't die; he can't. He's all
that's left—the last warrior. I need him. Everything he
knows about the Maklaks can't die with him. He deserves a
tomorrow. Please.*

She didn't know who she was praying to, maybe Eagle,
maybe Kumookumts, maybe Kiuka, maybe every entity the
Modocs—Maklaks—had once believed in. Warmth swirled
around her; she knew it didn't come from the sun. Giving
herself up to the warmth, she imagined that she and Loka
were again heading toward Spirit Mountain, only they
weren't walking as they'd done before. This time they
floated on the same wind currents that sustained Eagle. She
heard or thought she heard Wolf howl, crickets, a whirling,
whispering sound that must be the wind. Although she lis-

tened carefully, she didn't hear either Owl or Coyote, proof that all danger was gone.

In her mind, someone waited for them on the butte. When they were finally close enough, she took in the figure's painted mask, leathered hands clutching pristine eagle feathers. Kiuka, the first shaman.

After breaking free of the image long enough to assure herself that she still held the eagle feathers exactly as they'd been in the ancient drawing, she again concentrated on Kiuka. He stood with his arms uplifted as Loka had done before he collapsed. The sounds coming from his throat were those Loka, and she, had used.

He is in your hands. Yours and Eagle's. If you need him with you in your world, so be it. But I believe he belongs here. With me. Both safeguarding and sharing Wa'hash with those he trusts. Loving me. She faltered at the last but wasn't sorry she'd spoken the truth. Loka's life was up to Kiuka; she had absolutely no doubt of that. Mesmerized, she listened to the wind-borne song. Once, when the notes briefly died, she heard Wolf. His howl hung in the air, a lilting cry that seemed to have been alive since the beginning of time.

She looked around for the predator but couldn't see him.

Someday, she prayed, she'd gaze at the owner of those plaintive yet peaceful notes.

Wa'hash. Although the heat continued unabated, a cave-like coolness touched her nerve endings and eased her journey into the sacred place. Nothing of her sense of wonder from that first time had lessened. Again, awe, admiration, reverence washed over her as her mind's eye recorded each and every drawing, each ancient and telling symbol. But this time, instead of wanting the world to know what existed beneath the earth, she accepted it for what it was. A people's legacy.

This is your place, Kiuka. Yours and Kumookumts's. I feel blessed because I've seen it, but it isn't mine. I have no right saying what will be done with it. Wa'hash belongs to

*the ages. If that's how you want it to remain, I accept your
wisdom.*

Kiuka stopped chanting. Despite the distance between
them, she had no doubt of the message in his eyes. He had
heard her. But did he believe?

Loka moved, stole her thoughts. She lowered her gaze.
His eyes were open and clear, and he no longer looked pale
as death. "Kiuka," she whispered. "He's on Spirit Mountain."

"He waits for me."

"No," she told him with conviction. "He knows you
can't reach him. He—he comes to you through me."

"You believe?"

Emotion clogged her throat and made it impossible for
her to utter a word. Still, she trusted her eyes to speak for
her. After a few minutes during which the air remained full
from Kiuka's chanting, Loka brought her hands to his
mouth. When he saw the feathers she still clutched, a smile
touched his lips. "You remembered."

"That that was how a believer could be healed? Yes."

"It is not enough, Tory."

"Not enough?" Fear reasserted itself, but there was
strength in Loka's fingers and his eyes remained bright.

"Belief must be total. You as well as me."

"Me?" She hung on the word they both needed to hear,
the finality of it, the conviction. "Yes. Me, too." She
glanced up at Spirit Mountain, but Kiuka was no longer
there. She could still hear him and Wolf, or maybe their
songs now existed inside her.

Maybe they always had.

She helped Loka sit. He was no longer bleeding. The
day's heat beat down on her, but it no longer made her feel
light-headed and half-sick. *Something* had happened here
today. She might never put a name to it, not because it defied her comprehension, but because believing in the power
of the first Maklaks shaman belonged in her heart, not her
mind.

"I prayed for you." She couldn't take her eyes off him. "I don't know what I said. The words didn't make any sense. But it didn't matter. Whatever it took to keep you from dying—"

"I heard you."

"Did you?" A tiny white butterfly flitted near his dark hair. If Loka wasn't holding her hands, she would have seen if she could get it to land on her finger. "I was so scared you were dying. Then I saw and heard Kiuka, and I was no longer afraid. When I heard Wolf, the sound strengthened me."

"I felt your strength." He ran his fingers up her forearms, her shoulders, gently caressed the sides of her neck. "Here." He pressed his thumb against the pulse at the base of her throat. "And here." He covered her heart with a hand that could once again hunt and fish, and make love to her.

Echoing what he'd done, she placed her hand over his naked chest. Muscles roped it and sheltered his heart but didn't keep her from feeling its beat. Warmth flowed over her. This time, she knew, the heat came from him. Staring into his eyes, she believed he felt the same thing, because he understood her love for him.

"You couldn't die," she told him. "It wasn't time. Kiuka wouldn't let you."

"It was not Kiuka who kept me in this world."

He was right. He had been pulled back from the brink of death because he wasn't the only one who had been touched by Kiuka, Eagle and Wolf. He was no longer alone in that, would never climb Spirit Mountain by himself again.

"Kiuka trusts you, Tory," he whispered. "Eagle does, too. And Wolf."

"I—know."

"It is because they know I carry you within my heart."
His heart.

Epilogue

Summer's heat hadn't yet given way to cool fall, but Tory didn't feel the sun as she sat on one of the rocks that made up the dance ring. Miles away, tourists drove slowly over the park's single road, but she and the others were safe from prying eyes. She couldn't help but smile. If park personnel ever learned about the underground tunnel that allowed Modocs to come here undetected, they would undoubtedly add it to the list of attractions.

But the secret would remain safe until Loka and the other Modocs decided that the time for sharing had come. And it would be done in their way.

Loka, magnificent in his loincloth and sun-kissed flesh, turned in a slow circle as he addressed one Modoc child after another. Their looks of awe left no doubt that they were fascinated by stories of ancestors who'd survived harsh winters because they'd had the wisdom to gather and hunt during the generous summers. They loved to hear about Bear and Wolf, occasionally looking around with wide-eyed wonder.

"Maybe the time will come when they'll see Bear and Wolf and the others, when they fully understand."

Tory nodded to acknowledge what Black had 'said but didn't take her eyes off Loka. His wound was nearly healed. In every way that counted, in every way that mattered to her, he had recovered.

Loka had been pointing toward Spirit Mountain, but he stopped with his arm in the air and all eyes on him to look down at her. His smile, intimate and knowing, held for several seconds. Instead of blushing, she lovingly returned his gaze. He spent his days sharing his wisdom with the area's Modocs. She didn't resent a moment of his time and loved watching him emerge from his long isolation as both children and adults embraced him. At night—the nights belonged to them.

"You're sure he wants to do this?" Black asked when Loka returned to his storytelling. "You're going to be able to get him in a car? Into modern clothes?"

"Oh, yes. He believes as I now do that only Indians have a right to the Alsea site. We'll be going there next week. He's told me what he intends to say. His words are so eloquent, so powerful. They come from his heart, from an earlier time. Once the court hears him, I think they'll rule in favor of the Indians."

"It'll cost you your job."

"I don't care," she said, meaning it. "Black, you know what it's like to want to learn everything you can about ancient ways and beliefs. That's the way it is for me, too, now. The time will come when I'll know how to convey that to this generation. When Loka and I will do it together. But for now, I'm content to be a student."

"Hmm. That and embrace the last warrior."

The last warrior. Loka bent before a small boy so the child could touch the baby's cradle he carried. Boy and man locked eyes, and Tory saw, not grief for the son Loka had lost, but love for this child. Loka might be the last of a once-proud people, but he now lived in today. Loved in today. Was finding a place for himself in this generation.

Unconsciously, she spread her hand over her stomach. Next week she and Loka would travel to the Oregon coast. Just looking at him, feeling his pride and passion, she had no doubt that he would succeed in what he was determined to accomplish. The university and its staff wouldn't be the ones to uncover the Alsea past; Indians would.

Once their work on the coast was done, they would return here, he to continue introducing modern-day Modocs to their heritage, she to bring their child into the world. She intended to continue as an anthropologist, but from now on her focus would be on the magical, mystical world that sustained Loka and had been his people's most essential element.

The last warrior? With their son growing inside her, that was no longer true.

* * * * *

COMING NEXT MONTH

Take 4 bestselling love stories FREE

Plus get a FREE surprise gift!

Special Limited-time Offer

Mail to Silhouette Reader Service™

3010 Walden Avenue
P.O. Box 1867
Buffalo, N.Y. 14269-1867

YES! Please send me 4 free Silhouette Intimate Moments® novels and my free surprise gift. Then send me 6 brand-new novels every month, which I will receive months before they appear in bookstores. Bill me at the low price of $3.12 each plus 25¢ delivery and applicable sales tax, if any.* That's the complete price and a savings of over 10% off the cover prices—quite a bargain! I understand that accepting the books and gift places me under no obligation ever to buy any books. I can always return a shipment and cancel at any time. Even if I never buy another book from Silhouette, the 4 free books and the surprise gift are mine to keep forever.

245 BPA AWPM

Name	(PLEASE PRINT)	
Address	Apt. No.	
City	State	Zip

This offer is limited to one order per household and not valid to present Silhouette Intimate Moments® subscribers. *Terms and prices are subject to change without notice. Sales tax applicable in N.Y.

UMOM-995

©1990 Harlequin Enterprises Limited

Bestselling author

RACHEL LEE

takes her Conard County series to new heights with

A CONARD COUNTY Reckoning

This March, Rachel Lee brings readers a brand-new, longer-length, out-of-series title featuring the characters from her successful Conard County miniseries.

Janet Tate and Abel Pierce have both been betrayed and carry deep, bitter memories. Brought together by great passion, they must learn to trust again.

"Conard County is a wonderful place to visit! Rachel Lee has crafted warm, enchanting stories. These are wonderful books to curl up with and read. I highly recommend them."
—*New York Times* bestselling author
Heather Graham Pozzessere

Available in March, wherever Silhouette books are sold.

What do women really want to know?

Only the world's largest publisher of romance
fiction could possibly attempt an answer.

HARLEQUIN ULTIMATE GUIDES™

How to Talk to a Naked Man,

Make the Most of Your Love Life, and Live Happily Ever After

The editors of Harlequin and Silhouette are
definitely experts on love, men and relationships.
And now they're ready to share that expertise with
women everywhere.

Jam-packed with vital, indispensable, lighthearted
tips to improve every area of your romantic life—even
how to get one! So don't just sit around and wonder
why, how or where—run to your nearest bookstore
for your copy now!

Available this February, at your favorite retail outlet.

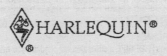

HARLEQUIN®

As seen on TV!
Free Gift Offer

With a Free Gift proof-of-purchase from any Silhouette® book,
you can receive a beautiful cubic zirconia pendant.

This gorgeous marquise-shaped stone is a genuine cubic
zirconia—accented by an 18" gold tone necklace.
(Approximate retail value $19.95)

Send for yours today...
compliments of ▼ *Silhouette*®

To receive your free gift, a cubic zirconia pendant, send us one original proof-of-
purchase, photocopies not accepted, from the back of any Silhouette Romance™,
Silhouette Desire®, Silhouette Special Edition®, Silhouette Intimate Moments®
or Silhouette Shadows™ title available in February, March or April at your favorite
retail outlet, together with the Free Gift Certificate, plus a check or money order for
$1.75 U.S./$2.25 CAN. (do not send cash) to cover postage and handling, payable
to Silhouette Free Gift Offer. We will send you the specified gift. Allow 6 to 8 weeks for
delivery. Offer good until April 30, 1996 or while quantities last. Offer valid in the U.S. and
Canada only.

Free Gift Certificate

Name: _____

Address: _____

City: _____ State/Province: _____ Zip/Postal Code: _____

Mail this certificate, one proof-of-purchase and a check or money order for postage
and handling to: SILHOUETTE FREE GIFT OFFER 1996. In the U.S.: 3010 Walden
Avenue, P.O. Box 9057, Buffalo NY 14269-9057. In Canada: P.O. Box 622, Fort Erie,

FREE GIFT OFFER

ONE PROOF-OF-PURCHASE

079-KBZ-R

To collect your fabulous FREE GIFT, a cubic zirconia pendant, you must include this
original proof-of-purchase for each gift with the properly completed Free Gift Certificate.

079-KBZ-R

TRINITY STREET WEST

where danger lies around every corner—and the
biggest danger of all is falling in love.

Meet the men and women of Trinity Street West in the
new Intimate Moments miniseries by

Justine Davis

beginning in March 1996 with

LOVER UNDER COVER (Intimate Moments #698):

Caitlin Murphy was determined to make a
difference at Trinity Street West. Then cocky detective
Quisto Romero shattered her world. He was willing to
risk everything to catch a young boy's killer—and to
conquer the defenses she had put around her heart.

Don't miss this new series—only from

INTIMATE MOMENTS®
Silhouette®

JDTSW-1